THE HARPY 3: DAMNATION

JULIE HUTCHINGS

inked entertainment

ALSO BY JULIE HUTCHINGS

Vampires of Fate

Running Home (Book 1)

Running Away (Book 2)

Crawling Back (Book 3)

The Harpy Series

The Harpy (Book 1)

The Harpy: Evolution (Book 2)

The Harpy: Damnation (Book 3)

Betty Bedlam

Book 1 Coming soon!

This one is for Lindsay and Colin. When you go through Hell, it shivers.

CHAPTER 1

"Hey, I'm Charity and it's been…108 days since I tore a dude apart and ate his flesh and organs."

A collective, stumbling, "H…h…hi Charity," tripped its way out of the mouths of the circle. I picked the most wide-eyed one I could find and focused on him.

"The longer I go, the harder it is to remember much about the guy I ate last…but I can taste his heart still. And intestines." I smiled at the guy whose mouth was sorta flopping around on his face as he listened. He was scared—but I couldn't smell the fear anymore. Those days were behind me. "I still get hungry, too, but a burger a day keeps the bird bitch away, amirite?" Strained chuckles.

"Uhhhh, thank you. Charity," the Guy Smiley that ran this group said after clearing his throat.

"Yeah, no problem," I replied with a toothy smile for

the crowd and strutted right through the middle to the donut table. Because they didn't replace man-meat, but they still were my biggest weakness. Well, behind booze. And blood and organs. What a stupid saying. Apparently most of my personality was weaknesses, but I was feeling pretty goddamn strong these days.

Behind me someone whispered, "She knows this is an Overeaters support group, right?"

"Sure do," I called back as I poured myself a cardboard cup of coffee and poured in a clump of powdered creamer. "I have an eating problem. We're a perfect match. You even set yourselves up to fail like I do! I mean, donuts? Seriously? What are you *thinking*?"

I may have become a *normal* girl who wears like, regular shirts and joggers and grocery shops and stuff, but goddamn did I still thrive when I could shake people up a little.

A brave lady followed my act and started talking about how hard it is not to eat too much at Christmas parties. I leaned against the church folding table and listened until the crying began. I wasn't at the stage of recovery yet where I felt like comforting people who could never understand me, no matter how many stories I told at any number of support groups— twenty-four now. I'd max out at four meetings when the leader would approach me, shaking, and say that I wasn't the right fit for fill-in-the-blank group. I wanted this one to be it, though. I wanted to be able to tell my story to someone besides Meat Matt at the butcher shop. Someone who could maybe make me feel listened to, and someone I could listen to, return the favor. I think you call them *friends.*

Everybody clapped, snapping me out of my thoughts, and I reached for a second donut. These people didn't need them. I waited for the next person to share, and made a conscious decision not to be judgmental of these losers.

I clapped too, sprinkle donut hanging from my mouth. Then I got a surprise.

"Charity, will you come back to the circle?" the Guy Smiley said.

Sprinkles fell out of my mouth as I said, "Sure. Sure I will. Thanks." I tossed the rest of the donut in the trashcan and went back to my seat. And some of these overeaters were actually smiling at me.

The next lady, Suzanne, started talking about her bitch mother-in-law and the stupid tuna casserole that she totally made on purpose to pick a fight with Suzanne, and the guy next to me patted me on the shoulder. It wasn't even weird. He smiled at me when I looked his way, as if to say I did a good job. But I hadn't really done a good job—of being supportive or opening up. I hadn't *really* tried. This guy had tried. Suzanne and the other lady with the Christmas problem tried.

When Suzanne stopped talking, I made a step forward, the first one I'd made in a really long time. "Suzanne," I said, "you're really brave. And your mother-in-law's a cunt."

~

*L*eaving there, I didn't even want meat. I wasn't hungry—maybe because I'd eaten three donuts, but that never stopped me before. I realized I was smiling as I walked home. And I gave myself a little credit for walking to the support group instead of driving, too. Fresh air and all that shit, especially when it's cold air and I'm driving an SUV with actual heated seats. Not mine, obviously, only on loan.

I'd moved. No more of Robbie's apartment for me. I'd gotten a sign that I needed to move on. An actual sign: *STUDIO FOR RENT.* It stood at the corner of the street right across from the butcher shop. And now that I was apparently capable of holding a job—been at The Full Sail bar for like almost a year, at this point—I could do it. I could really do it, without borrowing or living off my Robbie Trust Fund.

The twinge of guilt only lasted a second now. My inner sarcasm helped with the festering cesspool of feelings Robbie's death had left me with. Acknowledging that he managed to treat me like a charity case, even in death, helped me bury those feelings and turn them into a healthy ball of aggressive repression. Robbie had taken care of me for long enough. Now I was starting to take care of myself, not just survive.

Almost as if I actually mattered.

Almost like I was more than what I'd lived through, and had a life ahead of me.

Admittedly, I hadn't known what else to do after Psychiatrist totally lost his shit and wouldn't—some might say couldn't—confront Rose with me. He didn't agree with me, that she could be saved. He saw no way out for us or for her. *"The spirit has limits, too. Charity, she won't come out of this one."* Fucking coward. To think he was the one who gave me the courage to be this new, better version of myself. All that fire he helped me channel, and his sizzled out the second we needed it. Rose was his fucking responsibility and if he taught me anything it was that responsibility is purpose. And here he went and cried his fucking purpose away, leaving me to wonder *what next?*

Rose had solved what was next for me pretty quickly—she took my wings. Took me apart and stole them, took my choice to put them away. Forcing me into humanity, forcing me to leave her alone, really, because she could travel through time, and back and forth to the Wood of Suicides, and I was here.

I'll tell you what was next after that. Move on with my actual life. A human life.

My new apartment was actually pretty okay, considering I don't mind cold water and carpet so bumpy I tripped on it daily. A step down in size, which was a relief. I didn't want much of anything I'd shared with Robbie, didn't have much of anything before that, and the unicorn collection was a thing of the past.

They'd been such bullshit. Something to hide behind and cling to.

No more hiding. No more clinging. Whatever special thing I'd seen in them once, now they were reminders of beautiful myths that don't exist, and horrible ones that do.

Horrible ones that never rest.

"Hey, Mrs. Butter," I said, passing the little old lady who rented me the studio. Second floor of her house. I had my own set of very long stairs around the back, but it never stopped her from poking her head out every single fucking time I came in to say hi to me. I get that she was old and alone, but many days I had nothing to talk about, and most days she wouldn't want to hear about what I called a life. I liked my life enough for now, and I even liked Mrs. Butter, but I didn't want to share them with each other.

"Hello, dear. And it's Mrs. Bitters, honey. Bitters."

"Oh, I don't think your bitter. Okay, bye." I shut the door as fast as I could while she watched from below. Always watching. This must be what having a mother felt like. No thanks.

"Keegan," I cooed to my canary. "What did you do all day? Did you look for a job? Did you knit me a sweater? You know I don't wear sweaters, we've talked about this."

I plopped onto the couch, kicked off my sneakers and turned on TV, hoping for something new but knowing I'd end up watching The Office. For someone who would never work in an office, it was like seeing the monkey exhibit at the zoo.

Then the tapping started.

One thing about Mrs. Butter's house was that it was quiet. Really quiet except for old house groanings, and I loved those. Never had them before. Old sounds, new life. But this was not that.

This was intentional. Like at the window tapping scene in Lost Boys. Except a hot-ass Kiefer Sutherland probably wasn't outside.

"Mac and cheese for meese," I said and Keegan chirped. Bird never ceased to amaze me, that he knew when I needed any amount of reassuring.

I had the world's oldest stove up here, something that came from Butter's house in 1969 probably. I believe the color is called "goldenrod." But it wasn't a hotplate which made me feel just wonderful about my status in this bedroom of a home. I clanked around the stove with my single pan, sang Misfits to myself, anything to drown out the tapping, and eventually had a panful of mac and cheese in my lap. I didn't find The Office but did find some shit called Small Wonder, and went with it.

Tap. Tap. Tap. Tap.

I could go to work in two hours.

One thing that never seemed to go away was that anything out of the ordinary, anything that didn't fit into this come-home-make-mac-and-cheese-watch-television-maybe-masturbate life that existed within these four close walls legitimately unnerved me. The sound of trick-or-treaters at Halloween had scared me. I don't want to say I was scared, but okay. Okay. I was scared. The doorbell downstairs, the yelling kids, their voices high-pitched like shrieks, the darkness and excited tension in the area, even way up on the second floor...

I'd never been this person before. I'd never shown my fear of anything. I preferred to vent my negative feelings in fists and then later with teeth and talons. The Harpy was gone, and she wasn't coming back.

Tap. Tap. Tap.

"A woodpecker. Gotta be a woodpecker."

The metal spoon against the pan. Clanks and taps, clanks and taps.

Because what would a melodic tapping be? Someone trying to break into my house like a fucking jewel thief on a skylight?

But no matter how much I rationalized it, the tapping drove me mad and I wished like anything that I still had Psychiatrist to talk to. But he was still on "personal leave" in the cracker factory, and I hadn't seen him since we—well, I—decided we needed to make the first move on Rose.

Rose.

Tap. Tap. Tap.

Before I knew it my hands were knotted in my hair, pulling my ponytail out, my teeth were grinding, chest tight and expanding all at once, making this stupid mewling sound.

"I need to get out of here."

And that's the story of why I went to work early. One sound. One name. Total destruction of my psyche.

CHAPTER 2

I left so fast I forgot my keys and just walked to work, teeth chattering from the cold. I also hadn't worn a jacket, which got me a few interesting looks in the late days of November. My brain raced, a chorus of *tap, tap, tap* and a chanting of *Rose, Rose, Rose* in the background as my last conversation with Doctor Mortimer repeated itself in my head.

"She's always thinking a step ahead, way smarter than me. Like, regular smart people make a plan, but she's gonna have Frankenstein-level plans. You can't even call it a plan probably, it's like a gourmet meal of nightmare ideas. The thing is, the Harpies will do anything for her—she'll need to keep it that way. Even I know that. Best way to do that is feed them. The predators—or people she can see into, that they might become predatory dicks; they'll do whatever she says, too. At least the ones she showed mercy to. Some she might force, but most? Most would fall under her spell when

"

she showed them a higher path, gave them some reason to exist."

Mortimer had wanted to help me. He wanted to do the right thing, and even someone as good as him just can't always. Months later and he still couldn't, definitely not from the mental hospital I'd brought him to.

"Please, Charity. I don't trust myself. I'm too afraid, all the time."

I growled at the memory, got to work just as my fingers were getting numb, didn't stop as I went behind the counter, muttered a hello to my boss and started taking beer orders, most of which were done in the form of a nod because this was such a fucking townie bar. Good to have something to do.

Because if being the Harpy was good for nothing else, it was a kickass distraction. And now...I had nothing to distract me. Nothing to push itself into the space that Rose would erupt into.

I'd heard nothing from her. Nothing.

Every day felt borrowed, every minute like a countdown. And I'd been doing nothing except ignoring it. I'd traded in a life where I did some good for some people for a life where I waited, one minute to the next for something with a little meaning. I had no goddamn meaning anymore.

But you ignore the one thing you should be doing, asshole. Go to Rose. Stop pretending you aren't scared.

For what, though? She'd been quiet, she disappeared, and I took it as a hint that I wasn't wanted anymore. It wasn't my problem that she had some twisted idea of justice and a brain that was killing her.

"Holy fuck," I said out loud, scrunching a bar towel between my hands like I could wring the thought right out of it. "What if she's dead?" But the feeling that I would never be finished that easily wrenched my gut. It couldn't be that easy. *Real nice, Charity. Dead kid equals easy for you.*

Tap. Tap. Tap.

⁓

The tapping was gone when I got home around two in the morning, my pleasant tiredness fighting with how goddamn cold I was. My head was quiet. The house only creaked.

Half my clothes were off by the time I opened my door. Nothing grosser than walking in the cold with sweat stuck to you, the smell of stale beer and lemon cleaning stuff permeating everything. Straight to the shower.

I refused to think about Rose. I would not think about Rose and what she was up to. I wouldn't think about what she'd taken from me. I wouldn't think of her dead in the Facility or in the Wood. I would not give up these silent moments.

I mostly managed.

Stretching out in bed felt better than it should have. I'd worked harder many more nights, but tonight felt like I'd had all my muscles balled up for hours and the only relaxation they could get was between clean sheets. Unicorn bedspread was toast, torn through with claws and covered in blood stains. Now I had nice, grown-up Egyptian cotton sheets and a thing called a doovay, with zero animals on them. Just white.

Plain white sheets.

Plain white doovay.

Plain blonde hair in a plain ponytail.

Plain elastic-waist pants because your jeans are all too tight.

Plain Charity. Something I never thought possible, and it had felt like a vacation.

I closed my eyes tight against the needling thought that maybe, just maybe, the tapping was more than fear. Maybe it was *want*.

~

I'd been too hard on Mortimer, and that's why he'd locked himself up.

I came at him guns a-blazing, expecting him to pick up half the tab on my mistakes with Rose. Psychiatrists don't save the world.

Charity Fucking Blake saves the world.

No, that didn't sound right at all. I may have been reformed, but I'd never be a hero. I barely made it as normal. For nearly four months I'd been pulling my hair, no longer a halo of platinum frizz, into a ponytail to complement my casual normal girl clothes and go to my bar job, go to any support group I could find to get anyone to understand me, and the whole time Rose was there in my brain, waiting to be in my present, biding her time. And all the regular world shit would melt away once she showed up. The kick in the ass was that this small-town girl thing, where I passably blended into the real world, had worked pretty fucking hard to achieve, wasn't real. A bookmark in my shitty life story. Terrifyingly temporary.

Hell was eternal. And it would be waiting for me.

I stumbled to the coffee pot, which gloriously was only across the room. Checked my phone while I slugged down a cup, black. No messages. No texts. No emails. No calls. It was getting to be less pleasant all the time.

"You love me, right?" I asked the bird, dropping the phone and opening his cage door. He hopped on my finger right away, which was answer enough for me. I felt this bird more than I had most people in my existence. He hovered his tiny beak over my coffee cup. A Disney World mug that had been here when I moved in. "Coffee isn't for birds, babe." I threw back the rest of the Mickey mug as I put Keegan on his jungle gym that the pet store girl insisted was for bigger birds. I told her to think big, reach for the stars and give me the fucking jungle gym. Keegan was totally lost on the thing, but new worlds to discover and all that.

Tap. Tap. Tap.

"No. No no no no no." I couldn't hear that fucking sound again, was waiting for it and praying it wouldn't come.

That tap was a nail in the eggshell of my room. The pin to my balloon. It reminded me that something was out there, always something out there that wanted in.

The phone buzzed on the bed and I screamed, jarred from my crazy-ass morning terrors. I didn't know the number—I didn't really know any numbers—so I answered it because why the hell not.

"Is this Charity Blake?"

"Sure, why not?"

"Uh, Miss Blake, I'm calling from Beth Israel Deaconess Medical Center in Boston on behalf of Doctor Mortimer. He listed you as his emergency contact, is that right?"

I laughed so loud I heard her gasp. "I don't know what the worse emergency would be, but yeah, I'll take the call."

"It's not a collect call, ma'am, I'm calling because Doctor Mortimer is with us and ready to be discharged."

"Wait, why is he there? He was in the nuthouse."

She cleared her throat. "Well, yes, but he had an accident there and was transferred here. He was capable of signing himself out of the facility," my heart thudded at the word, "and would like you to come and get him, please."

Tap. Tap. Tap.

A trickle ran down my spine.

"Yeah, yeah of course. Um, Beth Israel, right? Just like, show up? Show up and come get him?"

"That would be fine," she said with a lilting laugh. "We look forward to seeing you."

I dropped onto the bed with the phone, the empty mug bouncing off the throw rug. Psychiatrist wanted to see me after all this time. Something had changed, something I was unaware of, and that did not fit into my routine. I wasn't ready. I didn't want to get him. I didn't want to know what he knew, what changed.

Except I did. Because I'd never know peace until this shitshow got started.

CHAPTER 3

*E*verything felt so fucking slow.

This was normal life. Driving to the city. Traffic lights that nobody paid attention to. Car horns. Parking and paying for that shit. Walking to the place you needed to go in Boston cold, which was a burning, sharp cold, unlike Plymouth's cold that settled into your bones. Why the hell didn't anyone in Boston seem to care that it was cold or they had to walk everywhere? Everything is wicked fucking inconvenient and yet all you hear is how convenient it is to live in the city. Sure, if you want to take two trains and walk six blocks.

More regular life stuff—retrieving a guy from the hospital.

"Hey, I need Mortimer."

The nurse sitting behind the desk I'd finally reached after more walking, had blue eyeshadow up to her fucking eyebrows, and that magnificent application had taken all her energy apparently. "What?" she huffed. All she was missing was Hubba Bubba.

"I need Mortimer."

"I heard what you said, what does it mean?"

"I'm checking out Doctor Mortimer, he's getting released. Is he ready?"

Not another word as she clicked on her computer, probably playing sudoku, and she didn't look at me when she said, "He's already gone."

"No, I just talked to a nurse about him like, an hour ago. You people called me."

"He's been checked out, miss," she snapped.

"Well who the fuck did you let take him? You let just anybody take a guy who's been in the mental institution? Don't you look at an ID, or, I don't know, ask any motherfucking questions before you let him walk out?"

"He was wheeled out, and I didn't ID you, did I?"

"Oh. So you're what, smart?" I leaned over the counter, shoved her Ring Dings aside, swiveled the computer and saw the room number he'd been in. I stomped past her as she yelled bullshit behind me.

"Hey, roommate," I said to the little old guy in the next bed. "Where'd this guy go?" I patted the still unchanged bed.

The old guy's voice was like Robbie's that time he had the nastiest flu in history. "How many pretty girls does that guy know, anyway?" he said with a dry cough.

"A girl came?"

"Pretty, too."

"How weird was she? Big burning hole in her belly or anything?" He narrowed his eyes at me. "Lady or a kid, huh? Answers, old man."

"Not a kid, no."

"Did he seem happy to go with her?"

"I don't think that man is happy about anything, young lady."

Seemed like he wasn't all better after his jaunt at Sunnybrook Farms. And now a Harpy had him.

"Are you okay?" the old man asked me. I'd sat on Mortimer's former bed, and found I'd been rocking back and forth like I was the one who should be locked up. But things weren't that bad, I was just…scared. I was scared. Of who took him, of what they wanted, of Rose, of this life…

"You know, young lady, if someone worried about me the way you're worried about that man who was here, I think I'd die happy."

I stopped moving. That got me right in the throat.

Because I did care about Mortimer, I did worry, and nobody cared or worried about me. Nobody.

"Yeah, I guess I'm worried. He was supposed to wait for me, and I don't know where the lady took him." *Yes you do.*

"He's lucky to have you." The old man's eyes were ocean-bright. He smiled wide at me, and it wasn't entirely unpleasant but I wasn't in the mood for more friends and definitely not any who needed me.

I sprung up to leave but stopped at the door. "Thanks. Get better."

"Where you going?" he asked.

"Why?"

"Can you get me a glass of water, please? That nurse..."

Who the hell was I now? Picked up the pitcher on his super convenient little rolly table—totally empty— went to the bathroom and filled it up because I was being nice but I was no saint and bathroom water was good enough. Brought it back, poured him a cup and tried to hand it to him but he just leaned forward like I was supposed to give it to him like a baby bird or something.

"I'll get you a straw, but this ain't happening. See ya, mister. Feel better."

"Already do," he croaked.

And sonofabitch if that didn't make me smile.

Blue Eyeshadow was in the same spot I'd left her. "Hey, Wet 'n Wild, wanna peel yourself out of that chair and get the guy in Mortimer's room a straw? He's been down there looking for water."

"I'll put the call in," she monotoned, and my blood fucking boiled.

I came around the desk and swiveled her chair around. "Get off your ass and help that guy. You're a nurse and all he wants is water. You know what I've done to help people? Fuck you if you think you're special because of those orthopedic sneakers, Saved by the Bell, get off your fat ass and bring him a straw or I'll break your fingers and you'll never put on blue eyeshadow the same again. Got it?" I shoved the chair out from behind the desk while she yelped and made mewling, appalled noises. But she got up—first to call security, which I gave her a no-no finger at—and then down the hall toward my old friend's room.

My day was just beginning, and I was so done with being a person it made my mouth water for raw chicken.

～

*B*road daylight, I'm contemplating eating a terrier tied up in front of a 7-11.

Where the fuck had Rose taken him?

It hadn't been Rose, but it had been one of hers, and she'd known he was at the hospital. Knew he was leaving and slipped him out. No violence, just total preparedness. Way scarier.

She'd been watching us, just like I knew she'd been. And she'd take Mortimer to the place she knew I couldn't go. She'd made sure I couldn't go,

The Wood of Suicides.

I closed my eyes, let the cold air soak into my face, wanting to stand there until my lips froze and everything in me stopped, just frozen like Jack in The Shining. My bladder felt full of ice, like I had to pee and throw up and my legs shook. My head got really hot and I snapped my eyes open so I wouldn't pass out but everything swam.

I can't do this. I can't go back there.

"God fucking dammit, why can't anyone just let me *not* be a murder bird!" What bullshit. I couldn't be a Harpy now if I wanted to be.

"There," Rose had said, blinking her big blue eyes innocently while she ripped my soul out. *"Now you're free."*

The surrounding pedestrians glared at me, but ear buds protect people from having to listen to the city crazies, of which I was currently one.

I half-jogged back to Mortimer's SUV in the lot four hundred miles away, still so wound up, running scenarios in my head. "I should not be driving," I said, eyes blurring with tears until I easily lost my way. Boston made it easy to get lost as it was. My throat sore from held-in tears and swearing, I parked illegally within sight of a coffee shop. Not Dunkins, some fancy place. I would have killed a man for a cup of coffee or a bottle of whiskey. They probably only had coffee at The Thinking Cup though.

I gotta say, the Monster Formerly Known as Charity Blake would have horrified the hipsters running around this place. As I was, sneakers and ponytail, I actually blended in. I *blended in.* The idea that someone like me could ever blend in with these fresh-from-pilates class acts and the bearded, jaunty-hatted gentlemen that thought themselves soooo unique was so nuts that it lightened my mood a little. These clowns had no idea what I was. Or had been.

Wouldn't be anymore.

I wondered how many of them I would have been drawn to destroy. Which one would have given me a run for my money.

"Miss?"

"Yeah, yeah, coffee, large. Come at me with all the fixins' and there's gonna be a problem. I want real coffee."

"Just coffee. Got it." To Beardie's credit, he actually smiled a little, I hadn't put him off at all. Maybe I wouldn't have turned any heads in a corset and fishnets in the big city, so good thing I aimed low like a townie. Maybe I'd thought I was shocking everybody but they just couldn't believe I was trying too hard. The name of the game had always been hiding from my past, not striving to stand out. Now here I was wishing for the stares and cringes. What the hell was I always trying to prove, anyway?

Psychiatrist would say I was growing up. Motherfucker would have been right. As exhibited by tennis shoes and freaking out over the whereabouts of a human being. Ready to save the world instead of picking it apart to the bones.

"Be happy to get you one," a smooth voice said. I followed a hand pointing at the bake case.

I curled my lips in, biting them so as not to snap at the guy. While I regretted not being looked at, I also didn't expect I'd be hit on, and I just wanted a cup of coffee. I turned my head slowly, probably looked possessed.

Cute. The blond hair mopped over like he'd just gotten off his surfboard and let it dry under the California fucking sun. Glinty little eyes, a smile that had used Invisiline. Stubble that didn't even look planned, but probably was.

"Hey, uh, thanks…Brady," his name had to be something like that, "but the last time I accepted pastries at a coffee shop from a rando hottie we committed a series of terrible crimes against humanity together and he went to Hell. I just got out, myself. So, no thanks."

He laughed really loudly and it made me laugh, even though I didn't want to. "That sounds awesome. Seriously, let me get you a danish. So good."

"Do I look like I need a danish?" I snapped, gesturing at my actually very normal body. I was so used to being disturbingly skinny, what with all my health consciousness. Raw meat, lots of booze, shit sleeping habits and flying kept me on the grosser side of heroin-chic. But now? Depression. And the *boredom*. Little Debbie and I had become good friends. I glared at the pretentious bake case. "What is that, repurposed wood? Jesus Christ."

"Here you are," the hipster behind the counter said, and the Brady about vaulted the three feet to shove a couple of bills into the pompadour's hand.

"Not necessary," I muttered.

"My pleasure," the Brady said, his face close to mine, and the scent of like, Old Spice and cookies, was a little too much for me. Because hell, it would be nice to just have sex with a regular dude real quick. I was hungry, I was pissed off, and kinda sad, and had too much to do but had no idea what to do, and I just wanted to do something not on the agenda. Like this guy.

But I took the coffee, walked out without another word. My vision got blurry for the hundredth time that hour, and I didn't think I'd make it to the SUV without having to sit down and sob.

If this was what emotional growth felt like, then stunt my fucking growth.

"Are you okay?"

Brady had caught up with me.

"No," I snapped, stopping and facing him like he had anything to do with anything. "You know, not so long ago I'd have hit on you first. Today I have to save a missing psychiatrist from Hell. Things change. Not your lucky day, Brady."

"It's Theo." He didn't smile, and I liked him more for it. I didn't want to like him or anybody, not even for a second.

"Theo. Cool name, actually. Now let me work out storming the castle, huh? Thanks for the coffee." But I was still looking at him, I didn't walk away yet. He was just so *nice.*

"No problem..."

I ran a hand through my hair, pulling it out of the

ponytail all crazy probably. "Charity."

His eyes wrinkled up like he'd laughed a lot in his life. "Charity. You're welcome. Feel better, okay?" He turned on his heel, took a few steps, and I stopped him.

"Why?"

"Huh?"

"Why do you want me to feel better? There are better looking women all over the place, look at her," pointing at a girl who scowled at me then pushed her hat down further.

He took a tentative step toward me again. "It's not about how you look."

"That's crap."

"I'm not lying. You seem different. And for your information, I would not have tried to sleep with you today. I'd have asked you to sit and have coffee with me, and if you did and it was as cool, I'd ask you to dinner tonight."

"I'm sorry," I said in a voice smaller than I'd ever heard out of my mouth, "but I'm not from around here and uh, I'm not dating right now."

When I looked up from my feet his face had fallen, the glittering smile gone. "Well, that's my bad luck then," he said huskily, sadly. And I wondered what on earth I'd done that he would be that disappointed.

"Yeah, it might feel like that today, but trust me, your luck would get worse with me. See you 'round, Theo," I said and took off like a shot to the borrowed SUV of a man I had to save.

CHAPTER 4

I wandered around my apartment, phone in hand, like I had someone to call.

"What do I do now, Keegs?" My little bird twittered like everything was the best it had ever been. Jesus, to be that happy all the time. I don't think I could've handled it. "What would you do if you lost your wings?" I whispered, and my voice broke.

Pouring Cheerios into a bowl and sniffling, like I'd been doing since I got home the day before, I mumbled to myself the same repetitive questions that I still had no answers for.

How can I get to Mortimer?

What does Rose want with him?

Will I be alone forever?

I slammed the cereal bowl down on the old oak table that had been here when I moved in. Cheerios scattered everywhere.

I was helpless. And alone.

Of course, I was alone by choice. This was no accident. It had been like, a year or something since Robbie died, and I still saw him in my eyes when I woke up. But more than that, I saw that there was no one else. Not just a guy, but like, anyone. Every. Single. Person. That came near me. Ended in a blaze of hellfire.

For a year I'd managed to fend off the guys at The Full Sail, the occasional creep at the supermarket, whatever. But this last guy…

It shouldn't have bothered me so much that he was disappointed.

It shouldn't have bothered me so much that I was disappointed, too.

But the longer I sat there at the old creaky table, eating my spilled Cheerios and listening to Keegan sing, the more I found myself imagining going out to dinner with Theo. A real date. Not like going to dinner with Evan, which was just a setup for ultimate weirdness to come. Not takeout with Robbie. Not a package of raw hamburger that would make me puke because I no longer had the system for it.

Dinner. A date. With a guy who knew nothing about me.

For the first time I thought of my boring life as maybe something exciting after all. Exciting because it was a fresh start. I'd done it before—Hazel Harrington was more than happy to become someone new—but this was a smoother, different kind of scary transition. I controlled this one for all new reasons.

I could be normal. I could forget what I'd turned into and focus on who I actually was.

Tap. Tap. Tap.

"Oh hell no."

The tapping showed up like the Grim Reaper.

Tap. Tap. Tap.

This time it was moving, across the roof, tapping in a vaguely familiar pattern and I wanted nothing, *nothing* familiar. All new, all better. No past, barely present, only future.

I wasn't ready to see what was on the roof. It was probably a woodpecker, I knew that, I *felt* it, and I refused to give into this paranoia that it was, what? Rose? The super dead Queen of Suicides? No, it was a fucking bird. It was nothing that needed facing.

What needed facing was this phone, that I had to call somebody to help me get Mortimer—from Hell.

Not this time, Blake. You're on your own.

Tap. Tap. Tap.

"Keegan," I said, shoving the cereal bowl across the table, "I'm missing something. What am I missing, birdie boo?"

Chirp chirp.

Tap. Tap.

"No offense, Keegs, but you talk nonsense to me. I need some serious food, I need to think like, hard. Can't do that with Cheerios, you read me?"

Chirp. Chirp. Chirp.

Tap. Tap. Tap.

It got louder and louder, the TV on in the background, louder and louder, my heart thudding in time with my forehead, louder and louder, the ringing in my ears, I was powerless, wingless, nothing, everybody and nobody.

I ran out the door, whipping on a coat even though sweat poured down my neck.

Something was coming for me, and I couldn't be sure if it was outside or inside my own head.

~

"I am not looking at the roof. Crazy people climb on the roof."

I'd actually put on a coat this time to brave the November wind, a step in the direction of making rational decisions. One regular person decision at a time, that's all it took.

Can't top off your rational decision with some raw meat to puke up. You gotta go to the grocery store like a townie.

"Fuck off I do. Not today."

More symptoms of crazy—carrying conversations with oneself habitually.

I stood staring at the SUV. Debating butcher shop meat at the top of the street, where I might get to puke up everything bothering me—before puking up all the raw meat. Or I could go to Market Basket, the fluorescent-lit haven of the elderly, where anyone who looked at you was a potential murderer with their carriage, and they didn't even have a self-checkout. I'd actually have to speak to a cashier. *And* a bagger. Normal stuff. No tapping. No missing psychiatrist, just for a while.

Chin up, I got in the car and drove to the supermarket, that freakshow of a food arena. This is what Hell should be modeled after.

I held it together through crowded aisle after crowded aisle, picked up a box of Christmas Tree Cakes, stomach turned at the scent of roasted chickens, white-knuckled the carriage handle at the ear-haired bastard who wouldn't move in front of the frozen pizzas, said excuse me a dozen times, bought bananas to turn brown, the whole time, convincing myself the thoughts in my head were no more or less awful than anyone else's around me. Theirs might feature the bitch at the soccer game who brought better snacks (cue lady frowning at everything on the pre-packaged snack shelf), or who would die in the nursing home next (in walks the oldest guy on the planet by himself), but Hell was the same for all of us. Blood ran through all of them. We weren't so different.

The deli case with all its off-colored meat and various stages of death sang to me like a goddamn choir. Even the dead fish, eyeballs staring blankly, gave me flickers of dead men's eyes, one asshole victim after the other, infesting my vision. The tang of blood flooded my mouth ever so briefly. All these people, and the dead things looked the most appetizing. I sighed. I was making strides.

It felt like running away again.

Roast beef, bologna, ham...

Shoving my hands in my coat pockets, I nodded to the deli kid. "Hey, can I get some Canadian Stab Bacon? Like a pound or whatever."

His little paper white hat and hairnet twitched when he furrowed his brows. "Do you mean...Canadian Slab Bacon?"

"It's not Stab? If it's not Stab Bacon, I don't want it. Gotta get your murder in somehow. Where's the Stab Bacon?"

"Ma'am, we don't have anything like that. No Stab Bacon."

My head fell back, giving the sigh a lot of volume while I tried not to kill this kid. "Fine, give me roast beef, but it had better be pink. Red, even."

I felt the eyes on me, and welcomed it. I rolled my head to the side to meet the eyes of a lady with hair so white it blended in with the milk bottles in the case beside her. "Hi," I said.

She scowled at me. And I really could have said a lot of things. But I bit my tongue, literally, stopped myself. I tapped my thrift store Converse, I waited for my meat. I smiled at a guy with a moustache so thick it had a life of its own when he grinned at me, like we had some secret joke. But he was laughing at me, wasn't he? Wasn't he?

"Anything else, ma'am?" White hat dropped a package on the counter. I could see the blood tinting the paper inside.

"I'm good. Thank you." I drawled it out, realizing how little I carried conversations like this. Just say what I needed to say and stop there. I always did have a flair for going too far. Saved me a lot of times. Distracted me a lot more.

Nothing could distract me from the ringing in my ears, a clinger from the panic attack before I left the house.

"Excuse me."

"Don't talk to me," I snapped.

"I just wanted to get by."

Deep breath.

The lady smiled, close-lipped at me. Soft, kind eyes met mine, closer to me than I wanted anyone to be, but she exuded warmth that I wanted to wrap myself in.

"You're doing great," she said quietly with a little nod.

I let out this gasping sob that felt like something breaking and growing inside.

She squeezed my arm, the ringing started again. She faintly ordered cheese but all I heard was the ringing, underwater voices, watched the scuffed linoleum floor blur and come into focus back and forth. Her hand squeezed my arm but the rest of me was numb. *Why is this happening to me?*

My stomach lurched when she moved me. Eyes

prodded all around me but how would I know that when I was looking at the floor.

"We've all had these days, honey," she said, leading me by the arm to a little row of chairs by a case of cheese.

"I don't want to sit in the deli," I heard myself say.

"It does smell," she said.

"I like the smell, I don't like the old people."

She laughed and I about died because it sounded like Jen's.

That's when I fell to the linoleum, a sea of orthopedic shoes surrounding me.

~

"Get them out of here," I heard the woman hiss. "The girl needs some air."

Shoes all around me again—still—not orthopedics, not as many. Regular sneakers, a pair of nice shoes or two… That meant a manager. And the lady who'd been so nice to me was toe to toe with him telling him that I just slipped and didn't need an ambulance.

I'd been pulled to a sitting position and was leaning against the lemon barrel. I was staring a bunch of dead fish on ice in the faces. I hopped up, brushed my pants off and let out a big sigh through my plastered-on smile. "Hey guys, thanks for the ambulance offer, but

I'm good. See? Good stuff." I shot a look at my lady savior and she smiled warmly.

"Would you like to fill out an accident report?" the manager asked me. "I believe—"

"—that we should forget this ever happened and go about our business. Okay, bye!"

I started to walk off but stopped at the woman. "You were great. Thank you for… I guess thank you for knowing I didn't want a big deal to be made of it, you know?"

She tilted her head, that same motherly smile. "Just remember that you've pulled through worse than a bad day at the deli, dear."

I threw my arms around her. Couldn't stop myself. I wanted to bring her out to coffee, or back to my nice little apartment for a drink, or get her number. But she was amazing and warm, comforting, full of sunshine, and I had none of that. I would only take from her. "Thank you," I said into her shoulder, and I took off before anyone else could stop me.

Knocked down a display of chamomile tea. Wished I had a minute to read the box to see if it would help with what were obviously fucking panic attacks. Raced out—foodless—to my—Mortimer's—car. I don't know if people were staring, but it felt like it. Didn't it always? Sitting in the driver's seat though, I noticed that there were a couple of women sitting just like me. Maybe not in a total state of confusion and panic, but one looked like she was ready to cry. One looked like she might take a nap right then and there. More dragged themselves to and from the store in a hurry or dragging their feet like they didn't want to do whatever thing they had to do next. It should have been one of those moments where I realize that we all have the same struggles, and nobody's lives are perfect, and women have it worse than men, and emotion means that we're processing it like Mortimer said, but it wasn't.

I just realized that when I was a Harpy, none of this seemed to matter.

This was the life I'd chosen? Where nobody's life matters more than the next person's and we're all in pain over our everyday worlds? How was this better than making a difference in the most definitive, solid way imaginable? How was this life of grocery store panic attacks more meaningful than destroying men who would pick these miserable women off one at a time?

Rose may have taken the Harpy wings out of me, but I'd planned to put them away for good anyway, be a good example for her. She just stole my safety net. I'd chosen wrong. The Harpy had been mine, I'd let this society of nothingness lure me away from it, and Rose had been all too happy to show me how little I was without it.

CHAPTER 5

At times like these, I was supposed to have a psychiatrist to talk to. Some drugs that I wouldn't bother refilling. Instead, I had Mrs. Butter downstairs, the mumbling of her talking to herself lulling me into a false state of calm.

I looked out the window, head still buzzing from the panic and the fall and hunger. My stomach turned.

This was not what a well-adjusted person looked like.

The tapping was fainter, like an echo, but there. Forever there. Like that crow poem by Edgar Allen Poe, never leaves. Or is it the heart one, that the guy hears beating under the floorboards? Robbie liked that one. Sounded a little more like me, except I'd be running toward the heart, ripping the floorboards up, salivating.

"Charity? Honey?"

Jesus Christ, I had to talk to Butter right now?

"Yeah?" I called out.

"Can I come in for a moment please?"

"Not feeling great, Mrs. Butter."

"Bitters, dear, and I'll only be a moment."

She came in on her own, holding an ancient Tupperware bowl, which she put down on the table.

"There's food in that, isn't there?" I said before I could think better of it.

Her smile was all warmth, zero judgment. "Chicken noodle soup, of course," she said with glee. So was that how one found happiness in this crap world? Being proud of soup? "I knew you weren't feeling well and thought it might do the trick."

I swung my legs off the wide windowsill, the wood groaning under my weight. "What do you mean, you knew I wasn't feeling well?"

"Your girlfriends told me you'd been at the hospital, dear! Now, why wouldn't you tell me you needed to go to the hospital? No young lady needs to endure that alone."

I was floundering for words, for so many reasons, but managed to get out, "My girlfriends?" My hatred for the term *girlfriends* as applied to just a friend who is a girl was overshadowed by the pit of ice that plunged through my body and into my bowels.

Someone was looking for me.

The old lady's eyebrows came together and she chuckled as if she couldn't quite believe I was this thick. "Yes, dear. They came by a few hours ago asking about you, said you'd been to the hospital and they wanted to make sure you were alright? I thought it was quite nice."

"I don't have friends."

"These two would disagree. They were quite eager to find you."

Tap. Tap. Tap.

"I...I'm not sick, I was looking for a friend, too," I told her, mind racing around all the things I should and shouldn't say, all the places I should check or avoid. "What did these girls look like?"

She rattled off descriptions of two women that sounded like nobody I knew, like nobody at all really, as she heated up the bowl of soup in the microwave. In my experience, when strangers are looking for me, it's time to run.

Mrs. Butter stayed with me while I ate, her warm soup and warmer spirit melting the ice paralyzing my chest and throat. She told me about her late husband, a Vietnam vet, and her long line of cats—she'd never been much of a bird person. Preferred the freedom and independence in a pet. And she laughed at my bad, under-the-breath jokes, which I thought was cute, because she's not my primary audience. For a short time, the tapping stopped, and I wondered if the tapping had been these "friends" of mine, scratching at the roof, looking for a subtle way in. These Harpies—because that was absolutely who they were, there was no other explanation—were either afraid of their own strength and power or trying to be subtle.

So either they're new, or they're trying to make a clean hit.

Before long, I'd lived through another day. A day in which I'd failed to keep Mortimer safe from the clutches of the Harpies.

Since when did they kidnap regular guys, living hostages for crying out loud? What game is Rose playing?

I went to bed wondering if I'd be strong enough to find out before it was too late.

~

*P*sychiatrist is focused on me with those sleepless-night watery eyes like I'm the god of good ideas. He's Quasimodo'd over the table, a cup of black coffee just under his nose, steaming, untouched. The little hair he has is all over the place. He looks like a chubbier James Lipton on a serious bender. But it's not the mess he's become that unnerves me.

What unnerves me is that I've got my back straight, my head on straight, sipping my coffee in a very put-together way, and Doctor Mortimer has come totally undone.

The walls of his house bow in on me, warp and reach for me as I realize that at some point in my time traveling murder sprees, our roles had reversed. I was the one who could accept reality now.

"You always have been," the picture of a bright-eyed kid says on the wall.

I slam my hand on the table, and Mortimer jumps with a little shriek. Hilarious. "Get it together, Psychiatrist, we have shit to do."

Rubbing a meaty hand over his face, he whimpers—actually whimpers—and my sad excuse for patience is at an all-time low. "I'm sorry," he moans. "You can't imagine how difficult it is for me, having had Rose Preston under my care, and not only failing her, but running from her. If I'd had more courage..."

The words echo, have a heartbeat of their own as I drink them in. The pictures laugh at both of us.

"No time for a pity party, Psychiatrist." But my fury couldn't be bridled. I grab his coffee cup, shower him with it from across the table. He yelps, jumping up, patting his clothes down like he's putting out a fire. "Shut up!" I yell. "Listen to me. You had a chance—you had the only chance to save her, Doctor, and if you expect me to feel bad for you, or sit here while you feel bad for yourself, while her memories have literally put holes in her brain, and she's been trapped in that shithole Facility, and now she's a..." I couldn't bring myself to call her a monster, but it's right there. I grit my teeth, sit, take a sip of my own coffee. I lower my voice but it's no less scary.

"The rage always wants out, the wings always want out, and he's pushing you," *Mortimer's kid's picture says and laughs.*

"She was so little, and you didn't just fail her, you threw

her away," I growl at Mortimer and he's shaking. "Now put some clean clothes on for chrissakes, and get your balls in order or I'll remove them. Because we lost Rose—we lost her —but we can't let her win."

The coffee drips onto the hardwood floor of this really nice house of his, paid for by patients he'd actually continued to talk to. I'd been one of them. It bores a hole through the wood, and below I see the Suicide Forest, blood-red and screaming, deformed arms of the trapped tree people clawing for me from that world to this one.

~

I Woke up screaming in the dark wood of my own apartment, wondering if Rose had been one of those reaching for me, begging me for help.

The dream—memory, really—had the soup sloshing in my gut and me craving the taste of cold, tough meat more than ever. Something terrible for someone terrible.

You're the reason Mortimer went away. You tortured him with your words.

The butcher shop wouldn't be open yet, the sun had just peeked through the winter clouds. Fuck it would be cold out there, but this was prime time for Meat Matt encounters.

Sweatpants, faded Rob Zombie t-shirt with the

sleeves cut off, flannel shirt of unknown origin, hoodie over that, ugly athletic sneakers, and I hit the street to the butcher shop, which I could see in all its glory as soon as I stepped onto my porch. Like a visual security blanket. A blood blanket.

In the quiet early morning, even before the little kids were walking to the tiny elementary school up the street, the crunch of a thin layer of snow under my feet soothed me, settled my brain from the nightmare. The nightmare that had been real, one of my own making. I was greeted with the slam of the butcher shop back door banging closed as I approached. My cheeks warmed up with a smile when I rounded the little building to see Matt, dumping guts in the snow.

"Miss Blake!" he said with a big smile, which frankly took me by surprise. Because—though it had been a while—I pretty much just ate his butcher dumpins' and told him all my gory secrets. Totally safe kid, and he was a great listener.

"Hey Matt, long time no see, right? You gonna—?" But I stopped myself. I didn't want the remnants of the innards, I just wanted raw meat, decent quality. And a chat.

"You want this, Miss Blake?"

"Holy shit, stop calling me that and no, but thanks. I could go for like, a big slice of pork, though."

"Well, I don't get that free, Miss—Charity."

"I know, I'll pay for it. I have a real live job. Caught it like a fish."

Blood spread out in the snow, turning pink as it sunk in. "You fish?" Matt said.

"More of a hunter, as you know." I sat on the freezing short brick wall beside the growing pinkish-red stain. The shock of cold to my ass was enough to distract me from the blood.

Matt had stopped to look at me like he was trying to figure out if I was an imposter or not. "It's been a long time. Are you alright, Miss Blake?"

"Not really, Meat."

"Please don't call—"

"Look. You're the only person I have. You know how sick that is? You're a child, and I'm a murderer and a fuckup besides, and somehow calling you Meat Matt makes it feel not as insane that I tell you all my secrets. So deal with it, kid. Anyway, no, *no* I am not alright. You know that psychiatrist?"

"Yes, you call him Psychiatrist."

"That's the one. Well, he's gone. Rose took him."

"She took him?"

I struggled to remember how much I'd told him, because yeah it had been a while, but I ran off at the mouth to Meat Matt like nobody's business. Tough to know when I stopped.

When I paused he asked, "Where?"

"The only place she knows I won't go. The Wood of Suicides."

I got up, paced in the snow, my ass numb, people

starting to walk by with their kids to school on the other side of the street. I avoided eye contact.

"Why is she trying to keep him away from you?"

That stopped me.

"You're right," I said in a breath.

"About what?"

"I'm thinking she's trying to keep him away from me, because obviously—"

"—it's about you…"

"Quit it. But yeah, what if it isn't about me? What if she's just trying to keep him *with her*?"

Chunks of unrecognizable meat fell from the bucket with a *slurp*. They plunked to the snow, now crystallized pink and red.

I didn't want to eat them.

"You think she brought your friend to…to…Hell?" Matt asked tentatively. Sweet kid, eyes kinda widened at the word though he'd heard me say it plenty and his dad said far worse while hacking up meat in the butcher shop I was guessing. I suppose it means something different when you're talking about an actual place.

"Well, you got me thinking, Me—*Matt*. If she was trying to make sure I couldn't get him back, yeah, she'd have taken him to the Wood. But if she just needed him with her, there's another place, right under my damn nose."

"Maybe it's a trap?" he offered, standing up straight from his blood-pouring position and screwing up his mouth uncertainly, a subtle suggestion that I probably shouldn't follow the bait.

But come on.

"A trap, huh?" and I felt my lips quirk up. Like I wanted to find out.

"It's self-defeating, Charity. Setting yourself up for trouble rather than try to find a better, though possibly more challenging, way out."

Psychiatrist always said shit like that.

"Miss Blake, I don't know if you should do whatever you're about to do," the teenager said.

I'd told him about the Facility, and a lot about Rose. Both dangerous, and both unavoidable if I wanted to get Mortimer away from her.

But Cleary is at the Facility, too. The very guy we'd wanted to find...I'd wanted to find...before Mortimer went on his mental vacation, leaving me with no card to play. Mortimer had the answers she needed, but Cleary could help me stop her. But if he'd been in touch with her for all this time, if the Facility really was where she'd been, he had to be part of her plan. I mean, he'd definitely fare well in it as her right hand, she loved him. And who would he be to stop her? She couldn't be stopped.

She couldn't be stopped.

Matt frowned at the phone alarm going off in his pants pocket, unable to reach for it with blood-yucky hands. "Time to open up," he said, glancing at the back door. We both knew his dad would be there any second. "But Charity…just, don't do anything too fast, okay? I know you aren't scared of danger, but…well, what if this is the time it doesn't work out?"

"Matt!" came the call from inside the shop.

"I'll be alright, Matt," I said quietly. I mean, it was touching, the kid worrying about me. And maybe a little jarring that a teenager had to tell me to slow down.

He pursed his lips, shaking his head before he said, "You don't know that. You don't know everything. Just—" another call from the shop, sharper this time, "don't make this be the last time I see you, Miss Blake."

The screen door slammed shut behind him, leaving me in the cherry slushie snow.

~

I went inside like a real customer, bought a bunch of beef which I fully intended to cook, and left.

If my walk home had been longer, maybe I'd have thought over what Matt said more. But my brain was already in a permanent state of belief that everyone would be better off without me—especially a teenager who balks at the use of the word *hell*. If I didn't go, Mortimer was stuck in a situation deemed even too dangerous for me, and that didn't fly. If it was a trap for me, then first, I was right and everything is about me all the time, and secondly, I was too curious to not dive in.

Regular life both bored and terrified me, and this…

Could be a reminder of who I was. Make me reevaluate who I am.

Who the hell am I kidding? I was going where the action was because it was *my* action, and *my* problem, and I wasn't running away and I wasn't scared.

"I'm not scared."

I'd wanted to pretend to be normal in a reverse dress-up way. I wanted quiet. I wanted to get over all I'd done, all I'd seen, who I'd been. But also, I was so fucking scared.

I raced up the stairs, threw the slab of beef in a frying pan (because I owned a frying pan at this point in adult life), and showered while I waited. It was a short shower because the smell of meat was enough to send me salivating. I'd barely dried off when I dropped the towel and slap-slapped to the stove with wet feet. Grabbed a fork out of the dish drainer, dropped it, swore because how was going to eat this thick thing with a fork, and grabbed the meat out of the pan, obviously burning myself. It seemed natural to just bite it, just bite the meat instead of putting it on one of my thrift store plates, just bite the fucking thing. Only parts were hot—and those weren't the parts I went for.

I'd been cooking meat and eating normal shit for so long, but the thought of going right back into the lion's den after all this time, of facing the past, and *giving in* made me thirst for the raw blood. Like drinking liquid courage.

Naked, hair dripping in tendrils hiding my face, meat juice trailing down my tits, chest heaving with the need and effort of tearing through the thick dead thing, I felt alive again, real, instinctual. Powerful. Myself.

Then the fucking knock on the door.

I threw the chewed-up chunk back in the pan. "Uh, yeah, don't come in, I'm not…" glance at the pan, at my naked body in beast juices, "decent."

"Just making sure—"

"I feel much better today, thanks Mrs. Butter, I just, uh, I gotta go out for a while."

I could hear her tension, how annoyed she was that I wasn't welcoming her in. "Well, alright dear. Don't overdo it, now." And she putted off.

Time to get decent enough to throw normal away, at least for a while.

CHAPTER 6

The great part of being an irresponsible emotional vagabond is that when you suddenly drop everything to go on a manhunt, nobody misses you.

No job mattered, not even the steady bartending one I'd hung onto at The Full Sail. My boss liked me, and I liked him, but I was under no illusion that he couldn't replace me in a heartbeat. If I didn't come back, he'd forget all about me in a week.

Rose hadn't forgotten me, and that was the important thing. *She* was the important thing. A sick part of me was glad that she found me worth sticking to, whether it was to kill me or whatever. But I was a live wire too, nerves jumping to the surface of my skin, sparking whenever I thought of what I would have to *do*.

Because what could I do, as just Charity Blake?

Well, that had been Rose's gameplan right from the start, probably. Take away my firepower first, take a breather, then steal Psychiatrist. How could I fix this? What could I fix without being the Harpy?

You don't have to fix everything today, dumbass, just get Mortimer. Get him and get out alive.

But my fingers were shaking on the wheel, and the gray and brick buildings of Boston loomed over the tunnel mouth, waiting to swallow me. Tapping in my head, and screaming in my heart. I was heading right for the worst horror I'd known in so long—that kid. That kid who I'd failed and sent to Hell.

Having made it through the tunnel, the orange-yellow lights amplifying the headlights, the horns and screeches and whipping-by of metal multiplied by a million in that concrete cave, I needed something. Coffee was the only acceptable thing. Maybe it would settle the meat scrambling around in my stomach like live worms and the needling headache closing in.

No, not a headache. A sound.

Tap. Tap. Tap.

"What the actual fuck." Whatever had found my apartment, my safe little cozy apartment, had found me, *me*, here?

Obviously not. You're just coffee-deprived and freaking out, and that sound is your Kryptonite. Still getting to you.

"Hey, uh…GPS? Bring me to that coffee place I went to before." No response. What the hell was the name of that place? "The Thinking Cup!"

"THREE LOCATIONS ARE AVAILABLE," the GPS voice monotoned."

"Uh, the one near the hospital. Fuck you!" I yelled at a piece of shit Volvo that cut me off.

"I DO NOT UNDERSTAND. PLEASE REPEAT."

"No, not you, the one near the hospital."

"I DO NOT UNDERSTAND. PLEASE REPEAT. THREE LOCATIONS ARE—"

"Yeah, I know, goddammit. Um, the one near Beth Israel Deaconess."

"PLEASE REPEAT YOUR ANSWER."

"The one near Beth Israel Deaconess Hospital!" Honks resounding all around me. I'd missed a light. I didn't even know where I was going, I just sorta went.

Tap. Tap. Tap. Hooooonnnkk!

My brain was squealing with the tapping and my stomach lurched and I felt every car around me like jaws trying clamping shut. Driving in Boston was this constant fight or flight environment that I could not handle today.

Turned out I was only six minutes from The Thinking Cup, and I felt like I was fighting a fucking pack of bulls trying to get there, just get there and get to the next place, just go somewhere you sorta kinda know, maybe see a friendly face, then keep going. Regular life again. Get through one moment (*hooooonkkkk!*), make it to the next until you die.

"Please let there be a spot, please let there be a spot..." Lo and behold, there were actually two, and when I inevitably couldn't get the Psychiatrist Mobile into one (more honking), the next one did the trick. I gave the finger to everybody who passed me as I got out.

Deep breaths as I walked, trying to think of a happy place like every online meditation site says. Yes, I had looked at online meditation sites because goddamn did I need something these days.

Trouble was, I had no happy place to think of.

A couple of people in line. I was cool with that, gave me a minute to look around, remember the scent from last time, try to be present and all that.

"Fancy meeting you here."

I popped my eyes open from my second-long visual break and look who it is. "Brady, what's up?" The smile was doubly perfect today. His whole face crinkled up, his eyes, his stubbly cheeks, even his forehead.

"Theo, and hi." Still with the smile.

"You been sitting here since yesterday in case I came back? That's fucking weird."

His laugh actually turned the heads of the now four people in front of me. "I'm here kind of a lot, I uh, bring my laptop and—"

"Oh no, are you a troubled writer? Starbucks too cliché for you?"

"Nothing that exciting, I'm afraid. But you, you're here again. Do you have somebody at the hospital?" Concern intensified his dark brown eyes and the smile lines faded.

"Um, I did, but now I don't think so. And I have to go to…" Shit, where was I going? I'd been on autopilot, knew I needed to get to the Facility, but I did not know how to get there. Pretty sure GPS would have plenty to say about that.

"You need help finding a place?" he asked with way too much excitement. "I'm happy to provide a guided tour."

Deep breath, this time one of…relief. My shoulders dropped some. Wasn't this why I'd come, for a friendly face?

A friendly face I didn't want to see removed from his body. "Theo…"

"Oh, I don't like the sound of that," he said, eyes twinkling.

"Your own name? Okay then, Brady, I'm on this Hell mission and I don't want to drag you to Hell today."

"I've been there, it's okay." Most seductive tilt of his head, soft expression.

"Not like me you haven't," I said, my voice meek. I dropped my head because I could not be seen in public with this defeated, watery-eyed sadness. The new panic squirrel tried to climb out of my stomach again, and I got really hot.

"Charity?" Theo said, even closer to me. "Can I bring you over there to sit down? Huh? I'm gonna take your arm now, okay?" But I couldn't move to nod or the tears would spill. Something bad would happen if I moved, my mind told me.

He led me out of line by the hand, my head still down, over to a round table in the corner. Cooled down enough to look up, I saw a dark wood cabinet right next to me, a sliver of sunlight reaching us from the window across the café, and it was quiet. Relatively.

"You must have been here since dawn to get this table," I mumbled.

"Very astute," he said, pushing a sad purple laptop out of the way between us. "They let me in early. After I wash the windows."

That got my attention. "What, you work here?"

"I work anywhere I can," he said with a self-deprecating chuckle I recognized from Robbie's humbleness. I waited for him to go on. "I wash the windows a few times a week, they let me hang out here. It's kind of a… hub…for people who need odd jobs. Like a living community bulletin board."

I barely let the coffee cup touch the table when a waitress brought them over. I slugged it back, ignoring the burn in my throat, the heat in my belly sloshing around.

"You're okay?" Theo asked, leaning down a little to try and look in my eyes.

"Uh, yeah. Yeah, I guess I am. You've got a natural way of calming a person, don't you?"

He laughed. "Some might say that just means I'm too relaxed. Should have been a psychiatrist maybe."

I choked on my second coffee gulp, waved away the usual are-you-okay, and gathered myself.

What the hell was I doing here, drinking coffee with a stranger while Psychiatrist was out there, waiting for me to save him?

Had I needed someone to listen to me that badly that I just attracted one?

"Listen, what are you doing today? Really?"

"Really?"

"Yeah. I mean, if your friend is out of the hospital and all. Where are you from? Didn't you say…"

"No, I'm not from around here. Plymouth."

"Plymouth, Mass or Plymouth, New Hampshire?"

"Mass. Obviously."

"Why is that obvious?"

"Because no friend would make me go over state lines."

That boisterous laugh again, like a Santa Claus-level of jolliness. "Is that the friendship standard for you? Well, I would gladly cross state lines to hang out with you for a while, but I'd rather maybe take you to the aquarium. If you have time. If you're not busy."

I don't remember the last time someone really surprised me, but Theo did it. Who the hell goes to the aquarium in the middle of the week with a dude they met twice? And one of those times had to help them to a chair like a feeb?

"Um, that sounds great. It does. And I would actually love nothing more than just to blow this day off, but I gotta say no. Thanks, though."

"Okay," he said, leaning back in his chair. The black t-shirt stretched across his chest and it looked pretty good. Really good. Add stubble and boyish smile and he was the perfect guy to have meaningless sex with instead of doing…the shit I was doing. Honestly, getting naked with this guy would be excellent, but the intersection of my former bird-bitch life and my regular life were overwhelming suddenly. New regular life was not supposed to come with mythological side projects like doing a soccer mom pickup of my psychiatrist. It had to be all regular now.

And yet.

"You know what, Theo? Fuck it. Let's go to the aquarium."

Kid on Christmas face. "You're serious? You're serious! Okay! Let's go!"

"That's it? We just go now?" I asked. Jesus Christ, did I sound *shocked*? I felt shocked. Like it was some impossible thing that we had to plan for an hour at least.

His laugh made everything easy. "Yeah! Before you change your mind. Let's go. You good to walk? That garage is kind of a lot."

"Walk?"

He slowed for a second, assessing my complete fish-out-of-water reaction here, pun totally intended. "Yeah, walk. Is that okay? It will be about ten minutes, but we can absolutely drive over there, my car is right outside—"

"No, no, let's walk. It's good for me, right? And you. We should walk."

We passed the SUV which was weird because it belonged to the guy I was supposed to be saving. And instead I was going to play at the aquarium with a strange man. It was the most exciting thing I'd done in over a year. And on the reckless scale, the aquarium was way lower than rushing headfirst into a Harpy trap.

Catch ya later, Psychiatrist.

CHAPTER 7

If I'd learned anything about Boston this week it was that city people have a much different idea of an acceptable walk than I do. Yeah, it was ten minutes, but through more traffic and past historic buildings and around so many people. It felt like a year.

But that all changed as soon as we got to the aquarium. Still a ton of people, even in the snow, but when we stepped on the wharf—because this aquarium is on a fucking wharf, like on the ocean where the fish come from—it was like I was going through some invisible tunnel or some shit into a parallel universe. It went from crazy city with too much energy to the smell of the ocean, the cry of the seagulls like at the beach near my apartment. These giant boats with wheels were driving around, and one drove right into the water.

Duck boats, Theo said. I felt like I'd been in a box my entire life.

"Wait for it…" Theo said, rounding in front of me and walking backwards with more childlike enthusiasm than I had seen in any child.

When he stepped aside, I gasped.

Right there on the wood dock, boats all around and ticket booths and kiosks like at the mall, was a huge fishtank thing full of *seals.* Right there on the outside of the building.

I couldn't help it, I ran to it, put my hands on the tank, bent down so I was below the water line as if I were swimming right alongside them, submerged in that silent ocean in the middle of this world of anxiety and horror.

A big round seal surprised me, glided right up from below where I could see, inches, mere inches from my face! I fell back on my ass and laughed like I hadn't maybe in my entire life while the seal swam away smoothly, sweet face disappearing into the green murky water, same as the harbor behind it.

Theo held out his hand and pulled me to my feet. Second time that day he picked me up when I was down.

You are not going to like this guy a lot. No side attractions.

But his face was inches from mine, and the magic of all of it, his smile, the seals, the quiet in the storm, almost had me. Just for a second.

"Look at that, you're having fun already," Theo said sweetly, not even trying to take advantage of the moment at all.

"Yeah, I am," I said. "This is amazing."

"We haven't even gone inside yet," he said through a laugh.

I was more than ready to be surprised again.

~

"You can't go to the gift shop first, that's a crime against nature!" Theo exclaimed in the animated way with all the walking backwards to show me the extent of his enthusiasm thing he did. But it wasn't an act. It wasn't to show me how adorable he was or to make me laugh, it just *was*.

"Hey, you don't know what kind of crimes I'm capable of, mister," I joked.

But then I looked up.

A whale the size of an airplane loomed overhead, suspended from the ceiling in this concrete haven filled with bubbling gurgles and serene splashing. It was crazy, that the place was all gray concrete but was cozy. The blues, grays, greens here were nothing like the bitter reds and oranges of the Wood; the smooth, cool water was a slap in the face of the brutally thorny human trees, the brittle, blood-soaked hay, the talons tearing flesh. Everything in Hell was sharp. Never really thought about it, but the whole place was millions of razors, every one slicing my soul more and more with each visit, filling it with heat and fury. *Furies...* Weren't they bird-bitches too?

When I looked away from the sea beasts hanging from the ceiling, sharks and skeletons and blue neon, I saw Theo had already gone ahead to lean over a wall. "Whatcha—"

But I didn't have to ask what he was looking at. Over the edge was a pool the size of the whole bottom floor below us, filled with hundreds of penguins on rocks and diving into the Hugh Hefner grotto-blue water. Some sped underneath the wall, swimming faster than the seals had outside, others were being thrown fish from a bucket by some lucky bitch in a scuba suit, and some ruffled their feathers being sprayed by fountains between the rock formations.

"I know, right?" Theo put his head on his crossed arms leaning on the wall. I'd honestly never seen anyone in my life so completely untroubled. I'd never been anywhere that beautiful, and he was the perfect person to appreciate it with.

I do not fucking think so, Charity. You're here for a day trip, not even, and this guy is not anyone you'll see again. Because if you do, shit will happen.

"Let's keep going," I said, and he pulled away reluctantly.

Floors and floors of huge tanks filled with seahorses more fairy-tale-ish than any unicorn, a bunch of different giant ugly-ass gray fish that looked like they'd been caught right off the murky Boston dock outside, poisonous frogs, all kinds of animals I'd never seen in person and mostly knew nothing about. A whole world of them.

I'd been all over the world and seen none of it.

I bet Rose has been here a bunch of times, I thought. I saw how amazing this place was for a little kid—they were running all over the place, squealing and laughing. I was jealous.

Tap. Tap. Tap.

Stifling a groan, I squeezed my eyes shut against the noise. It had no place here.

In the center of the aquarium was this winding circular ramp that wound around this ridiculous cylinder tank that went from the floor to the ceiling.

"You know what?" Theo said. "This tank is over 200,000 gallons of water."

"Seriously?"

Nooks were built into the sides of the ramp where I could sit on a concrete window bench and just melt into watching the ocean inside and the coral reef that made up the middle of the tank. We propped ourselves up in one of these semi-private viewing booths, him with one dirty sneaker up on the bench, leaning against the wall. He was nice to watch against the water. Like he could just slip through the glass and be part of that world like Ariel or some shit. I started laughing thinking about it, then had to explain myself.

"I just pictured you as a mermaid in there."

"Mer*man*!" he cried, fist raised.

"I love Zoolander."

"Everybody should."

A giant blue fish swam by him and he traced a finger along the glass with it.

Fuck, that was a burst of feeling I hadn't had in a very, very long time. A gushing crush feeling that made my stomach turn, but not like with too much meat in it.

"Tell me something about you, Charity." His voice was unintentionally sultry.

"Turns out I like long walks through the aquarium."

"Well, that makes me happy. How about something not related to today or me, or this aquarium?"

"Why ruin it?"

"Ruin what?" Cute puppy tilt of the head.

"This day. I don't…"

"Don't what?" he asked, leaning forward, that same concern from the coffee shop on his face.

"I don't get days like this. Or I never had a day like this, I guess. I mean, I could, but I never thought about it this year, like this year has been a totally new life for me, and I kinda like it but also it's boring as fuck, you know? And I never thought of doing something fun."

"I won't ask what you do for fun then."

My throat closed up. "I don't do anything for fun. Not anymore. And my version of fun in the past was… I have a new life now."

"A not fun life."

"Exactly. Your life must be nothing but fun, am I right?"

"It's pretty fun today," he said.

A shark with long needle teeth badly in need of braces swim by next to us, blank eye still and black.

"Jesus Christ," I whispered.

"I think it's a sand shark? Or a lemon shark? Nasty, huh? But not as nasty as that." Theo pointed at a hole in the reef where a moray eel the color of pea soup was showing off fangs and bloating up his gross gills.

"Thank you," I blurted.

"For what?"

Why am I talking like this? Shut up and look at the fucking fish. "Thank you for making me do this today. I didn't know what I was missing. I imagine I've been missing kind of a lot in the bottom of a bottle and in bad relationships and in Hell."

"I'm sorry no one has shown you this before. And that you haven't had an easy life."

"Well, it's not like I make life easy on myself or anybody else either."

He glanced down, as if measuring what he would say, and I hadn't seen him work that hard to come up with something to say yet. It would be a doozy, probably.

"I don't think life is supposed to be easy," he said, brows knitted together. "I think those of us who make sure it is tricked the system. Because it's definitely a system. Life is a pattern, we're all part of the pattern, and that's a system, right?" His adam's apple bobbed like it hurt to speak, and his eyes were as dark as that shark's when he spoke again. "I won't be part of a system that steals from me anymore. I'll enjoy what I have whether The Man likes it or not." Every tooth showed after that.

I leaned forward, a hand on the cold concrete bench, a school of fish shading the light of the tank. I wanted to kiss him. His lips were really soft-looking, and if he kissed like he smiled, it would be a burst of sunshine in winter.

"You want to…" he started.

"I do. Should I?"

"Should *I*?"

"You should."

Little kid voices went, "Oooooooh," when our lips met, as the sunshine seeped in.

It lasted only a second or two, and it was perfect. It fit in with the day instead of becoming it.

We continued up the ramp, round and round the tank, hand in hand. At the top, the tank was wide open, an uncovered fishbowl. Giant sea turtles grazed lettuce at the top, their speckly heads poking out of the water. The hollow of the reef descended into a darkness with flecks of magenta and orange fish darting in and out. The sharks that were so menacing in the lower levels blended in up here, bothering no one, no matter how scary they were up close. And we could see all the way down, rings and rings, deeper and deeper, layers upon layers of wild creatures that only became more beautiful with each tier, like a wedding cake.

Descending the ramps wasn't as nice. Going down, down, stopping at some of the windows to sit on the sills again, but none of them felt the same as when we were going up. Each level became darker, and my heart grew a little tighter when we reached the bottom. Those rings around that wound around the tank, when I looked back they seemed like they were squeezing the reef, not hugging it.

"Every ring has its reason, everything works together in there. A whole different ecosystem, right? It's amazing. A place where everything has a place." Theo's head was tilted back, looking the tank up and down one final time.

I kissed him again then. I don't know why.

He licked his lips when we parted, savoring it like he savored everything. "Come on," he said, and brought me to a low pool with another lucky bitch in a New England Aquarium polo shirt and mom jeans with a microphone standing over it, answering high-pitched questions from a couple of tiny kids. When a couple of people moved on, we weaseled up to the waist-high pool.

All glass so that if you knelt down—which I immediately did—you were right at fish-level. But there weren't fish in this water.

Stingrays. Or manta rays, something like that, but rays, gliding directly in front of me and far across the shallow water over smooth beach sand. A wide expanse, with only the occasional bushel of sea grass or tall rock formation that jutted from the water on top. Slight, slow beats of ray wings pushed them through the golden-lit water in huge circles.

My hands were splayed on the glass as one glided belly-up along the edge, showing me its white belly without a care in the world, unafraid to show its most tender skin, the whip-like tail a quiet warning that the creature was not defenseless.

This was my favorite place to be, under the water level, pretending I was in that silent water with them. Cool, quiet, the opposite of the worst place I'd ever been, wishing I could feel as at home in that water as I had in the Wood of Suicides.

I'd slipped into my head, but got jolted out when a hand appeared in front of my face in the water. Theo's.

"Holy fuck, you can put your hand in there!" I cried. Parents huffed as I shot to my feet and stuck my hand in the water beside Theo's. Cool, silky. I could dive right into that shit. It looked like Theo was about to, he was leaning forward so hard.

I saw why.

A shark.

Little, like the length of my forearm, with thick black stripes, sitting peacefully on the sandy bottom.

There were more, tucked away between the sea grass, a few swimming lazily with the rays.

Theo took my hand under the water, placed it on

the little shark who'd edged closer as if he liked it. Maybe I imagined it, but maybe I didn't. Couldn't this silent little predator want to be touched?

More high-pitched screeching from preschool children, and I was getting antsy that these beautiful animals should just be left alone by anyone but me and Theo. They were part of the regular world and we... I...was not.

For a brief, puke-worthy second, I envisioned grabbing that little shark and biting into him with all my jaws' strength until his pink insides showed through the crescent-shaped remains of his body.

That's when I puked into the tank.

"Ohhhh no," I moaned, lifting myself upright, though, as was my new habit, I sure as shit didn't want to make eye contact with anyone. Vomit spread like a disease through the water. Little sharks jerked out of their bottom-feeder daze to grossly gobble up the seeping sludge.

Screeching memories of Harpies, flocking to mutilated, undead bodies razor-cut across my vision.

I stumbled back, Theo caught me—again—and we raced out of there, followed by the announcement for cleanup on aisle five and a cacophony of disgusted cries.

*H*is arm wrapped around my shoulders tightly, we hurried out of the aquarium, him murmuring to me, but I couldn't understand what he was saying. It was all just twisting gut, red flashes of Harpy claws, screeches, puke, red meat in clumps, pulsing with a heartbeat, twitching, the ice-cold air, the simmering heat of Hell.

"Sit, sit, sit," I caught Theo repeating, pushing me gently onto a bench by the water. "Breathe, in deep through your nose. Charity. Breathe in deep through your nose. Yeah! Just like that, hold it. Hold it. Let it out through your mouth."

"Like puke?" I rasped, my throat aching from the heave.

"Yeah," he said through a laugh, "like puke in a shark tank. Stay right here, I'm going right over there for a bottle of water. Okay? Right over there."

Everything rippled around me, drunken waves of light and sound and brick and moving people walking on mushy ground, I focused on Theo, his jeans dark against the grays, the sure steps he took to the kiosk, not the sweat dripping down my back, the cold biting my fingers, the images I couldn't kick.

He jogged back, smiling at a passerby who caught his eye, twisted the cap off for me. "Slow sips for now, okay?"

Icy water shocked me back to the reality, made the moving fever dream around me solidify, and I became nightmarishly aware of the sickly slick on my forehead, the dryness of my lips, the burn of my stomach—

Rose.

Tap. Tap. Tap. Taptaptaptaptap...

"Hey, hey, you're alright."

My steps were slow, muddy, but I felt like I was moved by propellers with the city and the flurries of snow whipping past my face, more honking cars and sirens, until at the end of time we got back to the SUV. But I couldn't drive. I couldn't even think of it.

"It's getting late, Charity," Theo said. His voice was full of hesitation and doubt when he drawled out, "What do you want to do now?"

What *could* I do? Nothing about Mortimer, not now.

Guilt stabbed me in the chest. I'd played at the fucking aquarium while Rose did whatever she was doing to him. Gritting my teeth, I tried to convince myself I could go, that I had to *right now*, that he couldn't spend the night with her.

But the city lights blared, the noise changed, the streets I could barely navigate in daylight were slick with snow. And I was weak. Weak as fuck. Human and making myself sick, and scared, and how would I face Rose like this? What could I do now or ever? I shook off the rising wave of anxiety that would quickly morph into panic.

"You know about this place?" I said for no reason, because who the hell would know about a place in the city dredges called the Facility? "It's like, an old medical building or something? Maybe office building in parts, I dunno…"

"You're kinda slurry, there. I think we should talk about this somewhere warm where we can get you actual food. Pasta. You should have pasta, my mom always said, fills you up and sits in your belly like a pasta pillow. Trattoria II Panino is right—"

"No, no more public places. Sorry. I mean, today was awesome, but I blew it obviously and you've seen me freak the fuck out twice today or more. I don't always freak out, I… I kinda do now, but I have to get to this Facility—"

"Okay, okay, but you can't today, kid."

Kid.

"You called me kid."

"I do that, sorry."

"No, no, I like it. It reminds me of someone in a good way. I don't have many good memories left of her."

Tap.

Fucking hell, I couldn't keep a train of thought, I had to come across as absolutely mental, and the tapping…

"Charity. You can't think straight, and that's okay," he rushed to finish when he saw I got mildly offended —even though I'd just thought the same thing myself. "I lose myself in my head way too much. Way too much. I know how it looks." A wince, second-guessing his words. "And I know what PTSD looks like, too. You need food now. And rest. Listen, I'm gonna get you a hotel room, some room service, and you'll feel better tomorrow."

Everything stilled. Suddenly I was able to breathe in a whiff of the more heavily falling snow. I could see the lights without being blinded. And I could see him. Flakes clinging to his messy hair, the collar of his black coat.

"You would do that for me? You don't even know me," I said.

He shook his head, like he didn't get it. "I know you enough. It doesn't matter anyway, you need help, right?"

Dumbstruck. "Right. Thanks. Thanks, Theo."

After that it was really easy to give in. I sat in the passenger seat of the SUV which Theo said was "infinitely better" than his. The heated seat was the most fantastic thing that had ever been put into any car. The snow melted off me, the fear and sadness melted off me, and something else melted off me as I watched Theo jog with his head high, not stooped over like everyone else in the snow, to and from the Italian restaurant up the street.

"Room service takes too long, and this is as good as any home-cooked meal," he said, grinning like mad when he got in the SUV with a stack of take-out boxes. When I raised my eyebrows at the sheer amount of stacked containers, he said, "I know the chef."

"You didn't have—"

He stopped me, though. He didn't have to, he wanted to.

The unbelievably rich, mouthwatering scent of the food coupled with the warmth of the seat and the company put me at more ease than I think I'd ever been in my entire life.

"Why are you bringing me to a hotel?" I asked.

"Because you weren't in any shape to drive."

"But not to your place?"

"I didn't think that would make you feel comfortable. And also it's gross."

"I can't pay for a hotel, and you can't pay for one for me. You've done enough. Your place is fine. I like gross. It works for me. I guarantee it's a step up from places I've been."

He thought it over. "If you change your mind—"

"Theo, I'm good. You don't scare me and I can handle myself. I…trust you."

"Well, thank you."

"Now how fucking far away do you live because I'm about to eat right out of the container."

"Be my guest, it's your car."

At which point I told him that no it wasn't, and I needed to find Psychiatrist which is what I was doing in the city in the first place. To which he said that it seemed like a really inconvenient psychiatrist then.

"What's this?"

Seconds later, I mean literal seconds, we pulled up

to a dark parking garage. No lights, no attendant, just a card that he scanned and didn't answer me.

"Where the hell is this? This isn't an apartment."

"Relax, it's my apartment's parking garage. You're okay."

But my stomach was churning again and I gripped the pasta containers like weaponry. Without claws, was I anyone in a situation like this? What had I done? I remembered Meat Matt telling me this might be the dangerous position I didn't see myself out of. I didn't want him to be right. But I wasn't defenseless, I'd been in more fights than Mike Tyson. And I was resourceful. And fast. Fast-ish.

Theo told me not to panic, that this was his apartment, that there were plenty of people around and maybe his apartment wouldn't be quite what I was expecting.

Great. A dungeon then.

Once we got out though, I didn't bolt, I just followed through. I said I trusted him, so I would. Try to. I would try to.

"You live in a fucking mall?"

Out of the garage we entered a legit mall. Palm trees running down the middle of a narrow row of stores, but fancy stores. Fancy brick. Fancy benches.

"I don't live in a mall. Look up."

Balconies over the shops, that went up a few floors. "Your backyard is a mall?"

He laughed. "Yeah, that's more like it."

Into an elevator, up two floors, and his fucking apartment was the furthest thing from gross. It was insane. Huge windows, cornflower blue paint, hardwood floors, exposed brick, exposed beams, exposed secret that he was obviously rich.

"How is this gross? Are you kidding me?"

He fell onto a couch that looked straight out of the fanciest IKEA catalog they make. "Okay, it's not gross, but I didn't want to talk about me, okay? I wanted to talk about you. You needed it, I needed it, and all this is just an apartment."

And come to find out, his odd jobs that he performed were really more along the realm of building management because he owned most of Hanover Street. And he didn't earn it, he got fed it by a father with questionable morals.

"Your dad's in the mob."

"I never said that."

"Your dad's in the mob."

I ate baked ziti in a pair of pink sweatpants a girlfriend had left—a long time ago, he clarified—and the t-shirt I'd been in all day. The wall of windows framed by old brick gave a heavenly view of the snow, putting me in it instead of under it. Theo put a cup of tea from the café in his mall yard into my hand, even though I was pretty sure it'd been closed. I got the impression that mob boy didn't have to worry about stuff like that.

My eyes were blurring, and I was about to fall into the gentlest sleep, one I desperately needed, when Theo insisted I take his bed and he'd take the couch. I want the couch, I told him. He said he'd change the sheets though. I told him I didn't even remember the last time I'd changed my own sheets. And I definitely had never slept high enough to be one with the snow, with a fake fire in the fake fireplace, and I would be sleeping on the couch, thank you very much.

"We'll talk more tomorrow," Theo said as I nodded off on his surprisingly comfy sofa. And a kiss as gentle as the sugar sifter snow landed on my forehead.

Tap. Tap. Tap.

I'd slept dreamlessly but woke to a nightmare where the tapping had fucking followed me still, through the aquarium, through the night, out of that town and into this city and I knew I couldn't be going crazy. I'd been close enough and come back so many times.

No, this was from the outside. This sound had *found* me.

"Theo?" No answer.

I changed into my clothes from the day before, fast. I had not one more second to waste.

"Where you going?"

Theo came in, fisherman's sweater and jeans, looking more put together than any guy I'd ever associated with aside from Evan in the beginning, holding yet more food from his mall yard. Danishes. He had a thing for danishes. I took one and the coffee that came with it and tried not to slug it down. Because for as much as I needed to get on with my real, regular life, I'd be lying if I didn't say I'd fallen for this whisked away like a princess to a tower and given coffee treatment. The peace of it.

"I have to find my psychiatrist."

Big gulp of coffee for him. "So that wasn't the panic attack talking, huh?"

"Nope. Gotta find the Facility—been there a bunch of times, still can't ever figure out where it is—and get my psychiatrist back."

To Theo's credit, he didn't seem overly concerned. Mob boss kids, man. They've probably seen some shit. But he did start asking questions, and who was I to deny him that after how good he'd been to me?

Me. A rando at a coffee shop who looked like everybody else and freaked the fuck out at the slightest... anything. Like one of those wolf children from the rainforest or whatever, suddenly put into society.

So, I told him stuff. About Rose, that she was in trouble, that she was possibly definitely behind the kidnap of my psychiatrist, and no, I didn't care to go into that. Mob Boss Boy didn't even suggest calling the cops which saved me a lot of breath in argument. And the unbelievable shit of a hidden hospital or some crap and some off-the-books doctors didn't even faze him.

As a matter of fact...

"This place, it's called..." he asked.

"Here's the thing, it's called the Facility." And I described it to him, the stuff around it, anything I could remember because he was clearly processing it actively. He was really listening, not judging. Not waiting for the time he could say it wasn't possible. He just…believed me.

"I might know a guy who knows about this place," Theo said.

"Mob kid. You probably always know a guy, huh?"

He laughed, easing back in the leather chair across from my claimed space on the couch. "You meet a lot of people when you're—"

"Looking for odd jobs?" I finished with a laugh. "And yet you don't strike me as the real handy type? I see not one tool box or grease smudge anywhere around your little backyard mall palace," I teased.

His dark brown eyes glinted. "I think we both know those aren't the kinds of odd jobs I do best."

I didn't ask and he didn't elaborate.

We both made phone calls. Me on my shit phone to Butter, who was more than happy to feed Keegan and surprisingly sounded relieved to hear from me. Theo to who knows what contacts he had, and before I was able to raid his kitchen, he had a lead.

"This place, it doesn't have a pleasant reputation," he said.

"Yeah, whatever you've heard, it's probably worse."

He scrunched up his face like he'd stepped on a pin. "I won't let you…I don't want you to go alone. I know you can handle yourself, but you shouldn't have to. And I might be handier than I look."

"Even for a guy who actually owns a cake stand?" I said, brushing past him to the kitchen.

"I don't think that's what they're called," he said, a little shyness in his voice, as I lifted the glass dome and took out some weird muffin thing. Lemon something or other, but it was delicious.

"Fine, you can tag along, but only if you drive my psychiatrist's SUV and buy me food whenever possible. Turns out I'm a comfort food eater." I mean, if this wasn't a meat-eating monster hunt, I don't know what is, but all I wanted was carbs. Carbing up for the big game, maybe. Rose was nothing if not the big game.

Tap. Tap. Tap.

I dropped the muffin with an involuntary suck of breath, my body stiffening.

Whenever I thought of Rose—

TAPTAPTAPTAPTAP.

"Charity?"

Terror seized my throat, made tears spring to my eyes, or they watered because I couldn't blink, couldn't stop them from bulging. When I finally could suck in a breath, I said, "She's listening."

"*A*ll this time, it was in my head but *she* put it there…"

"You're freaking me out just a little, I gotta tell you," Theo said from the driver's seat. "You went white as a ghost, kid, and you're talking about someone in your head."

"All the time I was at home and thought the tapping was on the roof, I was so *paranoid*. But I wasn't always thinking of her when it happened, the tapping. There was—is—this tapping in my head, and the kid I told you about, well not to scare you but she's like, tele-pathic. More than that, but we'll start there. And she, uh, she's not happy with me. At all. And I keep hearing this sound, but I thought it was just a sound, but now, I think she's messing around in my mind. I haven't talked to her in like a few months, and she's got my psychiatrist, and she wants me."

Theo blinked a lot, let out a long breath. "I mean, are you sure she's doing this? I haven't known you that long but it sure seems like you're under a hell of a lot of stress…""This isn't PTSD. The kid has been in my head before, I know what it feels like. This isn't the same, but it feels like her. It's coming from outside, but it's an outside that knows me inside. She's coming for me *in my own fucking head.*"

She'd been in there before, but not like this. This wasn't the chisel, that sickle, digging. It was more of a powerful reminder of pain and a promise.

"You know where you're going?" I asked, clutching my head, waiting for the next round. "'Cause I don't remember. I got nothing. I shoulda drawn a fucking treasure map, but I was led there by heat, light, feeling. By her."

"Charity, you're not making a lot of sense. My guy told me where to go. Just…close your eyes, you'll need your head clear. I get the feeling we won't be welcomed warmly."

"Never am." I took his advice, closed my eyes against the ricocheting sun, snow, guardrails, cars. *Deep breaths. Get angry, because you're walking right into it, just like you knew you were.* Rose had probably planned it all along. Drawn me in, and she had all the advantages now.

I had nothing. No talons to claw their way out through my toes, ready for ripping. No beak to render flesh, no needle-feathers and dry, hard skin on my legs, only this unending restlessness and fear. And sadness. Feelings I had to use as a weapon when I had nothing else.

Like someone who actually had listened to their psychiatrist once upon a time.

A psychiatrist that was now a basket case, and I had to rescue him. Crazy fucking world we live in. Not the one I wanted. Not one I *didn't* want—the aquarium had changed that droning, pitiful struggle to like normalcy for me—but one I didn't have. I didn't get the life I thought I would after being the Harpy. Once I turned away from the Dark Side, shouldn't I have gotten some reward, some kind of *win* for once? At least the knowledge that I'd helped the kid? Instead after a year, it was all on the attack and nothing of reunion. Nothing of love. Love I felt like I had fucking earned. That I'd started to believe I was worthy of, and then it was ripped away from me, and from her.

Pissed me the fuck off.

Try to do right by women of the world, and get everyone I love killed or worse, make the only thing that made me feel worthwhile feel disgusting—making me feel disgusting for wanting it so badly—and what do I end up with? A nosy old lady, a dive bar job, and interchangeable panic and anxiety, along with a meat-covered teenager that I told my woes to.

Suddenly, a screeching crunch assaulted my ears.

Glass beat my cheeks and eyelids.

Theo let out this howl of shock, and I realized I was screaming too. I'd thrown my arms up—not soon enough to save my face—and my elbows smacked into the roof.

Car horns blared from every direction. Tires squealed. More crunching and metal crashing outside.

Theo's hands, covered in blood, still gripped the wheel, swinging it crazy. I reached over and steadied it.

"What is it!" he screamed.

"We're still moving forward, keep us steady!" The windshield was demolished, leaving a monstrous hole, so at least he could see out. I looked up to see the roof crushed in, with three—no, four—giant holes over my head.

Four more near his.

Another rush of metal and screaming when the pounce came again. Talons pierced the roof, each as long as my finger. This time, the space where the windshield had been closed up like an envelope, blinding us to the outside, and we'd stopped. Outside my passenger window cars had stopped, faces paralyzed in silent screams as they took in the monster ripping its way through the SUV roof toward Theo and me.

"Harpy!" I cried out.

"Harpy? What the—what?"

"Giant bird lady, she's not nice, just, just…"

It pushed off the mangled roof, jolting the SUV.

"Is it leaving?" Theo whispered, wide-eyed. Purple bloomed around his eyes.

"No, it's getting ready to pounce again, get out!"

But the SUV was crushed like a beer can, doors included, and we stood no chance on the outside anyway.

The Harpy smashed against my window, a mess of feathers and burning eyes, shrieking wildly, and nabbed my shoulder with one nasty talon, ripping a hole right through it.

Bursts of blinding pain took over where the glass shards left off, turning my vision red. But that sharp stab was nothing beside the slow build of agony racing through my blood, a hot stove burning that crept up until it was all I knew.

My legs twisted, the bones knotting and unknotting, as fast as the skin splitting on the backs of my arms was slow and meandering.

Outside, more screeching of both wheels and Harpy, but all I could register was the torture of being in my own body, and a sneaking fear of the next massive crack against the car that would drag me into the open.

Theo was calling my name, but I couldn't look at him, couldn't see past the Harpy inside, destroying regular me to claw its way out.

"—to run!" Theo cried right into my ear.

Sirens approached, louder than the bird-bitch squawkings.

"Where is she?" I mumbled, my voice like IHOP syrup. My mouth stretched, ached, begging to become the beak.

"Hey, stay with me," Theo said in a voice so solid and quiet that it drowned everything else out. "You've lost some blood, but you're tough as nails, Charity. Stay with me and let's *go*."

I blinked hard, focused on my limbs. He was right. My body wasn't changing, nothing was breaking below the skin; there were no Harpy parts left. Rose's Harpectomy had left me...human. Defenseless. And blood-soaked.

Twisting to the right I could make out the Harpy—

now two—at a distance, clawing and gouging each other in the sky.

"Yup, time to go," I said, and forced myself onto my knees in the seat as Theo pounded the door that was never gonna open. I smashed the rest of my passenger window with my fist in the tight quarters. It crumbled and I scrambled out in a mess of knees and elbows and bloody hands and fifteen pounds ago it would have been a lot easier. Taller, more muscular Theo couldn't get out, would never be able to wrench himself into the position that I could, even in my heroin-not-so-chic body.

The cop cars and an ambulance came to a halt skirting the edges of the clusterfuck of encircling cars and trucks and an eighteen-wheeler on its side.

"Get out of here," Theo said, when I ran to the driver's side. His words struggling, sweat drenching his forehead with no traces of those laugh lines now behind two black eyes.

"I'm staying. The cops and fire trucks are here, they'll get to you fast."

"But you—"

"I'm good, I can take multiple hits. Just stop moving, take deep breaths, they're coming for you."

And that's when they came for me, too.

A different they.

"No!" I yelled, like the bird-bitch would listen, like I stood a chance when it grabbed my shoulders and hips at the same time and picked me up like a pill bug from my crouch. In seconds I was higher than the overpass, looking down at the wreckage of the highway, claw tips scraping my shoulder bones, watching people run around through a blur, shadows and ants, shadows and ants as I struggled not to pass out from the searing pain.

"Shut up," it hissed, voice alarmingly human. I took that as my cue to stop fighting, tried not to let Carl Painter pop into my head telling me to do the same, always popping in to add his two cents, and blurred my eyes to the terror.

Painter drifting away, highway drift away, Theo and Mortimer and Rose drifting away, I let myself drift away, over the occasional tree and the rows of city buildings. I was gone, and I let myself be. Eventually I'd end up somewhere and I'd fight again. That was inevitable.

CHAPTER 9

*I*didn't anticipate that when I burst into consciousness after being flying-monkeyed away, that I'd be snuggled in a comfy bed.

"Dude, am I in the Facility?" I said like it was the most magical thing ever, like I'd woken up in fucking Disneyworld.

"Yes, now lie back down. She'll be here soon."

"Where's Theo?" I snapped, suddenly jarred into memory. A sensation like broken eggshells being poured into my veins. "Right now, tell me where the fuck he is."

"I don't know a Theo, miss. But she will be here soon."

I'd wait, but not long. In this bed, with an IV, with ginger ale on the cart-table thingy.

"Was this blanket seriously warmed up in the dryer?" I asked the nurse. Regular nurse. Regular IV like every other time I'd been to the ER, same smile all nurses gave.

"Would you like some tea?" she asked.

Heavy sigh. Heavier fears. "I would. I want the tea. I like the blanket a lot. Super comfortable. Why?" Why were they putting me back together and welcoming me like this just to turn around and murder me? Because I was definitely getting murdered. This entire transaction reeked of murder. They'd probably murdered Theo, the poor bastard, he had nothing to do with this, should never have had anything to do with me. I'd let him. I'd let him even though I knew better.

I gasped when the nurse reached out and put a hand on my head, looked into my eyes, that sedate, lovely smile reassuring me. "It's okay," she said with full, red lips. "I'll be back with tea in a minute." I watched her walk out, the pretty thing, like a movie nurse, and it wasn't until the door clicked—and locked—shut behind her that I looked around the room. Big. Brick walls on two sides, and a window. A *window*? Had to be some kind of crazy glass that didn't break and nobody could see me through. Like the one-way mirror on the wall to my right. Bed was in the middle of the room, tons of space around it but I felt at ease, not exposed. Safe, even though I was being watched.

"What the hell is happening?" I muttered, and wondered if I'd been miked somewhere, alien abduction-style.

As promised, in came the nurse with the tea in this

little plastic mug the color of mud. I took a deep sip of it and wished the mug was bigger because goddamn if I didn't feel like a fucking princess wrapped in a warm blankie with a cup of tea, being doted upon and having nothing around me, nothing to do, nothing to run from, nothing to save, nothing to be, except right here being taken care of.

The nurse sat on the edge of my bed, same sweet smile, laid the back of her hand on my forehead in a way that I knew would tell her nothing about my temperature that she didn't already know. It was to comfort me, lure me in. This was a setup to draw me in. "She's not your enemy, you know," she said warmly.

"Doubt that's true." She could have been talking about anybody, my answer would have been the same. Nobody was this kind without wanting something.

"Would she have brought you here if she wanted to hurt you, Charity?"

The use of my name stopped me mid-sip because I knew that ploy. Psychiatrist—before I called him Mortimer—used to say my name like, six dozen times per appointment, to lure me into believing that he considered me a real person, keep me coming back.

"Just because you know my name doesn't make me want to join your murder team."

Then the super nice nurse leaned close, her breath smelling of mint with a hint of red meat behind it. "You're the team captain, darling," she said.

"No fucking way!" I said, excitement rivaling seeing

Little Debbie's face in the back of a cabinet after too long without a meal. "You're a Harpy!"

She quirked an eyebrow, ruby lips puckered. "In the flesh." She savored the last word as if tasting it right then and there.

"But you're…"

Her laugh was guttural, nothing like the laugh of this svelte beauty before me should be. "Normal?" She stood with grace, held her arms out on display, untalony fingers poised like a hand model. "This is what can become of all of us, Charity. We can rise from the ashes the way we were always meant to be."

This was some kind of crazy-ass magic, this wasn't Harpy realm at all. The hunched half-humans and feral cannibals of the Wood of Suicides couldn't have normaled this much with a script and a stylist.

What did you do, Rose?

I already knew, though. Rose would do whatever she wanted. No, more than that. She'd do whatever it took.

"Tell me more," I asked the nurse, who now seemed preoccupied with her own body, watching her arms move. "I bet the air feels good, huh?" Considering that where she lived the air was so *chunky* feeling, meat soup to breathe in, not to mention the color of fresh blood.

She stopped to take me in, her watchfulness definitely a Harpy's. "The child did this for me. She has given me a life again and I would follow her to the end of time."

Yup. That was some Charlie Manson shit right there.

"You got like, wing holes in the back of that old timey costume?" I asked. I mean, the nurse outfit even had that little hat that I'm pretty sure they used in Dubya Dubya Two. Her wings—black, nondescript as far as Harpy couture goes—sprung from her shoulder blades. Not like mine that erupted from the backs of my arms like mutant goosebumps. The feathers ran down her arms, Teen Wolf style, stopping at normal hands. Slender, human legs. Nothing special about her, not really.

"Remember," she said, grabbing my hand, "she can offer you more than the world."

And she left me with my warm blanket and warm tea and a sickening cold in my gut that had me wishing for hot blood to smother it.

Every fucking time I got scared, the first place I went was the thirst for blood, for the love of shit! Who the hell wants *to eat living things and taste blood* as their comfort food? Well, anyone who knew how strong it would make them feel, that's who. And I sure needed some inner strength real fast.

Silence but for the distant hum of the air conditioning—which paired with my warm cocoon like Pabst and steak.

Steak.

The smell of red meat filled my nostrils out of nowhere, and Rose sailed in through the door, never even reached out a hand to open it. Her movement was so slight, she could have been floating, ghostly in a loose white sundress. But Rose was no damaged kid anymore.

The glow of fire in the pit of her stomach that used to show up when she was angry was just *there* now, showing through. Her bare arms, her thin legs, her round little face, made me wince.

Every inch of her skin was a searing red, like the hottest sunburn, her blonde hair even brighter yellow against it. She couldn't have looked more like Satan himself if she tried. That white dress was probably the only thing she could wear that didn't hurt. But the worst of all this hot horror she'd become, was her eyes. Because her eyes—they were cold.

"Looking hot, Red," I said weakly.

"You look good," she said back, and it shocked me. Her voice was just a kid's. Barely more mature than when we met. Despite the inhuman terror she was now, I got teary, goddammit. I turned away, spilled the tea on myself and cursed, which always made me feel better.

"Yeah, thanks, been working out," I muttered.

"My mom used to do aerobics at the Gloria Stevens—"

"I haven't really been working out, kid. Look, what is this? You run the Facility now? Harpy nurses and stuff? Hardly seems like the lofty goals you had your sights set on." Might as well get right to it.

"I'm just...staying here, I guess." She swished her bare foot back and forth, avoiding my eyes.

I was not prepared for her to talk to me like a kid, as if we'd not been through everything ever, and she wasn't a murder monster, but a *child.* I'd had every intention of coming here for a showdown until I eventually was killed, and maybe then, if she regretted my murder, Rose would see the error of her ways but at least hopefully I'd get Mortimer free. I'd tried to abolish the thought that Rose was as good as my own little sister, my only family, even if I'd made it up, and now she was that kid again. Alone, fragile. She was...

Manipulating me. She was manipulating me.

"I'm not manipulating you," she said.

"Get out of my head."

Her voice cracked when she said, "I can't stay out of your head." She swallowed a lump in her throat, frowning. Shit, she was in pain. *Don't let her get to you.*

"You've been tapping around in there like you're cracking a fucking egg, kid."

"I can...see...when you're in familiar places, or when your guard is down. I see," hard swallow, "when you think of me. Not always. Only lately, if I'm too close. I can't be too close." She put a delicate hand to her temple. The one simple motion tore a hole in my heart. With a deep breath, she gathered herself, brought her chin up, became the powerful girl I admired. "I don't want to fight you, Charity. You've hurt me, left me, gave up on me, but it doesn't matter. I still want you with me," she pleaded with very, very convincing tears in her startling blue eyes.

Tears hit my cheeks, I grit my teeth and sneered them away. "You wanted me with you, what have you been doing for the past like, 200 fucking days?"

"Planning," she said simply. "Planning how to make the Wood what we wanted, remember? Release the trees, make it better for the Harpies, but I can go so much further than that. I can take what we wanted for the Wood and make it so much bigger, go deeper. I needed time...to think over what happened. And I thought I could heal myself, so I tried, over and over, but...some things I can't do. My brain, it wants the memories."

There was so much ambition there, destroying her, but I couldn't get past her clear sadness. She had to have been so lonely, so afraid, trying to fix her brain. "I never wanted to hurt you, Rose. I was trying to do what was best for you, kid. I could have been with you all this time."

"You would have held me back. You weren't ready to see what I wanted you to see, how much we could do together below."

"Fine, but you coulda called for chrissakes. You didn't have to make me wonder if death was around every corner for months, then send the brigade to goddamn pulverize Psychiatrist's car, and take my friend."

"I didn't mean to hurt Robbie."

"Don't!" I screamed. Then quieter, "Please. Don't say his name." I couldn't take the emotional fucking teacup ride going round and round, flashbacks and future messes and present confusion over and over. "This isn't about him. I meant my new friend, Theo. Where is he? Is he okay? He's a good guy and your goons could have killed him, you know."

"Sorry," she whispered. Too soft a word from such a demonic-looking thing in a young girl's body.

"It...he wasn't your fault. Completely. I know you didn't mean to..."

"But I did."

"But you did," I agreed.

The truth of it hung between us in deathly stillness. We'd never be able to make that better, no matter what terrible things she did next, no matter what kind of a kid she could become if she just *turned away* from this power. She would never escape that she'd murdered the best of us.

I hated that Robbie was the best of us. Rose should have been the best of us. If she'd been taken care of, if Cody Reese hadn't...

If never got me anywhere, and it wouldn't now.

"You think I can't be helped," Rose said.

"Not true." I meant it.

"But you think I need help," she said, a dip to her head.

"And you don't?"

"Not the kind you're thinking of."

"Enough word games and bullshit. Where's Theo?"

"He's resting. He's fine and he knows you're fine. Don't worry, I don't want him."

"Why do you want me though?"

"You were coming here anyway."

"Then why did you bring me here like *that*? I know why *I* was coming here, but seriously? Why the murder squad?" And the question I wasn't ready to ask: What the hell had she done with Psychiatrist.

The calculating glimmer brightened in her eyes, she couldn't hide it from me. Pre-planned...anything... wasn't really my forte, but I knew conniving when I saw it. She swaggered closer to me, and I yanked the IV out, ready to run or fight. I'd not have gotten far. I barely stood a chance against her as a Harpy, what in hell would I do as a regular loser?

"You know why I brought you here, Charity. Sister. Because we're better together than we are apart. I can see how much you love me—it looks like how I love you. If I take it apart, I see nothing underneath. It's pure. Maybe the purest thing either of us have felt since being tortured the way we both were. We never deserved that, but we do deserve this." When she sat on the bed and took my hand, I didn't pull away. But there was something behind her words, something I couldn't put my finger on. "For as much as I condemn you, I also want to thank you for protecting me. It wasn't enough, but you tried, and it's not your fault that you've never known enough real protection to emulate it. But I can show you protection now." She swallowed, the one she did to quiet her feelings. Or to pretend she had feelings to quiet.

"Kid, there's a problem with that. The only thing I need protection from now is you."

Her tender skin rippled like the shimmers over new pavement in the sun. Instead of reminding me of the freshly poured stuff in the beach parking lot, it made me think of the bugs that got stuck in the old stuff. How they went from burning in the sun to being smothered in the darkness.

Holy shit, when did I get so philosophical? It had to be this fucking ponytail.

She jumped up like the bugs were under her skin. "Wrong," she spat. "You need protection from the pitiful life oppressing you. The constant cloud cover you search for sunlight through."

"That pitiful life isn't so bad, and you're the one who made sure I had it! You're the one who showed up when you didn't have to, and you took me apart! You took my wings, Rose!"

"Only to show you how much you'd miss them. You need a purpose, and you found it, as a Harpy—then turned it away, because you were misguided and small-minded."

. . .

"You…are making me feel *awesome*. I mean, this is one hell of a motivational speech. Go on."

"The Queen *kept* Harpies. She didn't lead them. These great, powerful women, prey turned predator turned prey again, to a life of pointless enslavement and untapped potential."

"Can you just talk without the riddles?"

"No. I won't be lesser ever again. Can you rise to the challenge?"

Goddamn kid.

"Fine. The Harpies were held back by the Queen. But Rose, you've got Harpies in this world now. Walking around, with fucking jobs? A nurse? They shouldn't be here, they should be—"

"Eating the limbs of suicide victims? Sent to Hell because of archaic ideas and an endless cycle of victim blaming?" She wandered the room, trailing a finger here, pausing there. Spinning on me, her hair whipped around her like licks of flame. "I will raise these beauties up from those treacherous depths and show them how to take charge of a world that was ripped from them."

"I know you want to purge the world of predators. I mean, it's a good idea, you can see who might become a rapist and have your Harpies take them out, I get it." I had to meet her halfway here. "But Rose, the entire world isn't at fault."

"And the entire world won't have to fall to us. I don't want to destroy Earth," she said, brows knitted, shaking her head. Disappointed that I'd think this of her. "All I want is for us to live in the sun again, on a safe Earth, *if we choose*. I want us to have choices, and not be damned to serve this hunger and squander eternity being punished!" Her voice rose with every word, rage escalating, the room warming.

"How safe is it if you'll kill anyone who might turn out wrong?" I yelled back.

"Safe for the right ones," she replied.

"You don't have to be one of them! You can turn it away, just like I did. They don't have to be your safety net, let me be."

"I choose them! I *am* them. Has anyone ever fought for the Harpies before? Shown them that they aren't castoffs, dehumanized by humans and made monsters by monsters? I can make a difference to them and change this world for the better with their help! Imagine it, Charity. Imagine a world where *we* make the choices, and *we* decide what's best. They're failing now out there," she said with a sweeping arm toward the window. "More innocent people are ruined every day, and more predators grow, thrive, come into power, while the Harpies, infinitely stronger in every way and tried, tested, continuously suffer like *they're* the animals!"

I had to hand it to her, she had my attention.

Pacing, she didn't give the impression of being fanatical, she was passionate, logical. "The existence of Hell is undeniable now, correct?" I nodded my agreement, though I hadn't really thought of it one way or another before this moment. I just *was* where I *was*. Where I'd been was Hell. "It stands to reason that if there is Hell, whether or not there is the opposite pole of Heaven, that divine intervention does exist. It must, because those who go to Hell are not random; they're chosen. Right?"

"Yeah, right, sure." I tried to play it off like I thought she was talking nonsense, but I was absolutely intrigued, and she knew it because of course, she couldn't stay out of my head.

"If divine intervention of any kind exists then that means there is a Plan. A capital P Plan." She stopped in front of me, across the room now, looking every bit the angel from Hell in her white dress and sunshine hair, with that red skin. "Then Charity, it means that I was given the abilities I have for a reason. It's part of the Plan."

"Okay, okay, it's convincing, and you definitely have a godliness about you, but you think—"

"I don't have to think!" she boomed. "I *know*. I have seen Hell, deeper than you have. I took it apart and saw all of it, and there's more. More than me, more than you, and nothing is there by chance, least of all me. These gifts of mine, and even my ruination, were all instruments to bring me to this purpose that began in Hell. And I embrace it wholeheartedly. The question is —will you embrace that Plan and be the archangel at my side? I can return your wings to you, Charity. Make you more powerful than you can dream of. Will you be with me? Or will you find yourself waiting for Hell to claim you once again?"

I got up, dropping the IV tube I'd pulled out, realizing I'd been changed into a johnnie—though still wearing underwear, which was a plus. Not that they covered much. "Before you work any harder to induct me into your Harpy cult, I want to know—where's Mortimer?"

She narrowed her eyes. "He's here, and here is where he'll stay until he gives me what I want."

"Are you fucking torturing him?" I snapped, lunging forward but stopping myself before I grabbed the hot little mess. "He's not against you! Let him go, we want to—"

"Help me?" she shrieked. "We've been over this. The help you want to give me is not the help I need."

I whipped the plastic water pitcher against the fucking wall. Not the same effect as glass shattering, let me tell you.

"No more fucking games, Rose!" I screamed, ass hanging out in the hospital dress. "You—" banging a finger on my temple way too hard, "tap into my head, drive me crazy after months without a word? After taking my Harpy clean out of me? You steal Mortimer, torturing him? Right? Making him tell you what you can't remember?"

"I'm not torturing him."

"Shut the hell up! Now you know, you fucking *know* I'm coming to get him and—oh you shut up when I say it—and *help. You.* And you have to like, throw your weight around? Show me who's boss or whatever by destroying the guy's SUV? It had heated fucking seats, Rose!"

She was suddenly avoiding my eyes, and the thing I knew was there when she'd been talking, I kinda got it.

A purse of the lips, a rapid blink. She was deciding whether or not to lie to me. I had the same tell. "I won't lie to you," she said. "I can see that you know I was considering it, but there would be little point. I didn't send the Harpies that attacked you."

More surprises. No shit. "So, what, they came without you knowing? Why would they do that? Are they just that unfuckingsocialized?"

"They weren't mine," she whispered.

"Oh shit!" I said with a laugh. Dumb move but I couldn't help it. Not everyone was on board with the kid. There was resistance to her ideas. I could work with that. Poke at the tender spot. "They came to get me then so I wouldn't get to you."

"Stop smiling, it's not funny!" Rose screamed, and the bed burst into flames. The wings—holy shit they were scarier than ever. Giant razor-blade beasts, way bigger than I remembered and she didn't seem to have any control over them. They burst up lopsided, and her red body hunched under their weight.

"Nope, no, no not funny, put the razors away, kid. I'm not prepared for a knife fight," I said, hands up, but she just growled, anger reddening her skin even more, to a scarlet that emanated heat waves. "Look, Rose, I'm just a fucking person! You made sure of that. I can't even break a plastic water pitcher, for fucks sake. And you need me. Right? You need me."

This was a wild card to play, but why not. My plans were...well, I'd never had a plan actually.

Her skin simmered down, like when you turn off a pot of boiling water, and she squeezed her eyes shut.

I was more scared of the idea that she was in more pain coming down from the anger than she was getting there.

When she opened her eyes, I took a couple of steps forward and she didn't try to murder me, so I went with it. "Now before you go dark and dirty and red all over again, we have to get to the bottom of some things. Right?" She nodded, so I pushed more. "I'd like to do that sitting down." A glance at the pile of metal bars and ashes that had been the bed. "This room's closing in on me, how about—"

"No," she snapped, clenching her fists. So, too far then.

"Cool. But I still don't want to stand here."

After a few terrifying moments of her staring through me she finally nodded at the one-way mirror once, and in seconds two guys in white mental institution scrubs wordlessly brought in an old wooden end table and a couple of big puffy chairs that looked just like the ones from Psychiatrist's office. I laughed nervously, but it didn't take long for me to register how fucking twisted this could be.

"Ha, you're not like, recreating a therapy session or anything, are you?" I pictured what that might look like for Mortimer. Him gripping the arms of that chair until his fingertips hurt. Her tying him to it when he couldn't take her digging in his head anymore.

And Rose didn't say a word.

I swallowed and sat down easily, not my usual plopping motion. It made me feel like I could run at any moment, but I knew I had nowhere to go.

"Who's on the other side of the mirror, Rose?" I asked quietly. But I got nothing.

She sat facing me over the end table that if I'd checked, knew would have a deck of playing cards in the drawer. Because fuck if this wasn't the exact end table from Mortimer's waiting room. She started. "Some Harpies don't want you talking to me, it would seem."

"Interesting. That's not what I got out of my Mile High Club abduction. I think they wanted to drag me to Hell."

"Why do you say that?" she asked.

"I remember the sky melting, that's what it looked like as I passed out. They were opening a portal," I said.

The rapid blinks again. It was easy for me to tell when I was giving her new information. She was such a little kid that way. A weird combination of total honesty and knowing too much. "They want you back," she said in a rumbling low voice.

"You know, we think a lot alike. You didn't think they wanted me—just that they didn't want *you* to have me. I thought the same thing about Doctor Mortimer and you. You only want him because I do."

"We're not talking about that."

"*Him.*"

"That," she hissed. And I was getting bristly.

"Whatever your plan is in the Wood, kid? Not all the birdies are on board. Enough so that they'd want me back even though I was pretty goddamn clear that wasn't an option. Are you sure you've got the right idea here? 'Cause here's what I'm thinkin'. If there are enough Harpies against your plan that they'd organize and send a sentry out for me, your arch enemy and occasional BFF, then they were prepared for a fight. This isn't a one-bitch operation. You got enough fire-power to come out on top in a civil war?"

She smirked. An ugly thing on a baboon-butt red face. "How do you know it's the Harpies I'd be warring with?"

"Welllll, if you've got Harpies against you, and you're planning a war with someone else? That's like, two wars. At the same time."

"I'm capable of war," she snarled. "I *am* war."

"And here I thought you didn't want to fight. You want me to round up the rogues? Is that right?"

"In a nutshell."

"Kid, you aren't gonna like what I have to say. I wasn't on my way here to join your murder cult, and I'm sure as hell not a thumbs up for letting Harpies loose on the world. I can't be your right hand. I need to leave Hell behind or it will never stop coming for me, can't you see that? You thought I'd miss the Harpy too much to not go along with you, but it's just not true." I didn't think it was true. Not totally.

Her sneer reached for me like claws. "If Hell is the only place that always wants you, why run from it?"

That was tough to swallow. "This isn't about me. It's about you, having too much power and nobody to hold you back."

The walls on either side of us became curtains of flame. I screamed, the heat reaching me from halfway across the room.

"How dare you?" she screamed over me. "I've been held back all my life, until I was useful, and it was *fun*. When someone thought up sick enough experiments, then the script changed. This world can't handle me because I was meant for *more*. This is my time to meet that fate."

"Hell isn't the only place for you, kid. You're a fucking miracle! Look at what you can do!"

"And look what they can use me for," she spat, pointing at the one-way mirror.

Deep breath. "Rose. I'm gonna ask again. Who's behind the mirror?"

"Nobody you need to worry about right now. All you need to worry about is picking the right side because you cannot stay out of this, Charity. You don't get to choose—"

My turn to get motherfucking angry. "You have *got* to be fucking kidding me!" I screeched, knotting my fingers in my hair, pulling the ponytail even more out of place. "You just fucking said how it's our turn to choose or some bullshit, but that means you get to be a fucking dictator? Is that right? It's a fucking bullying technique if I ever heard one." I figured getting that out would make me feel a little better, but it wasn't enough. I stood up, whipped Mortimer's Office Depot catalog armchair at the one-way mirror. That felt better. But it didn't put a crack in the glass and for whatever reason, that was a metaphor for my entire fucking life right there and it was too much for me.

Everything went silent except for the crackling of Rose's fire licking up the walls.

I started crying.

Rose's bright blues bore into me, like she was in shock. Her mouth hung open. Shit, her lips were so pink and babyish when I first found her, and now it was like she'd been sucking on hot coals.

I cried harder.

"Fuck you, Rose! I've busted my fucking ass trying to give you, I don't know, some kind of normal life, like trying to fucking make up for shit. It's not even my shit! I didn't do anything to you, Rose! You're not my responsibility, the Harpies aren't my fucking responsibility, not even Psychiatrist—" I felt like a child throwing a tantrum the second I thought of him. He was who the hell knew where in this place, right here under my nose, and I was letting a kid stand in the way of him. She was the reason for all of it, and I was trying to help *her*, too! "I fucking quit, kid! You hear me? Fucking digging yourself in deeper all the time… You got dealt a shit card, yeah. But it wasn't all bad, Rose, and you take every goddamn opportunity to make it worse!" Like I was talking about myself, for chrissakes. "You're not taking Mortimer and Theo and anyone else along for your death ride. You want to wage war on whoever, go for it. Leave me the fuck out of it, give me them back and take control for yourself. Move *forward*. Stop reaching for what's behind you and for people behind you."

My brain sizzled like Robbie tossing burgers on the grill. Rose was yelling for me to shut up but I couldn't stop screaming, who the hell would be able to stop screaming?! A sheet of red not unlike the sky in the Wood overran my eyes, the abysmal fucking tapping came, more of an icepick now, and the red got thicker and darker until I couldn't see, couldn't hear past my own burning brain. I smacked my head on something metal, so apparently I was convulsing.

Hands grabbed both my arms, lifted me off the

floor. I couldn't see but I felt them go through the door with me when they banged my flailing leg on the doorframe. I didn't give a shit as long as they got me away from Rose. Sick bitch that I am, I was worried she'd feel bad for hurting me.

Spoiler alert: she didn't.

Painfully fast, my brain-banging stopped, leaving me missing the sound like a dead limb for a second. I blinked hard, whipped my arms and legs so the dudes in scrubs had to put me down, one of which yelled, "Fucking bitch" as I connected with his nose.

"Thanks for the lift, now get the fuck out." They'd brought me to a bathroom, super conveniently. I locked the door behind them and peed, still unable to see past the red globs in my vision.

After fumbling for the tp and the faucet handles, I wiped my eyes with wet hands.

They came away with more blood than I'd seen on my hands in a very long time.

In the mirror, thick streaks of red and little globs of pink covered my face, like pieces of my fucking brain had bled out my eyes.

Shit. Pieces of my motherfucking brain had *bled out my eyes.* Takes a special girl who can handle a shit ton of torture to stay awake through that. I could only hope it wasn't brain matter I needed.

The linoleum swapped places with the popcorn ceiling with the toilet with the sink and I was down. More blood in my eyes.

Oh my god, I'm gonna die in a bathroom.

I forced myself to sit up through the black and red and swirling consciousness, because like hell would I die in a bathroom. And I'm really proud of the fact that my next thought was of Mortimer and what must be happening to him, if this just happened to me because she was in a bad mood. I mean, that was supposed to be a negotiating kind of talk. My heart sank a little. Looked like negotiating was out of the picture.

I pulled myself up on the edge of the toilet, only slipping off and hitting the floor once. I washed my face, spat a bunch of blood into the sink and pulled my hair back, blood and goo with it.

I didn't know where Rose was now, but this was my chance to sneak around and find Theo and Mortimer, and get the hell out of here. First place I was going— the other side of that one-way mirror.

CHAPTER 10

Limping is the shittiest feeling. It's the number one marker of the hurt and defenseless girl, best when paired with a hopeless sob or two.

I wasn't quite there yet, and the blood blanket I was wearing had me feeling far more Carrie than First Girl Killed.

First step was to find a weapon. My choices were limited. Sink, mirror, toilet. Toilet tank lid was pretty bulky, I wouldn't be able to hold it up and open the door at the same time. Paper towel dispenser was bolted to the wall. I poked around at it and found a thin metal flap, same size as those shitty brown single-sheet paper towels it dispensed. I ripped that thing off and waved it around. The metal bent with each swish making a kind of flapping noise. It would have to do.

"Hey," I said. No answer, so "Hey!" louder.

"Yeah?" came the guard's voice from the other side of the door.

"Can you open the door, I need help." Wrong thing to say. What the hell would I need help with that I'd take from this jimook?

"Uh…uh…" he stammered, obviously not trained for this kind of request.

A second later the door handle pushed down a little, and I yanked it open fast, pulling the big guy in and smacked him in the face with the metal plate.

"What the—" His free hand flew to his cheek and I took the opportunity to slap him in the nuts with the stupid thing and I don't think it even touched him. He yelled at me to fucking stop it, I knew someone would be coming really soon and that I was probably being recorded right that very second with some spy shit, so I kicked him in the nuts next, which should have been my initial move, and when he doubled over I drove my elbow into the back of his head. He hit the floor, and I was gone.

Grunting with anger, effort, annoyance, I dragged my stupid leg down the hall following the blood trail, past the open doorway where I'd come from, to the wall on the other side which I was guessing needed a key card from 1996 or some shit. This fucking building was both a time capsule and weirdly almost technologically up-to-date, equally wicked disorienting.

The door was one of those solid pieces of laminated "wood" with a silver handle you only ever see at doctor's offices or on The Brady Bunch. Yet right there, a goddamn keypad had been fitted to it, of course.

I crouched down in a bad attempt to hide myself in a wide-open hallway, hearing loud voices around the corner that could only mean trouble for me, and started punching keys at random. Again, planning is not my forte. The buttons lit up red with every wild punch, but sometimes blue. So I slowed down, tried for the blue ones again but how many? And which ones were they? God I was so bad at this.

Didn't matter when the door swung open and I fell on my face to the floor into a dark room. Silently, I was pulled inside.

~

I jumped to my feet, falling on my knee once, screamed an obscenity or six, and took in my surroundings like I'd been whisked away to Gryffindor or whatever the fuck. There's wasn't much to see. Old school cafeteria table, a glass of water, a coffee mug. And the one dude who apparently used them.

"Tell me who the fuck you are right now or I'll kick you in the nuts too," I said.

Except this guy didn't strike me at all as the guy who needed a nut kick at the moment, even though his hair was impossibly slicked back in a stylish, not greasy way, and he wore a black suit and skinny tie that shined of money. The white shirt was whiter than anything white had ever been, and his ridiculously masculine and handsome face was the stuff GQ was made of. But goddamn if he didn't just give off the air of honesty.

"I'm Rose's father."

"You're not. No way."

He lifted his arms in a shruggy way, tight smile, raised eyebrows.

"Oh my god, you are, aren't you?"

"We don't have a lot of time, Miss Blake."

"I don't get. You're, what? Working with her? Why is she all grabby for Mortimer if you're here? Where's Cleary? What the actual fuck…" I snapped my fingers at him for an answer.

"Bob."

"Bob? Seriously? I guess you can't look like that and have a cool name too." I straightened my bloody johnnie, strode to one of the crappy chairs and sat, taking a slug of his cold-ass coffee. "What the fuck are you up to?" And I choked out the hardest question, "How can you look at her the way she is and not help her? Why did you leave her?"

He opened the one buttoned button of his blazer, like any good-looking guy does when he means business, and sat across from me, leaning forward like I mattered to this operation. And I did get the distinct impression that this was an operation.

"I went to find Cody Reese, I had to. But when I

did…I couldn't do what I needed to. He was a kid, too, just a kid—"

"That raped your little girl."

"Don't you think I know that? I wasn't strong enough to do what a father should for his child, I couldn't. And yes, I was afraid to go back without having done it. How could I look my wife in the eyes? How could I look at my baby… She wouldn't have needed her abilities to look through me and see that I failed her."

Well, fuck it all if I didn't feel really, really horrible for him then. He couldn't kill a kid and he couldn't face his own because of it.

"There had to be another way."

"Bring him to court?" he spat. "Torture my family by reliving it again and again? No. She didn't need to know he survived, and I didn't deserve to have her in my life. Then, it was too late."

Too late. Rose's mother. Annie. So much death. So much pain and loss. Too much for a child to understand or cope with.

"Tell me what happened next," I said, wanting the pain, wanting to know it all so I could feel it with her, and him, and be in it.

"When the government came to me, wanting her, what else was I to do, Charity? I wasn't the man she needed me to be. And now, Rose must be stopped."

"No shit, Sherlock, where have you been? No literally, where have you been all this time? Why are you here now?"

He hung his head, his shoulders rising and falling with a frustrated sigh. When he looked back up, his face was a mask of grief, eyes darker, lines visible. "It doesn't matter—I haven't been here. I couldn't risk being that close to her. Mr. Cleary came to me a week ago because her need for answers that only I could give was becoming too much. And yet, she isn't ready for them."

"You can't possibly know that. You don't even know her," I spat. "She's more than you give her credit for, obviously."

"I know her!" he yelled, his voice gruff, eyes alight with defensive anger. "Who do you think orchestrated this place to contain her, keep her occupied? Keep her safe from—"

"From dickheads who would do experiments on her and turn her even more into a weapon, even less than a child?" Tears clogged my throat.

He smiled wryly. "I don't have to tell you that there's always someone worse out there, with more sinister intentions, and Rose needed the means to expand her mind. She'd never have been able to live with herself outside of here, being so different, after what she'd done. The lives she took."

"What do you mean, you orchestrated this place?" I wouldn't be swayed by the rest of what he'd said, no matter how true it was.

He met my eyes with the determination of a man who'd convinced himself he did the right thing, every time he didn't. "The government wanted her, and either I could work with them or keep her running from them as much as she ran from herself."

The keypad made its beeps outside, and in seconds the door had shut quietly and quickly behind a frantic-looking Cleary. "She's cooling down in the tank right now. Hi, Miss Blake." He waved a little hello like this was totally normal, and that made me even more nervous.

"The tank? You put her in a fish tank?"

Cleary nodded once, sweat dripping off his brow. "For lack of a better word, yes."

"Who's side are you on, Cleary?" I asked. I had no interest in pretending there weren't sides, and Cleary had been Rose's real father for a long time. At least that's how Rose saw him.

"It's not that simple," Bob said.

"Is your name Cleary?" I snapped. "No, it's fucking *Bob*." I turned back to Mr. Cleary who had a little sparkle in his eye and that was enough of an answer for me.

He cleared his throat. "I think there's more than one answer to this question."

"Just looking for one, though," I said.

He trained his eyes on Rose's father, didn't look away for like ten seconds, and that made me respect him even a little more. "Rose's side," he said.

I tried not to smile. "Do you think she should remember everything?"

Once again, Bob answered for him. "If her subconscious wanted her to remember, she'd have taken this place, my mind, apart by now. Nobody can hide from her, and yet here I am, like she wanted, and now that I am, she won't see me. She's scared. That part of her brain that's hidden from her, once she acknowledges it, her memories—"

"And you," Cleary put in.

"—and when she acknowledges me, I'm afraid that she won't be miraculously healed, she'll be…"

A cold seeped through me. "That she won't be Rose at all anymore." I couldn't even picture what would become of her next when she understood the full depth of the lies, the hiding, and whatever we didn't all know. What she'd be like when there was no humanity left, only this fire monster with an army of Harpies.

"But if she doesn't remember, her brain will burn her out if her emotions don't first," Cleary growled. "She can't go on like this, she's a live wire. You're worried about what will happen if she remembers *you*."

"Of course I am," her father said sadly, and turned away, hands in pockets. "I really did put her here with the best intentions. The government promised me her brain would get the enrichment it required. It couldn't be allowed to run free, can you imagine that? A little girl with murders under her belt, no ability to control herself, no way to understand what was happening to her? *I* couldn't help her! But I could watch—"

"Watch?" I huffed. "She needed a father."

"And she got one!" Bob yelled, spinning on me. "Do you think it was easy for me to see how attached she became…" he waved his hand toward Cleary.

"It was necessity," Cleary said, not unkindly. "*I* was here for her, helping her grow without losing her mind."

"Didn't work," I interjected.

Cleary went on, "She grew to see this place as home, as I hoped she would. We needed to contain her as much as we needed to nurture her, and with those two warring objectives, the expected results were blurry."

"Meaning you didn't know what to expect," Bob said.

"Did you?" Cleary snapped at him.

"That was your job," Bob said quietly.

"Funny, I never saw Rose as a job," Cleary said.

"Maybe that was the problem," Bob said, and I was in no mood to get in the middle of a dad fight.

I said, "We need you to talk to her, Bob. We don't care if you get caught for being the weirdest absentee dad ever."

"The Facility exists because of me! She'd only ever have seen the inside of some isolation cell for what she'd done, if she lived through it at all. I'm only a man, for the love of God! They—" he nodded at Cleary, "were going to help her!"

I shook my head. "You knew eventually that it wasn't *help* anymore, it was exploitation. Experimentation."

Deflated, eyes empty of willpower, body slumped, Bob admitted, "I wasn't strong enough to take her away. What if those experiments could..."

"Could what?" I prompted.

"Cure her," he said with a mirthless chuckle.

Cleary said, "She wasn't a disease. She is an extraordinary child."

"She's not normal!" Bob snapped. "I wanted her to be normal, a regular girl, and maybe being here could fix her, and make her forget."

"Fuck, like longer, weirder shock therapy?" I said. "After all that she'd been through—"

"And done," Bob interjected, like some lawyer. "She killed people. She killed *my wife.*"

"So that's what this was about? Punishing her?" I asked. "She was a child. She'd lost everything, been violated by that sonofabitch, and your answer was to make her forget? Make *her* the problem? Actually hope that the Facility could take part of her brain away?"

Bob gulped. To go with missing a part of her past is a small price to pay."

Cleary punched the wall, and it shocked the shit out of me because he was totally not the type. But he straightened up, spoke like a civilized man. "The missing memories are literal pockets in her brain. They grow deeper with each passing day. And if the pockets aren't filled, her brain will disintegrate. Do you under-stand?" he barked, voice rising. "Her brain will *disinte-grate*. We owe her the opportunity to fully understand what she's lived through before we condemn her to die from it!"

I couldn't stop the tears from burning my eyes. "She shouldn't have to pay a price," I said, even though I knew it wasn't entirely true. "It's not fair," I squeaked out, now pissed that I sounded so stupid. "She's had this fucked-up life! And now she has to just *die* before ever having anything normal, this fucking terrible life? This is your fault," I growled, in Bob's face, his smooth and steady face.

"The time she had with her mother was perfect. And the time we were a family." His voice cracked. My heart cracked.

"She was happy here, I think," Cleary added, sympathy softening his voice. "For a time. I think it shows in that she's come back here."

The residual Psychiatrist talk worked in my mind. "More like she has a Stockholm Syndrome for the place."

They both looked at me in surprise, but I knew my fucked-up terminology.

"I know why she wants to rain Hell on Earth now," I said, nodding. "Being cast away from it before she could ever really enjoy it. Having that little bit of nice home life, then having it torn from her? How could it be any worse? Then brought here, nothing spontaneous, nothing natural, and her in a way, more natural than anything on earth. You say she was allowed to grow here, but I think it's because you love her, not because it's true," I said to Cleary. Then to Bob, "There may have been no other options, I get it. Who would know what to do? No wonder she hates this world and wants revenge. The Harpies will let her have it, and they love her too. She's a hero for them. She's not a hero to anyone else, is she? But there's an entire other world of girls who've had their lives distorted, she wants to help them, they're just like her."

Mr. Cleary shook his head, eyes on the ground. "Not like her. Nobody has ever been like her." It hung between us, the eulogy.

"What now?" I said, falling back into my chair. What could we possibly do that wouldn't turn Rose into an even bigger nuclear reactor?

Mr. Cleary leaned against the wall, hands hung at his sides. "Rose wants to cure her brain, and thinks—knows —that her father and Dr. Mortimer have the answers to help her. With her brain whole, it's true, she will become more unimaginably powerful than anything we could dream up. I know this because the weaker her mind becomes, the more erratic her powers. She can't control her wings, for instance. They pop up without her willing. She's completely unsafe to stand within ten feet of, which makes her feel altogether more inhuman. You've of course seen the fire. And she's dipping into people's minds unwillingly as well. It's a fact that with her mind at its full potential she will be unstoppable, but," he pushed off the wall, "she will also be clear-headed! Unstoppable, and that could be *wonderful*. We can't assume that she'll be a monster once she's been helped and treated like the incredible person that she is."

"It isn't a chance we can take," Bob muttered, head hung.

"So you want to let her die," Cleary accused Bob. "And have you considered that with a disintegrating brain she'll become even more unpredictable? Her powers won't fizzle out like a cigarette in an ashtray, they'll fire off like missiles."

I hated myself for saying what I did. For even thinking it. "But then it will stop." I had to keep going with it. "Yeah, it will be horrifying in that moment, and it could do more damage than a fucking atom bomb—but then it will be over. And she won't be a threat anymore."

Cleary said, "If we take our feelings out of it, yes, that's most likely the case."

And yet we couldn't move from our spots. Because for as much as we were at each other's throats over it, we all knew that her just not existing was the safest thing for the entire world.

"Charity," Bob started, "only you can get to the Wood of Suicides and raise the—"

"Nope. Stop right the fuck there. I can't to the

Wood of Suicides, I'm not a Harpy! Does this ponytail say Harpy to you?"

"All the blood does," Cleary said and I shot him a look.

"If you don't go, Rose will bring Hell straight to Earth!" Bob yelled gruffly.

"Rose took the Harpy right out of me. She took me apart," I said, kinda embarrassed. The two men side-eyed each other.

Gently, Cleary said, "We know that the Harpies came for you, that they planned to bring you to the Wood of Suicides and form a plan to overthrow Rose."

That stopped me. "How did you know?" Nothing from either one of them. "I said. How. Did you know?"

With a deep sigh, Bob said, "We convinced one of the Harpies Rose brought above to be a sleeper agent for us, to gather some of her less enthusiastic supporters in the Wood and strengthen their hold."

"With me," I said.

"With you," Cleary confirmed. "We acted together on that point. We've truly tried to think of everything. Stopping her by any means necessary was never our first choice, and it still isn't one that I stand behind, but you must see that we both have exhausted our options. You're our last hope, Charity."

"That won't work out for you," I said.

"I disagree," Cleary said with that air of hopefulness that he commandeered so well. "Rose will listen to you if you become part of her plan, or the Harpies will listen to you if you convince them to oppose her, but one way or the other, you're the only one with the power to end this nightmare. You, Charity. Not the Harpy, but you."

It got me right in the feels, but the idea of the Wood, of going down the path again that I'd sworn off, sucked. "What do you even expect me to do down there?" I choked out, my voice thick. "Convince the Harpies to what? Turn on her? Not only would she know I was there, she could take them apart like fucking Thanos."

"Thanos?"

Head shaking with my disbelief, I threw my hands up. "I gotta get out of here."

Bob said, "You do. But not without an agenda, because this problem will only keep coming back for you until we're all dead. Everyone. Only you know the way in and out of the Wood. Only you have what it takes to negotiate with the Harpies. You think the Harpies will listen to me? Cleary? Who am I to them, even if I could get down there?"

I snickered, "If you got down there you'd be in no condition to do anything but scream."

"Exactly. There's only you, Charity." Bob grasped my hands that had fallen back to the table. "You have to save everyone."

"Jesus Christ, Bob. Listen to me. She already wanted me down there to get the defectors on board with her. She'll obliterate the Wood of Suicides if she thinks they've rejected Team Rose Takeover." I remembered a time when Rose was a fresh-faced kid, ready to disassemble the Wood in a good way, showing the Harpies how she could take the trees apart like a real-life magician. They'd never known hope down there. And now, they'd seen what hope could become—an unreachable, untouchable demon child.

"But—"

"No buts, Bob. Me going to Hell won't save Rose and it won't kill her either. Plan B. Go."

"There is no Plan B," Cleary said.

I wanted to bang my head against the fucking wall. "Did you honestly think that she didn't see this coming? That somebody would try to stop her?" I scoffed at them. "This was your big idea. Send me to Hell—me, of all people, who abandoned the Harpies, swore I'd never come back—and ask the bird-bitches, who eat human trees, to be on your side? Bad idea. Desperate."

"Indeed we are," Bob said.

"Well, you have no more ideas but Rose is nothing *but* ideas. Letting the Harpies come above is her step one, and whether or not it works, she's got the next level planned." My breath caught. What she'd told me finally came clear, all the shit about the bigger plan and having seen more than me in Hell. That she'd been planning to make more than just the Wood bigger—to go *deeper*. That was what she said. "I know what she wants." The words hurt coming out: "She wants to take over down below."

~

Cleary and Bob started rambling about some dude Don Tay while I raced through in my head what it meant for Rose to rule Hell.

She'd change all the rules, whatever they were.

Apparently, Don Tay wrote a book about Hell, and the shithole went a lot deeper and taller than the Wood of Suicides, and while they geeked out over this book I figured out that each part of Hell obviously had its own monsters.

Fuck, did I need to read a book?

"Is it getting hot in here?" Cleary said.

"I am not taking off all my clothes. Who am I kidding, I would kill to not be in…a blood and brain-soaked ripped johnnie, I guess."

"It is," Bob said, eyes narrowed, sweat beading on his upper lip.

"She knows," I said. My stomach turned, I got hot like I was about to pass out, and quietly, subtly, there was one single *tap*. "She's peeling me apart inside, but it's real quiet."

"We aren't ready for this," Cleary blurted to Bob. "If she knows we're talking to Charity without her she'll kill us both."

"Nope," I burped out. Nausea in a flood of fire

threatened to ooze from every hole in my body. "Not you, Cleary," I said. "She loves you too much. You're the one she'd forgive anything." I was kinda jealous. He knew it was true, and I could see why—he looked directly at me, not denying that she'd save him of all of us, and the love he had for her shined like the gleaming metal of her nasty wings. He loved her the way she wanted to be loved—like a father, but one who would let his child take the lead and give her endless tools to do so.

Tap.

That one didn't hurt as much. She didn't want me to know she was in my head. Too late, Red.

Mr. Cleary took me by the arm, out of the room, down the already clean hallway which showed no traces of my brain blood, and sat with me in an all-window room thingy, like where they bring old people to stare at the sky. A nurse walked by—different nurse, possibly human but who the hell knows—and I snapped my fingers at her, asked for some clean clothes, seeing as my ass was sticking to this window seat. She brought me a pair of blue hospital scrubs which I put on right there because Cleary had seen just about everything with me in this johnnie anyway. I'll be goddamned if hospital scrubs aren't the most comfortable thing goin'.

"I have a question," I said, sitting down again. "Why haven't you made Mortimer and Bob tell Rose everything?"

He thought on it for a second before saying, "Because I've made those decisions for Rose for too long."

"Tell me, Cleary," I whispered, like it mattered, "who's in charge of this place now? You, Bob, or Rose?"

He smiled. It was charming. "Bob was never in charge. I make sure everything runs smoothly. She lets me take care of her, but Rose is the tiger and we're all in her cage now."

Blonde hair in wet tendrils hanging around her arms, red skin now looking softer, not dry and ready to crack, Rose padded down the white hallway in a light pink giant t-shirt. Still little girlish, but now with boobs. She looked happier than before, like the cool water of her Little Mermaid tank had eased more than her skin. I thought of the sharks and rays at the aquarium, how she'd have boiled the water they lived in.

"How was your swim?" I asked.

"It's not really a swim, more of a float," she said, bouncing down beside me like a child. "How are you feeling?"

Like she hadn't exploded part of my brain. "Um, actually okay," I realized, considering I no longer had all my brain chunks. "You? Are you fixing me?" I gasped.

Rose smiled sweetly. "I did discover a few new things while trying to heal myself."

For chrissakes, I didn't know feelings could get this complicated. One second she wants to burn me alive, the next she wants to take over Hell, the next she's healing me and asking me to be by her side. And I loved her. I just did, that's what this bullshit was where I knew it would end badly for me but I still wanted *in.*

Her eyes sparkled like the Atlantic. "I can put things back together too, you know," she said, nudging me with her shoulder. I shifted my eyes to Cleary who looked like he was watching his puppy die. She couldn't put herself back together, though.

"I need to think," I said, and shit did I ever mean it. In truth, I didn't know, I couldn't know… Even if I could end her life, would I?

"I know," she said lightly, taking my hand. Her palm was light pink like her dress, like the pads of a cat's foot against her red skin. "Come back soon, though, okay? I don't have much time."

My chest ached, my throat hurt, my eyes blurred.

How could she talk about the end so easily? With too much and too little understanding?

"I won't be long," I said, voice thick with tears again, exhaustion in my words. I kissed the top of her head as she placed it on my shoulder. My lips came away tingling like I'd eaten Red Hots. Time to break this moment that was as simple and pleasant as it was horrendous. "And I won't be far. Try to stay out of my head, Rose. I know you can do it. You can control it."

She lifted her head, turned my face to hers with pink fingers. "I will," she said. "I know you need privacy, a little space. I'll always give that to you," she promised, as if making a contract with me for our impending life in Hell.

"I need you to give me the guys back, too," I added.

"Just one," she said. "Take the nice guy—he really is nice, Charity, I like him," she said with a knowing smile, "but the doctor has to stay here."

"No."

"Yes. How else do I know you'll come back?" As if she couldn't make me. "And he has to help me remember. I can't make a difference anywhere, to anyone if I'm dead, and I'll be ever stronger if the holes," she squeezed her eyes shut, slapped herself in the temple, "if they're healed." Very cut and dry, seemingly clean logic. It was easy to see how it made sense to her tortured mind, but her need for vengeance, her ache to hurt those who hurt her, the pain, the trauma and denial, not to mention the time-jumping and time in Hell, and facing the men who stole from her and were the only love she'd known... Not to mention that she thought releasing the Harpies on Earth would do some good? She was all short circuits and live wires. She was gonna blow. There was no way she couldn't.

"Kid," I said quietly, "just look into Mortimer's head and see what you need to see then let him go."

Her face hardened. She bared her teeth like a wolf. "He doesn't deserve it to be that easy," she said. "Besides, his mind is too human. I can't get close enough, it's too muddy in there."

"My mind isn't human?" I said, my fingertips icy suddenly.

She tilted her head at me in a condescending, Regina George, "oh sweetie, no" manner.

I glanced at Cleary who blinked rapidly but I didn't know what it meant, not exactly.

"You know Mortimer isn't the only one here who can help you remember, right? You remember that, can't you?" I said.

She stiffened beside me and said, "What do you mean?"

"Charity…" Cleary cautioned.

Looked like denial wasn't just a river in Egypt. The kid asked to have her father brought here and now she couldn't even admit that she knew he was. That level of repression was beyond anything I could comprehend. My habit was to let the hard stuff take up prime brain space then run away from it. But to block out what was right there in the building with her? No wonder Cleary was afraid to push Bob onto her. He was probably wondering if it was a good idea to bring him to the Facility at all. I looked at him for a second. His good-natured face showed lines around his eyes, weariness in the set of his jaw. He was just plain tired.

"I asked what you mean," Rose said again.

"Nothing, kid. Just promise me you'll be nice to him no matter what."

"No matter what?" she said coldly.

I pushed her away from me a little, turned to full-scolding position. "Rose, if you want to remember everything, if you *really* do, you cannot take out on him what you learn. Do you understand m'e?"

"What if he won't tell me at all?"

"No matter what. You have to be nice to him no matter what."

With a snarl, she said, "Fine. But you have until tomorrow."

"What? No way, I need to sleep until tomorrow, my brains got blown out. I need more time."

"Don't try to get out of this," she said in a creepy as shit sing-song voice.

"I won't. I'll be back, for you *and* for him."

"Two days then! See you later, Charity! I'm going to get some Froot Loops. If you're hungry, Mr. Cleary will make sure you get something to eat, okay? Bye!" And she all but skipped down the hall, slightly frizzed half-dry hair swinging.

I couldn't help my mouth hanging open when I looked back at Mr. Cleary who was literally twiddling his thumbs. I didn't think that was an actual thing. He looked so *heavy*.

"Dr. Mortimer says she's regressing," Cleary said. "Whenever she gets out of the tank especially, she's like this," he said, lifting a heavy hand to gesture after her down the hallway.

"Damn, kid has more psychological issues than one body can hold, huh?" Immediately I felt bad for saying it, because her body actually couldn't hold them all.

"She doesn't know, does she, that her father is the one who made this place happen?"

"Of course not."

The Facility had this air of hospital quiet but there were no beepings and hushed voices. Just the emptiness of people trying to help other people. Even the occasional passing nurse seemed saddened by it. Maybe it was the part of my brain that Rose had healed, but I understood that they were all here just for her. Just for Rose, to help hide the lie that she was the only patient. The inmate running the prison.

Theo, worry creasing his forehead and wrinkling his eyes where laugh lines were supposed to go, came stumbling into view at the end of the long hallway.

"Theo!" I jumped up and ran to him, throwing my arms around his neck in a highly-unlike me gesture that I don't care to ever analyze. He wrapped his arms around my shoulders, his chin digging into the crook of my neck, his breathing jagged.

"A red kid…"

"Yeah, I know."

"We have to go," he drawled, and I hoped all his brain matter was in place. He would need it over the next two days.

❧

I couldn't even think of going home, which was the sickest part of it. I didn't want to be alone with my thoughts, with Rose's brain interfering when she wasn't even trying, with the bone-deep knowledge that Mortimer's life was on borrowed time.

If I agreed to help Rose the entire world would be doomed, and I'd probably be right there with it the first time I said anything that she didn't agree with. She was just as close to evil overlord as she was to mentally deranged young adult.

If I didn't help her, we'd all pay the price. Everyone on Earth including me, Mortimer; she'd probably drag Cleary to Hell to hang out with her though.

"Have I mentioned that most of my friends end up dead in Hell?" I said to Theo as we got into the car he'd sent for.

"Have I mentioned my family business?" he muttered back, eyes half-closed. "God, what did that red girl do to me, I'm so tired."

I sincerely hoped she hadn't rooted around his head. Not only because Theo didn't deserve that, and didn't know anything anyway, but because Rose hadn't told me. The idea that even now she might be lying to me would have been a nail in the coffin. Couldn't say whose coffin, but it would have meant there was even less left of the Rose I knew than I'd thought.

By the time we got back to Theo's little castle in the sky, I was the tired one and he was positively energized. I mean, it was not that long a ride, though I'd nodded off more than once during it.

"You seem better," I said as we got off the elevator.

"I feel a lot better. Maybe I just needed a fifteen-minute car ride," he said with a laugh.

"Fifteen minutes? You said *fifteen minutes?*"

"Yeah, we're really close to that place it turns out," he said. "Lie down, you look like you've been—"

"Don't say it."

But for the second time I fell onto Theo's couch, feeling like shit and I just plain didn't remember feeling like this as often when I was a Harpy. And that was a dangerous memory when possibly the best choice I had ahead of me was to go back there.

"You're crying," Theo said—gasped, really, like he'd never seen anything more shocking.

"That's so unusual?" Then I got pissed. I was just tired maybe. Definitely. Maybe more. "Isn't part of being a goddamn human that we get to cry, like it's some wonderful thing to *feel?*"

He held his hands up in surrender and I wish I'd felt bad about yelling at him but I was just so fucking sick of everything.

"I didn't mean anything by it, Charity, really."

"Yeah, well nobody ever does when they say something stupid. Hey, have I told you that you're definitely guaranteed to die by hanging out with me?"

He *laughed.* "Have I told you that yet?" Then we both laughed. We laughed until I was crying from laughing and I don't think I'd ever done that before. I'd like to think I'd have remembered but who knew what I was blocking out? Who knew what memories I'd hidden away? It didn't matter though. I was tasked with saving the world basically. The chances of that going well were pretty slim.

We drank about three pots of coffee between us, while I confirmed that Rose was indeed red, and it wasn't the drugs he thought she'd slipped him. Whenever I told him not to ask questions he'd insist that I tell him everything. I didn't go into the depths of my childhood, I just started with that I'd been through some shit and it turned me into a Hell bird. When he asked me to show him, which of course he did, I couldn't. But I could show him the scars. Well, the newer ones. I'd never scarred when I changed before, but Rose made sure I wouldn't forget what I'd been. The whitened welts on my legs where the hardened skin would take over when I changed. The toes, black-tipped, nails even blacker, the mottled redness of the skin. Covered those up quick. Then he ran a finger up the back of my arm, from my wrist to the blue sleeve of the scrub top.

"And these?" he said.

I flipped my arm over, then the other, looking at the long red lines dotted with smaller slashes all over. "Yeah, those. That's where the wings would come from."

I told him how I became a Harpy one day because

I'd been hurt too much and I was "special." I told him about the bird bitches, and the Queen a little, but not about everyone else, like Jen or Painter, or Evan. Those wounds didn't heal and weren't up for discussion. As expected, he couldn't believe it. He asked questions that I answered poorly but seriously, how the hell could I sum up any of it? But he did ask me the big question.

"What are you gonna do, Charity?"

It was near dawn by this point, and time was running out. "I'll sleep on it. Maybe tomorrow everything will be different."

"Hate to tell you, it's basically tomorrow."

"Nope, not until I've gone to sleep and woken up again."

He stood up, looking really good, like Rose had done some solid reparation. Nobody asked her to, she just did it. As a way to show me what she could do? Or had it just been because she wanted to make him better?

It was that thought and a kiss on the forehead that lulled me into sleep, where I hoped to dream of a world where Rose Preston was a little girl again.

~

"Charity!"

I rolled over, fell off the couch. "Ugh, what? Why are you waking me up, do you not know how I react to that?"

But Theo's face was a mask of worry and fear.

Then the front door shook like a bomb exploded on the handle.

"Charity, that doesn't sound friendly."

He was right, it didn't. But only one thing I knew could make that much of a ruckus.

Another great shake of the door.

A Harpy. But they were definitely not the sort to show up for a visit and use the door at all.

"These goddamn backwards birds," I snarled, tearing the blanket from around my legs, getting to my feet poorly and with grunting.

Just as the door shook again, I swung it open without even a look through the keyhole. "Do you have any idea what time it is?" I barked, then set eyes upon the monster.

She was a Harpy all right. She wore a human face with about as much elegance as I'd wear an evening gown, either at my heroin-chic skeleton best or my Little Debbie exaggerated hourglass. I'd never seen anything so inhuman, so terrifying in at least a year.

The flesh of her face hung off until it was apparent that it wasn't her face at all. Some corpse was missing her smile, I was guessing in the Wood. Her black hair was matted and half of it was feathers. She was bony, frail, covered in bruises on her mottled skin. I'd seen bruises like that before and knew something or someone had been beating on her. The outfit was the dead giveaway that she came from Hell: oversized acid-washed jeans and a paisley-print sweater.

"Looks like you ate Madonna's ugliest sister. What the hell are you doing here? Get in here before someone sees you."

I yanked the thing into Theo's house, which I probably should have asked about first, and felt her skin *come off* in my hand.

"What the fuck!" I sloughed it off my hand to the floor where it landed with a wet *splat*. Her "hand" was a mix of bones and scaly skin like birds' feet. "You had to go Leatherface to come here, huh? What the hell is going on? Can you even speak?"

"Ye…yeee…yeessss," it crackled out in a witch voice.

"Oh my fucking god," Theo said behind me. I swear, any other guy probably would have peed his pants at the sight of this bitch, but Theo held his own. Point for Theo.

"Yeah, these are the kinds of things we'll be getting a look at if Rose has her way," I said. "What are you doing here?" I asked her but got only a blank black stare. "You got a name?"

"No name. Message." Hell, I never wanted to hear this voice again. "Must…come…to Wood. Or will c… c…come g…get *you*," she finished with a point of her finger, which was now just a bone that turned into bird skin at the end.

"Oh really? And who exactly is that? Who will be coming to get me, because I have to say the Harpy methods aren't at all meshing in this world. Between the highway incident and your shitty trick-or-treating costume, I'd say you all aren't suited for Earth."

"Not. Harpy," it managed to spit out, and its black eyes glimmered like oil. "*Him.*"

"Him? Him who? There are no hims in the Wood that have control over shit, let alone—"

"Not. In. Wood!" it said painfully, its neck twisting as if the words were clawing their way out. "Him."

"Charity," Theo said behind me, "I think I know who Him probably is."

I spun on him, scaring the shit out of No Name, and she fell backward with an ungodly *splat*. "You do *not* mean what I think you mean," I said. Whipped back around to the flailing demonic mess on the ground in the hallway. "Is *that* who sent you? The big guy?"

But the Harpy could only choke and spasm, leaving splatters and gobs of black goo around her until she melted into a fizzy pile of bones, feathers, skin and teeth.

Theo was at my shoulder. "I think I'll call the cleaning service," he said, and I slowly shut the door.

CHAPTER 11

The Harpy had been sent by Satan himself to…ask…me to go to Hell? I mean that was kinda what I got from it, that he was politely requesting via ill-suited Harpy that I go for a quickie, but he sure didn't send me adequate transportation.

"I need to go home," I said, shoving my hair into place, failing, ripping the elastic out and just letting it be a horror show. "I don't have much time, my bird misses me, and I don't know if I should go hang with the dude before or after I get back to Rose and she starts letting Harpies loose up here." I had nothing with me, never carried a purse, my ID had been shoved into the scrub top pocket, no cash, not even keys since they'd gone with the SUV. Wherever that was.

Nothing tied me here. Nothing but my bird that would gladly live with Butter downstairs.

A year into being just a person, and I had nothing. No one who'd miss me for long. No loose ends to tie up, no trace of my existence. It was getting harder and harder to convince myself that Hell wasn't more welcoming.

Theo once again weighed in, and in keeping with my annoyance of Earth and rejecting its amenities, I was getting suspicious. He asked why the Harpy had fizzled out like that, why it was such a mess.

"Well, I'm guessing she wasn't built for visiting Earth. Tell me though, why are you asking? Tell me for real, Theo, why haven't you thrown my ass right out the door, why are we still talking after you've nearly been killed, I've had like eleven panic attacks, crashed on your couch, eaten all your food… What the hell do you want?" I mean, he hadn't even tried anything on me and I'd slept at his house twice. He picked me up at a coffee shop for crying out loud, and we'd done nothing since that wasn't utterly terrifying. What was he up to?

He stood there, in the perfect little kitchen of dark wood and light furnishings and cabinets, this really hot guy in a white t-shirt and sweats, and looked at me like I'd hurt his feelings.

"Seriously, what do you want with me?" I asked with gritted teeth.

Shifting his weigh to one foot, he snickered, looked away with an eye roll in disbelief. "Can it not be enough that I like you?"

"No it can't. Nobody likes anybody enough to withstand this kind of bullshit." *Robbie.*

"I want to get to know you and the best way to do it is to withstand exactly this kind of bullshit," he said, the slight but genuine smile returning. But when I didn't immediately gush over his unearned loyalty, he continued. "I'm twenty-six years old, I've seen more dead bodies than just about anyone outside of a morgue, half the city works for my dad which makes it pretty tough to get a date who isn't terrified or on payroll, or gold digging as the best case scenario. And honestly, every girl I've dated, employee or not, has been so fucking *boring* I couldn't bring myself to ask for a second date most of the time. I get whatever I want, like a prince. I try to work for it, but it's a lie. So, yeah, if you want to know what's in it for me, the answer is two-fold: fun and somebody else's danger. Good enough for you?"

It had been a few days of me talking about myself and my shit and I'd barely asked about his life. But this seemed like a pretty accurate summary of what being a mob kid would be like. And who was I to turn away a friend who actually wanted to be part of this shit show?

"All right, Goodfella, but don't say I didn't warn you." The smile on my face couldn't be controlled. Because for once, I felt like I was gonna have some fun.

"Your SUV is being worked on, but for now my driver will bring you home—if that's what you want to do—but I think it's kinda nuts. Rose is here, we're short on time, obviously Satan considers this your work-space, so might as well…"

"When this is over you should be in my new band, Satan's Workspace. But for now, I need to at least check on my bird, call the landlady."

Theo pulled out his phone and was already talking to someone before I could ask him who the hell he needed to talk to right now.

"The driver is going to get your bird for you, bring him here. How's that sound?"

"Um, great," I said, letting it sink in. "But I mean, I should get some clothes maybe?"

"You have all the clothes you could need downstairs in the shops."

"Let me guess, free of charge?"

He flashed me a winning smile. Pretty sure that was the reason he didn't have to work for anything, not quite as much because his family owned Boston.

Breakfast showed up like magic, and I never ate so many eggs in my life. The need for meat had dwindled, which I hadn't noticed. I'd gone back to eating in fits and spurts by necessity instead of making it necessary to eat for the past few days. The more Hell that was in my life, the less I struggled with overeating. Dipping my toes in and out of Hell kept me in fight or flight mode, surviving on barely anything. I don't know which was less healthy.

I dropped my fork on the plate with an ear-splitting

echo, but it was less intrusive than the sudden screeching in my brain.

Theo's voice was a thing underwater beneath the high-pitched wailing in my mind that could only be Rose.

"...told her to stay out of my head!" I finally heard the end of my own words. "Fuck that was like a knife to the brain. How many times is she going to rip my head apart and wiggle it back together this week? Shit, my head!" I clutched my skull as the screech rattled around it again, this time shorter.

Then the flashback came.

Pinned to the ground, frozen by fear and something else, a disconnection. The shush of grass rubbing under my head. The trees above. The grunting. And the words. *Undo you from the inside.*

Screaming, the flashback snapped away like a slap, replaced with a bird, dismembered, blood on my tiny hands.

Rose. I was remembering with her. In her mind.

Image of waking up in a puddle of urine, crying for my mother.

My mother.

Then a picture of my own mother. Needle in her arm, hanging half off the couch. A line of drool, thick, tinted brown down her cheek from her mouth.

My mother, eyes bloodshot and bleary, smoothing my hair. She didn't have to kneel this time, I was older. Almost as tall as her. And I hurt all over. In places I hadn't wanted to think about. It had not been the first time.

Me, staring out the window, seeing nothing. Nothing. Feeling nothing. Wishing I was nothing.

Like a needle being pulled out slowly, the images went away leaving me on Theo's kitchen floor. Piss streamed down my legs, but I saw blood when I looked, then piss, then blood, then the pain of being touched, no more touching, please. "Please," I was saying out loud, but no one would hear me. Painter loved when I said please. "Please." What else was there to say? I had no other words. I had nothing.

"*Charity*," I heard, and moaned. I hated when Painter said my name. But then again, "Charity," and the hand I was punching away was Theo's. I remembered where I was again. "Charity, should I call an ambulance?" he was asking me, holding my hands. I'd scratched his face, it was bleeding.

But I couldn't answer him, I could only cry and cry and never not cry again.

He held me when I knew my body didn't actually hurt anymore, that I could be touched again, that he wasn't Carl Painter. When the memory that wasn't my memory of Cody Reese had burned itself away, leaving me scorched. He held me even though I'd peed on his floor like a fucking dog. And I had to tell myself all over again that I was not nothing. I had to remind myself what Psychiatrist always told me, that I had intrinsic value and nothing I did could remove it.

Psychiatrist. "Theo," I said, my voice cracking, my throat cracking. He let go of me, I heard the fridge open and quietly clunk shut as I stared out the window. Remembered staring out the window in Rose's head, in my own head after we'd been hurt so badly.

The ice-cold bottle of water he placed in my hand snapped me back to the moment. "I don't know what to say," I said after a long, painfully cold swig.

"You don't have to say anything. It's nothing."

Nothing. Nothing. Nothing.

The tears came again but my throat hurt too much to let the sob happen. I grit my teeth, a reminder of where I was right then and there. Just me and Theo.

But Rose had been in my head.

"She's—Rose—she's reliving memories," I said. "She must have cracked Mortimer. Fuck, what did she do to him?"

"You can't worry about him right now, you need a moment to gather yourself. Get in a hot shower, you'll feel better."

I couldn't tell him I didn't want to be alone because that was an invitation to shower with me and the memory of how much I shoved away through sex, through drinking, through eating, through murdering as a Harpy swelled in me like a tidal wave. He wasn't that guy, and I didn't have to be that girl.

"Hot shower. Yeah. And maybe some more coffee."

It was full daytime now, and I felt like a countdown

clock was ticking in my soul. Everything needed to be handled like, yesterday. Before yesterday. Everything...

Mortimer, held captive...by Rose, who was reliving memories, and inflicting them upon *me*...Rose, who had given me an ultimatum to help her or lose the psychiatrist basically. And fucking *Satan* was looking for me. That should have been the least surprising thing ever.

I'd barely gotten out of the shower when I heard the scratching. Not like a cat scratching—thicker. By something bigger. One guess what it was.

Emerging as decently as I could in a towel, I found Theo's back to me at the big picture window that I loved. Hard to love it when on the other side was a Harpy, much more put together than Satan's shitty messenger, this was one that fed well in the Wood of Suicides. The big question was which team was she on? How many teams were there at this point anyway?

I pulled on my new clothes (pink jogging pants and a hoodie with a Boston Strong t-shirt), as I stumbled over to Theo's side.

"You didn't think of a bra, huh?" I said, our shoulders touching, looking straight forward where a Harpy hovered inches away on the other side of the glass, powerful flaps of her wings ruffling her blonde hair.

Eyes still on our new friend, Theo responded, "Maybe I did and decided against it."

"Comfort is key," I said. "Shall we let the birdie in?"

"Meh, why not? These windows don't open though. She's gonna have to use the door like everybody else."

Surprise, no she didn't. She imploded in a black butthole of a portal and reappeared beside me as it reverse-burst open, spilling her out.

"Holy crap, that was sick!" Theo gasped.

"Charity Blake," she said in a voice much slicker than most Harpies. She'd held onto her humanity. "A word?"

"I'll leave you two to…talk," Theo said.

"So," I started. "Which team are you on? We need shirts now, or ID cards."

She smiled. Real teeth, that didn't look too disgusting, as if they'd been brushed once or twice. She was intriguing. "I believe you might remember our mutual friend, Loretta."

Loretta. The Harpy I actually had fond memories of. Elegant—or as elegant as she could be—all black and flapper-esque, definitely made a Harpy in the twenties. I bet she'd have been cool to hang out with. But I never recalled another that was as put together as her.

"I'm Sandra. You certainly wouldn't remember me this way. The last time you saw me I was no more civil than any of the other creatures in the Wood."

"What happened?" I asked, dumbfounded.

"Rose did," she said.

I asked her to sit down, like she was a guest, but she just happened to be the nicest guest so far. She folded in her wings—simple wings, seagull-white, not completely clean or dirty—and she was suddenly not so different from me. She glanced down at her Harpy feet, the talons alone the size of one of my hands.

With a sad smile she said, "I cannot fully transition the way you do. I don't know if anyone can."

"The way I *did*," I corrected. "I'm clean now."

Her laugh was part cruel, part hurt, part civil. "Clean," she said. "Is that how you feel now?"

I sat up straighter. "Clean*er*, how's that? Not soaked in human blood most days. Now how about you take it down a peg and tell me what you're here for. We're all on borrowed time here."

She folded her claws in her lap. "Rose was able to take apart all of my memories, bring me back to myself. She undid so much damage, it changed me entirely— though not enough to remove me from the Wood of Suicides. Not enough to make me human again, living again."

"Okay, I follow. So you're here to…"

"Loretta and I, some of the others, we became Harpies upon death. We came from this world; most of the Harpies did not."

She said this like it was supposed to mean something to me, but it didn't. Thankfully, Theo had been listening from the hallway like a creep. He approached us, clearing his throat and I told Sandra that it was fine, to back down. Obviously not a big truster of the menfolk, this one.

"I kinda think I know what she's hinting at," Theo offered shyly.

"Enlighten us, boy," Sandra said.

Unfazed, he said, "That one who came before, she didn't look like she had one human thing about her. She wasn't supposed to be here. Like in alien movies how they can't adjust to Earth's air, she couldn't stay here."

"Ooooooh, I get it," I said.

But Sandra didn't look like she followed. "Who came earlier?" she asked.

"Oh, she wasn't with you guys," Theo said.

I leaned over and whispered, "The big guy sent her," hoping she'd be super impressed.

She leaned back, eyes wide, her mouth a perfect O. When she finally closed her mouth, blinked the fear away, she said, "I must go."

"Oh hell no," I said, "you're staying right here. Tell me why you came."

"He has stepped in and you expect me to stay? The Devil himself."

"Yup, that's the guy, and you're already here. Hey, I'll put in a good word for you. He wants me to come visit."

Sandra let out an actual cry at that one. "You cannot!" she gasped.

Mocking her was fun. "But I can!" I gasped, a hand flying to my throat.

"Wait, Charity, you're going?" Theo said.

Truth was, I hadn't planned on it but once I was told I couldn't, that changed everything. Finally, I felt like I was in the driver's seat on this one. "Yeah, I mean we're talking *Satan*. Who turns that down? Besides, can you imagine the bands that must play in The Devil's place? All the good ones, so much metal."

"Bands?" Theo said, "How much more of this do you think you can handle?" I thought he was finally coming to his senses, would stop seeing the cool side of my once and again lifestyle. "I don't think there's any coming back from seeing…Him."

"Then I'll be quick," Sandra said. "Certainly I don't want to disappoint you—you, who Satan has chosen to speak with. "As I was saying, Rose has done something incredible for me—given me my humanity back."

"But…"

"But now I live in Hell," she said with a laugh. "I'm able to come above, and if Rose has it her way then I'll be accepted here. If there is a 'here' to return to when she's done with it. What you must understand, what you certainly do, is that Hell is my home now, the only home I can truly remember, the only home where I felt powerful, and I despise it. She damned me to live there, now with the idea, the *hope* of who I could be on Earth."

I swallowed hard. "Yeah. Yeah that sucks. I'm sorry." Not human anymore, but wanting to be and being stuck in Hell *fucking eating people.*

"That's not all," she went on, glancing over her

shoulder as if expecting Satan to show up. "Not all of those who had their memories restored are as, let's say, well-adjusted as I am. Truly, they will be her avenging angels on Earth, with a vendetta that won't ever be sated until they've eradicated everyone. And they all love Rose. They all love her like the child they wish they had, or had been."

Theo made a noise. I couldn't look at him.

"And the others?" I asked.

"Like I said, there are some of us who went to Hell upon death—but the majority of the Harpies are simply monsters, Charity. I...I can call you Charity, right? Would you rather Miss Blake?" I shook my head and she went on. "They were created in and for the Wood of Suicides. Unleashed upon this world they would do nothing but tear it to shreds."

"Until they implode," Theo said.

"I don't know what you mean by that," Sandra said.

"The one the big guy sent was a mess and she was here for like, seconds before *poof*. Or more like a splat-fart thing," I said.

"I don't know that this is what will happen to all Harpies who come above, but I can say that they will bring a level of destruction that the world has never seen," Sandra said ominously.

No shit, Sherlock. I knew that, But I knew something else now, too: Once Sandra heard Satan was checking me out, she started being extra polite. She wanted to call me Miss Blake—and there was a flicker of fear in her eyes. I hadn't seen that fleeting fear since I'd given up being a true predator.

This felt like an open door begging me to sashay my ass through.

"I hear what you're saying," I said, unleashing my inner diplomat, "but that's not exactly breaking news. Harpies no bueno on the upper crust."

"Are you offering a solution?" Theo said.

"Wait, I've got this one," I interjected. "You want me to kill Rose, right? You think I just magically can murder her. Or you want me to peace-talk her."

"No, actually," Sandra said.

"Oh a new idea? Like me leading the Harpies in a revolt? Haven't heard that one before." Except I had.

"I want you to convince her…" Sandra said, pausing to take a hard, deep breath, and reaching over to grab both of my hands as if she was pulling me to shore to save me from drowning. "I want you to convince her to end it all. Charity, convince her to take the Wood of Suicides apart."

CHAPTER 12

My time was—nothing. It wasn't even short, it was non-existent. Hours until Rose wanted an answer about fighting by her side. Her memories forked into my brain here and there, until I'd run out of bile to expel. If I fought against her with Cleary and Bob, it would have to be decided like, yesterday. Mortimer was waiting for me to rescue him, and if Rose was hurting me from a distance, I could only imagine what she was doing to him up close. It felt like a year ago that the Harpies had destroyed Psychiatrist's SUV and tried to abduct me back to the Wood, the place I'd tried to escape successfully for over a year. Who did I answer first? Who the hell would I side with?

Pretty sure I'd better check in with Satan.

"From whence you came," I said to Sandra after her

big idea was revealed. "Total props on thinking outside the box. I mean, convincing the devil baby to just shut down shop when she's right on the brink of franchising? Bold. Now that I'm in the loop, from whence you came. Go. Go now."

"You're not taking this seriously," she said. "Please, listen to what I have to say, I've come all this way."

"Didn't look too hard for you."

"I assure you, getting out of the Wood undetected is quite a feat. No sooner did she afford us the opportunity than she decided who went where and why."

I sized her up for a second. "Were the ones who tried to take me to the Wood before, the ones who trashed my car, they yours?"

"No. I knew nothing of it."

"Is *anyone* on the same side down there, for fucks sake?"

She sneered, and it was the first sign of the ugliness of the Harpy that I'd seen from her. They were all alike in some ways. "Nobody is on anyone's side in Hell," she spat. "The Wood needs to be brought down, finished, not expanded to the world above..."

She kept ranting but a jagged knife tore through my head, someone else's scream from inside sliding out of the brain wound like a tongue. *"You knew!"* she wailed. *"You kneewwwwwww..."* in a moan erupting with agony, blame, disbelief.

This. This was terror. The need to scream, cry, fall

over, kill myself before she made it to me first, the knowledge that Rose had learned something I could never defend against about me, something I could never come back from. It didn't matter what it was, the accusation was enough to make it true. It was real to her, and it was real to me.

What had she learned?

"Oh. Oh, shit." Theo's quiet words popped like a tiny bubble through the din of my destroyed brain, my quivering body. "Oh, shit," he said again, with more fear this time. I felt it, I felt everything from everyone at once.

This was what Rose had become.

With a sound like rusty, heavy metal being dragged across a sidewalk, the pain, the anger was gone leaving me with only my fear of Rose, a fear unlike anything I'd ever known. A fear more debilitating than any monster I'd known on Earth. My body loosened, a flopping mess in my seat, my bones liquefied.

"...can never unite the Harpies," Sandra finished. A glance behind her and I saw that Theo was on the phone, worry lines taking over his face, rapid blinking betraying his fear. He was afraid. That wasn't good.

And it wasn't good that nobody noticed I'd just been rent from top to bottom, that everything about my consciousness had changed, been demolished and rebuilt in the wrong shape. A bloody puzzle being squashed together badly. I held my torment inside, the teetering meat tower crumbling with every millisecond for only myself to see.

This was what Rose had been her whole life.

Of course she wanted revenge. I wanted it for her.

"I have to go," I croaked.

"What?" Sandra said. "Where?"

"Charity," Theo interrupted, shoving his phone into his pocket. "I'm so sorry."

"What?" Everything was happening at once, around me and to me. "Sorry for what?"

But it only took a second for me to remember what we'd been waiting for. What should have been here by now.

Theo crossed the room to me in long strides, scooped me up under the arms and held me close, and everything else disappeared for a blink in time. Until he said, "That was my driver. Your landlady..."

"Butter?" I gasped, even while I felt relief that it wasn't Keegan, that the little life I'd been missing and brought me peace and loved me right back was safe.

He pulled me slightly away to look in my eyes. "She's been killed. And...and..."

"No. No and."

"She knows!" Sandra cried, and so help me if I didn't want to kick her down a fucking flight of stairs for tearing me away from the evils my life had been turned into, my inner meat tower swaying precariously. Sandra splayed her fingers out in front of her, creating a beautiful portal that glimmered at the edges like one of those rocks you smash open to find crystals inside. And as quickly as she'd fucked up my day, she was gone through it, leaving behind one more thing for me to do, one more consideration, one more option without even the time to weigh it. All the choices, all the consequences were on me and I couldn't even take a fucking breath.

I never should have left the Wood at all. Everything didn't fall apart at the same time, instant by instant, when I was there.

"I'm so sorry," Theo said again. Normally I'd have wanted to punch anyone who apologized so many times for something they'd had nothing to do with. Such a sign of weakness.

"You really are, aren't you?" I said.

"Yeah," he said, eyes darting, "of course I am. Way too much happening at once. I don't know how you handle it. How much longer you can. So much death, it's gotta take a toll on you."

I straightened up, threw on my brave face. "I've *been* death. I know how it works and how easy it is to come by."

"Granted, you sound badass, but I know you're hurting. I wish I could—"

"Don't," I snapped, holding up a hand. "Savior complexes don't fit in my world."

He squinted, shook his head. "Savior complex? I just wanted to—"

"No guy sees what I've shown you and 'just' wants to do anything. Look, I get you've got some blood on your hands, but I'm not your ticket to absolution, got it?" I knew I was being a royal douche, but niceties weren't coming to me easily at this point.

Dropping his head, he muttered, "Got it."

A knock sounded on the door and I groaned, praying for a blackout. I couldn't hear Keegan's name, or see his fragile little body, another body I was responsible for.

Theo set me down on the couch and went to the door as I watched, wondering if it would be the driver alone or if he'd brought the body of my little bird that had been free if he wanted but chose to stay with me.

"No," I moaned as I saw the cage dangling from his left hand.

But Keegan was in it. Alive. "Alive!" I screamed and jumped up, ran to them and fell to my knees, pulled open the miniature door that kept him safe as the man stayed still, letting me do whatever I needed to. I cooed his name, "Keegan, baby, come on out," and he came right to me, the little watermelon-sunrise-fire bird, curled right into my open palm. This was bliss. This was happiness. Simplicity.

Wait. Keegan still cupped in my hand I looked up at Theo whose sadness had turned around at seeing me so happy. Impossible not to be happy with that sweet chirping in the air. "Theo, you...I thought you were going to say Keegan was..."

"No. No," he said, as if he couldn't say any more.

"Rose, she was sending a message, she killed that poor woman—" I was distracted by the driver's quickly sallowing face at the mere mention of it. I did *not* want to know what Rose had done to the sweet lady who'd cared about me for some unknown reason. The message had been clear—Rose was pissed, more furious than any furious thing ever could be, and she'd makeme pay.

But under it all, she was still a little girl who couldn't kill a bird.

"Oh god," I cried, the agony too much to think of. The reality another gash in my soul that couldn't hold any more pain or guilt or anger. "Oh my god, no!"

The driver pulled a piece of paper from an inner pocket of his coat. I noticed how chapped his hands were, from the bitter cold. I noticed how his wool sleeve bunched up a little as his hand disappeared to the hidden pocket. I noticed his gold watch get covered again as his hand emerged with the note meant for me, the note that would say something I couldn't bear to hear. It crinkled, a thick sound.

It was on butcher paper.

~

*B*lood stained the white paper. It showed when I unfolded the neat wrapping, letting out a burst of laughter as my stomach unclenched—because shit, at least she'd had the decency not to wrap up a piece of Matt's body in here, even though it lacked a bit of follow-through. I mean, how perfect would that have been? The body parts of the butcher's kid, butchered and wrapped in butcher paper?

The laughter kept coming as I fell against the door frame and the tears came, pouring down my face, splashing onto Rose's note:

You knew. This is your punishment

Nothing little girlish about that note. Even the damn handwriting. I didn't know what she was talking about, but it didn't matter.

Rose. Killed. Matt.

I couldn't live like this, knowing that kid, that sweet kid who I had no right to even talk to, was dead because of me. How in fucking hell could Rose *do* that to him? Such an innocent if there ever was one, such a gangly, thoughtful, quiet kid who worked with his dad for fucks sake.

I slid down to the floor, and Theo sat beside me. I handed him Keegan; I didn't deserve that comfort. I didn't deserve the love he had for me, the soothing nature of his little soul. Not a soulless beast like me.

"You're sure?" I said, voice hollow.

"I'm sure, miss," the driver said above me.

Part of me wanted to say, "prove it." Part of me

knew that he'd have proof and I couldn't ever, ever handle seeing it. Never.

I'd been an asshole in my life, and I'd done some terrible shit. But this was the worst by far. There was no coming back from this one. I didn't want to be in a world where kids like Matt died simply for knowing me.

Once again, I was saved from knowing what to say or do, was saved from hearing how sorry Theo and his driver were, because there was another glimmer in the air where Sandra had transported back to the Wood. It glimmered, glowed like it was full of radioactive chemicals now, and it grew wider, bleeding at the edges rather than expanding. Then it exploded like a zit and out came a Harpy. I didn't have the energy to react. Just a regular bird-bitch, nothing exciting. Brown wings, haggard face, dead behind the eyes. Still stronger than me. Still hadn't killed as many people as I had.

Rose might have killed Mrs. Bitters and Matt, but I was the one who'd given her the taste for blood.

"You knew." I heard Rose's words repeated in my head as I went towards the hissing Harpy.

Theo jumped in front of me, eyes wide, practically begging me. "Charity, you can't possibly mean to go with her."

"Enough with the savior complex."

"You keep saying that, but I think you're the one with a savior complex."

"*What?*" But shit. I hadn't thought of that. "What-ever, either way, I'm stronger than you think."

"No, I think you're pretty strong. But what kind of friend would I be if I didn't point out how fucking mental this is?" he said, leaning in.

"What choices do I have, Theo?" I answered as gently as I could. There wasn't a whole lot of gentle left in me but he didn't deserve the nastiness I was giving him. "Whether I go with Rose or I go with Sandra and Loretta, or I go with Rose's father, they're all death sentences and I'll end up in Hell one way or another." His head dropped, and my heart went with it. "Hey, I'm coming back. I'm coming back, I swear. I need to do my part. I'm going to Hell but I've already been there and gotten out—I can do it again. Besides, I'm no more damned down there than I am up here."

He put his hand on the side of my face, like someone who really cared. I couldn't get over the fact that we'd just goddamn met. I hadn't even slept with him. The thought that maybe sex wasn't the only factor here brought a smile to my lips and he smiled in return, just as small.

"You know I'm a little afraid, right?" he said with a laugh.

"Oh shit, I should hope so. It's good, makes you less of a hero. But I can't just sit around and think about things anymore, I have to move. These clowns," I said, gesturing to the average Harpy, "haven't had their say yet, and I think it's because they can't make their brains work up here. I'm just going to chat. Really! Then I'll see what's going on down there with my own eyes."

"Will you come back...different?" Theo said, eyebrows raised.

The Harpy grabbed my hand. God, she was cold.

"I'm already different," I said. I kissed him, soft and lingering. "But I might come back with upgrades."

CHAPTER 13

hud! We hit the hay-strewn ground, face-first. "I never get tired of that," I bitched after I tore myself up. Gobs of gore clung to my hair. I ripped the elastic out.

No more ponytail.

The Wood of Suicides. It had been months and it felt like longer. Looked like longer, too. This place, that had been unchanging, forever stuck, was different.

Still blood-red, the sky now had huge white rifts across it, as if ginormous claws had tried to gut it open. Sparks, like wires shorting out, spit from the rifts and set fires in the hay below. All around, Harpies flapped away, screeching.

The Harpies had never been friendly with each other, not even the best of them, but now it was worse. Some huddled together, pecking at each other even in their own groups. Others had barricaded themselves behind torn-off limbs from the human trees. Grotesque braids of arms and legs, ending in ever-bleeding stumps, hiding the very monsters who fed off them. More hid in the breathing tree knots, feeling safer peering out from between distorted faces in constant screams than among their own kind.

"All right, all right, wherever we're going, get me there fast. I didn't miss this place as much as I thought I would."

"Still think you're too good for us, huh?" she said. Sounded a whole lot smarter down here. So it was true, that they couldn't hold their shit together on Earth.

"You don't like it up there, do you?" I said.

"That's not where we're meant to be," she said simply.

"But don't you think it's like, better? I mean, you could eat so many different kinds of meat—" I sucked in a breath like I'd been punched in the gut at the thought of meat.

Matt.

Fuck, why had I called him Meat Matt when I knew he didn't like it?

I choked back tears. There was no place for them here and I didn't get the luxury of shedding them anymore.

The Harpy whose name I never got because it didn't matter, craned her neck back and up, throat bobbing as she let out this crazy bird call. It bounced off the invisible walls of this place, too terrible to let out. It worked though—a half dozen Harpies came ape-walking to us, and encircled us with their wings like a shield.

Damn, it stank in that huddle hole. Raw meat and ancient body odor.

I yelped when they all like, locked wings, and lifted both me and Nameless Harpy up, up, up, taking me unseen to some relatively safe spot. No spot is safe in Hell, obviously.

When they slapped their wings back ungracefully, I grimaced at their sanctuary.

A craggy cliff heaped with trampled skulls and still-blinking, half-crushed human eyeballs. They all seemed to be blue, giving a late night TV glow under the black hood over us—which turned out to be the former Queen's black nest, overturned. It was held up a couple of feet on one side by a few femurs, tied together with blackening intestines.

Talk about making a statement.

"Who *is* your decorator, she's a genius."

"It is a disgrace," one Harpy snapped. "Our Queen's throne, salvaged from the wastes. This is our only memory of her now."

"Didn't find her crown, huh?" I said. Because shit, that thing was beastly cool. Black, glittery, defiantly tall and spiky.

"Not true," another said. She looked war-ravaged. Deep scars running down each cheek, one eye milky. She produced the beautiful thing from under a—oh, man, from under a Harpy wing, clearly torn off at the shoulder. These Harpies loved symbolism. She held it up, the others taking turns ogling it and looking over their shoulders for threats.

"We want you to have it, Charity," she said.

"We want you to *earn* it," another growled, glaring at me.

"Coulda fooled me. You nearly killed me trying to get me here the first time."

"Harpies aren't built for the world above, not a one of us," the one who took me from Theo's said. "For those who believe Rose's propaganda, it will spell disaster."

"Would you say it was a suicide mission?" I joked, badly. But it did raise the question, if they didn't survive the vacation, wouldn't they just end up back here anyway? What would it hurt to try? I chose to keep that to myself.

"There are worse places in Hell than this one," she said.

Another piped up in a jarringly soft voice, "We were born here," eyes roving around the circle, "and we don't want to leave. To be torn from our home after seeing it fall into chaos like this, that would be Hell to us."

"Hell is different for us," one murmured and they all agreed with clicking nods of their heads and gnashing of teeth.

"True that," I said without wanting to. "Listen, what do you want me to do? You want me to fight off Rose, or what? What's your idea?"

The thing about Harpies—and especially ones born in the Wood, it turns out—is that they're just as bad at planning as I am. Maybe that's why they like me so much.

They looked back and forth at each other, like they never expected that I would ask something like that, and it was probably true.

"We—*ahem*—" she actually cleared her throat, something I'd never seen a Harpy do, "thought you might have a plan," the first of the ten little monkeys said.

"A plan, like a leader would have," another added.

"And before you object," another said, "yes, you are a leader whether you like it or not. You're the first one to change anything here, the only one that the Queen wanted until Rose came along. You're the rightful heir if there ever was one."

Well, that went right to my head. It had been a long time—over a year, to be specific—that I'd felt in control of much of anything. It had been that long since I'd felt like myself.

"You all thrive on chaos, though, I mean look at this place you set up. Nice."

"We need a leader, someone to keep us from killing each other!"

"And someone to keep the Wood the same."

"Rose will change everything!"

They went on to tell me how they love Rose but she needs to be their child, she needs a big sister or a mother, *meaning me*, and that she'd never be welcome above again.

"Well, you might be right about that, but I cannot—will not—stay here. I can't run the Wood. I don't belong here, not anymore."

They all looked genuinely hurt, their eyes darkening as they gaped at each other, none of them talking over each other anymore.

"She'll destroy this place, won't she?" I said. *And some want her to.*

And with a faraway look that spoke of doom and other dimensions, something beyond what I could understand or see, a place she saw all on her own, a Harpy said, "Even if she doesn't mean to."

I fell to my side from the crouch I'd been in—standard Harpy stance—because an earthquake rocked the ground.

"You guys get earthquakes here?" I asked as another shook us, the nest held up by bones, everything judging by the alarmed screeches piercing the tomato-soup air.

"It's her!" a short, round Harpy cried and bolted from the nest, possibly afraid of being caught.

Speaking of being caught…

The ground shook harder, faster. The intestines unraveled from the bone tent-pole, sending everything crashing down. The Harpies underneath it left me, and the nest toppled down, pinning me.

"She's here," I heard in a crisp, frozen in fear voice.

The nest vaulted off me and went spinning through the air, tearing white streaks behind it.

Through the white streaks Rose's memories appeared to me, or her version of them. Death in lightning-fast pictures, each punctuated by an assaulting slicing sound and brilliant flashes like metal in the sun, *crack! Flash!*

An old woman, burned to a crisp with blackened wires and tubes hanging out of her in a hospital bed.

Crack!

A tiny child's hand, palm down in the grass. Her fingers curl into the dirt. A fuzzy peripheral vision shows flowers set aflame.

Flash!

The same mutilated seagull, the air slowly deflating from it.

Crack! Flash! And then…

Matt. Splayed on the white ground like he was making snow angels. Rivers of red ran from his hands and feet, trailing into the slushy, icy gutter and mixing with clumps of dirty innards.

He lifted his head, his eyes gone, leaving only red holes. He croaked out my name.

As the lightning flashed and the sound tore through my head I screamed, "Is this real? Is this real?"

The shaking stopped. The flashing, the visions, all stopped. But that *feeling,* that inability to see anything but the decay under everything, in everyone, the destruction they wrought…

The images stopped, but Rose never would. She couldn't. There was so little left of her now.

High in the air like a nightmare star, the red girl blended right into the thick red haze around her, but for the pulsing of her entire body, like a thudding heartbeat, expanding and contracting. And of course, there were the wings. Great, vicious mass of razor edges, not a work of art as much as they were a flying junk drawer of knives.

When Keegan's feathers shed or whatever, it was like little single flames falling to the bottom of the cage. But this…heavy, deadly blades, thick and ugly, rusted with blood. Razors, knives, sharp slivers of metal, fell from her to the ground below. Some of them dangled, used and damaged, rattling around her, cutting her all the time. The gashes up and down her arms and legs gaped open, fresh.

"You knew!" she shouted at me, voice cracking like the lightning in her mind. She sounded so hurt still, always hurt.

"Knew what?" I shouted back. "I can count on one hand the number of things I know."

She folded the wings back with a deep clanging sound. They were more like the Ghost of Christmas Past's chains than wings. Such a lie to her, that they could free her. She was the picture of damned, her wings clattery and falling apart, though they still carried her. In one fell swoop, she was in front of me, a flurry of blades falling around her. Good lord, she reeked like an old charcoal grill. The Wood was just chock full of smells that I didn't notice as much when I'd been a Harpy.

"I can't believe you didn't tell me about my father," she moaned, eyebrows knit together. "The Facility. He made that place to keep me! He held me there!"

That threw me, because that wasn't one of her memories. How could it be? She learned that. *This isn't a memory that she dragged out of Mortimer.* The faintest relief that she hadn't messed with Mortimer like we sorta agreed upon, mingled with the realization that she still didn't have all her memories, then. That she was still dying. "He didn't know what else to do, Rose."

"You're defending him!"

"No! Well, maybe a little! Kid, how could anyone know what was best for you, especially after what you'd been through? There's never been a kid like—"

"Do *not* say there's never been a kid like me. There's never been a kid like any kid that's out there. Everyone is different, everyone is hard in their own way, it doesn't give their family the right to lie and imprison them, force them to be alone. My *father*," she spat, "didn't even try to learn how to be a father to me after I'd been hurt. He contained me. Like I was the problem, not that boy who raped me." She said the word too casually, even making *me* wince. "He turned me into a lab rat and didn't even watch! He's ashamed of me! Of *me*," she said, scoffing. "He's *ashamed* because I'm not just different—I'm better."

I gulped, because she wasn't wrong. The dude made a prison for her and left her there for another guy to raise because he was too scared and too helpless. But it didn't change anything. "Your past sucked, but holding grudges like this, taking revenge, none of it matters now, if you just change *yourself.* Stop thinking of everyone else, kid, think of yourself! It didn't have anything to do with—" I couldn't say his name. *Matt.* Then I felt guilty that Butter got pushed out of my head to think of him. "Rose, how could you do what you did to Matt? And that little old lady?" My eyes filled up.

"You needed to be taught a lesson," she said with a shrug. "I also needed to remind you of what happens to those who defy me now."

"Dressing for the job you want, I guess," I said, anger overtaking my sadness. "Satan-red doesn't really suit you, kid. Neither does irrational murder."

"How about rational murder?" She grinned. "You know, Dr. Mortimer has been helpful to me—after some persuading—but I think you've gotten the point. So *have* you thought about our discussion, about returning here and changing this place for the better?"

My heart stopped. "You're saying you'll kill Psychiatrist if I don't stand at your side." She only blinked slowly in response. Scoffing, I looked around to see that most Harpies had hidden themselves, barely peeking out at Rose. Hell beasts that were afraid of a kid. It had been just fine without her.

"Why does it have to change here?" I asked. "Look around, kid. They're scared of you."

"They are not all scared of me!"

"Uh, yeah they are. Definitely. Some might want to go above, act out your fantasy of killing all the sex predators before they've ever thought about sex, but all these Harpies are afraid of you. On your side or not, you've terrified them, Rose. They're from Hell for fucks sake, and they're scare of you. A kid. Is that what you want? To scare them and change their world on them?"

She shifted feet, then back again. "You see why I need your help, Charity. You question me."

"You literally just said though that you'll kill people I love if I defy you."

"I admit that's a fine line. But to answer your questions, yes and yes. I want them to be afraid of me because otherwise I'm prey. I'm a child, and they love me for it, but I can't be weak. Some of them will never see me as more than a child, and that's why you could be of such help. They respect you."

Same reason the Harpies that didn't want her in charge wanted me. It was starting to look like I was the rightful heir to the throne or whatever. I could see the kid's point, too. Between the two of us we'd be the Wonder Twins down there. A little something for everyharpy.

She turned away from me, making me dodge a stray

razor, and addressed her people far below the cliff. "Harpies, come out and hear me."

It took a second but tentatively they emerged from behind gnarled human limbs and out of the treetops, eyes wide.

"You are creatures of ancient myths. You know this, correct?" Murmurs from the crowd. "And yet you're afraid to walk among those who write epics about you. And there are those of you damned here because of your rage, your pain, the insurmountable horrors you've faced. That pain has made you powerful. I ask you this—are you the monsters?" The Harpies crowded closer, to better see her raised chin, the violent pride. They roared in applause and inhuman calls when she pounded her heart with one hand and cried, "ARE WE NOT HEROES?!"

Fuuuuuck, she was good at this.

Harpies jumped with actual joy, drowning out the moaning of the trees. There was no screaming because every Harpy gathered around Rose, nobody tearing them to shreds. Rose took advantage of it.

"I may not be able to end your pain," Rose called out to the trees with a warble in her voice. "Even you couldn't do that up above, that's why you're one of us now. We are all part of the same machine, the human machine that cycles us, turns us into monsters and damns us. I wouldn't return you to that world if I could," she told the suicide victims, with so much emotion in her voice that I choked up, too. "But I can untwist you. Set you free of each other," she pleaded, "and I can give *them*—" pointing at the horde of Harpies, "true monsters to feed upon!"

Unanimous howls and glorifying cries rose up from prey and predator alike, a din of fanatical cultists united in the worship of a single deity.

Except this deity was coming apart inside, and would take everyone, above and below alike, down with her.

Loretta slowly raised her head down below, catching my eye. She stood out among her ecstatic sisters, stone-faced and focused on me. Her message was clear:

She must be stopped.

"Sooner than you know, we'll rise above and take what's ours! It will be our choice, whether we stay or leave, and we'll rectify the wrongs in that world one monster at a time!"

Oh, I didn't like the sound of that. *Sooner than you know?* The Wood had no sense of time, time was its enemy if there was knowledge of it at all. Soon could be right now for all they knew.

Once the roar had quieted, Rose tried to wrap things up. "Before we're ready, we have but one thing to do," she said. And she turned to me, crouching out of sight behind her where I preferred to stay and saw no reason to leave. "Charity," she said, and held out her hand. Her palm wasn't that demon red of the rest of her. "Come on, Charity," she pleaded. "I need you."

I didn't know what to do. But Rose knew what to say.

"I could forgive all of it, Charity, forget everything. Forget that you ever left me," she said so earnestly that it was clear she wanted it as much, more, than I did, "forget you kept my father from me, or that you wanted to take Dr. Mortimer from me. None of it would matter, and we'd be together. Don't you want that?" She winced, and twitched like the words hurt to say. When she grabbed her head, I knew they had.

She'll die without me.

Not because I could save her, because I probably couldn't—but I thought, when she dies, I won't be there if I don't stay with her now. And I loved her. God help me, I loved the kid and I couldn't leave her alone. Not again.

I took her hand, stood up beside her and went to the edge of the cliff. Jesus Christ, was I forever on the edge of a cliff or what? It was where I was most comfortable. When they saw me, the crowd roared again. Asshole that I am, the swell of pride made me lift my head and smile. The Harpies saw it. Rose definitely saw it. I could feel the waves of heat from her, a differ-ent, *sweeter* kind that felt positive.

How fucking twisted is that?

This place...it twisted everything. Up above, the idea of helping Rose was out of the question. It would mean the end of everything on Earth eventually. But down here, faced with the kid where she was at her most comfortable, with all the Harpies festering without sunlight or air or horror, I could be swayed.

Weak.

I couldn't afford to be weak. More depended on me than I wanted to acknowledge.

When the Harpies had calmed down and gone about their day of just being gross, tearing sinewy muscles and flesh from bones and fighting amongst themselves, I tried to snap out of it, remember that this wasn't where I wanted to be. Who I wanted to be.

Right? Did I know who I wanted to be any more now than I ever had?

But thinking of Matt, Mrs. Bitters, Theo, everyone who had suffered and would, and even her father and Cleary, and—

"Rose, we need to talk about Psychiatrist."

She stiffened. The simmering warmth of her became a boiling again, but she tried to hide it. The turn of her body was a metamorphosis of inspirational leader of evil to child to manipulator when she set her eyes on me.

"Do we?" she asked with an innocent tilt of her head. "Now that you've made your choice, I don't believe you have to worry about him any longer."

"Oh, that doesn't sound right," I said, laughing with poor timing. Her eyes blazed with fury. No flames or anything, but a pissed off kid can be just as scary. "I know you, Rose." I stepped closer to her, challenging, before I lost my nerve. Even though I was a human being with no special anything. Might as well go all in. "You won't be able to stop looking for memories. You won't stop until you've retrieved them all, and you'll kill him to do it. Even if you don't want to, you'll root in his brain so hard that you'll tear him apart."

"He'd deserve it," she said with a sneer.

"Nobody deserves to be *violated*."

The word made her eyes narrow, size me up. "Don't even think of using that word to compare us and him. Looking in his mind for *myself* is not violating him. Him holding my past hostage is a violation! My father, protecting a rapist because he's too scared to own up to his own weakness is a violation. Do you know what my father did? Do you?"

White streaks scratched the air again, smaller, between us, showing memories of Cody Reese behind them like panels from the worst comic book ever.

My stomach went cold.

Her turn to laugh. "He wanted to kill Cody Reese—but he couldn't do it. He was too weak. He had sympathy for that *thing*! After carrying my bloody, despondent body home, after watching me fall apart, he couldn't do it! My great protector." More slashes in the sky around her head, and pain flickered across her face in grimaces and squeezed eyes. "Instead he stashed me away, threw money at the bad situation, hid from me and my mother, and wallowed in his self-pity." Her eyes glowed an electric blue that made me squirm. "He chose a monster over his own child."

That was a tough one to defend. And why exactly was I defending him?

"Yeah, that's unforgiveable. I feel you. He didn't have to kill the kid but he needed to stand by you better."

She leaned away from me, taken aback. "Thank you."

"Yeah, no problem."

Heavy quiet between us though the Wood was far from silent. It was never silent.

Rose suddenly screamed and fell to her knees, white rips in the atmosphere around her head as she clutched her ears and screamed.

Blood poured from her eyes.

Her wings shot out, one, then the other, sloppily as she huddled on the ground, rocking back and forth with slash after slash of hidden memories surrounded her, forcing their way out of her head.

Then with each of her screams, her body…faded. Became less solid, less real. Back again, fully there, in and out, like someone walking in front of a projector.

"R…Rose?" I approached her, halting every step. *This is it,* I thought. *She's dying.*

The white streaks riddled with memories tore out of her brain, that brain which never got a second's rest. Images that I didn't understand, more like feelings given form. The knife wings twitched, spasms sending a blade flying here, there. Any second she could fucking decapitate me, but all I could worry about was that I was losing her. Not an ounce of relief that the world would be safe, only crippling sadness that made me want to melt into the ground and stay there in a puddle, feel nothing, see nothing, never speak again. She deserved so much more.

"Put them away," I said in a voice she couldn't possibly hear. "Rose," I spoke up, "try to fold in your wings. If you can hear me, you have to try, kid."

The words, or my voice, reached her, and the wings flapped around, falling all over themselves like drunk living things, until they retracted. I fell to my knees, held her in my arms as she shook and screamed. I thought of how coherent, but how insane she sounded, how it got worse every time she spoke to me. I wondered how much more there was to her mind, what else was fighting to find its way out.

I wondered if she'd find peace in death.

And I wondered where her soul would go.

She shook, but the screaming slowed, and the white gashes in the air stayed, but there was nothing behind them. When she stopped screaming altogether, a deep shudder wracked her body, and her body went limp against mine.

CHAPTER 14

*T*he sky never darkened in the Wood. Nobody got hungry because they were always eating. A person like me down here was oblivious, like in a casino but instead of fresh air being pumped through it was fucking blood-tinged smog and screams.

It could have been a day, two days that I sat there, holding Rose until my screams turned to nothing, and the nothing turned to crying, and the crying turned to staring. It all blended together in that place. The entire Wood was grief, who would notice a little more? Even if it meant that their beloved daughter was dead?

Turns out it couldn't have been that long.

Rose cracked her neck, stretched out an arm, then two.

"Holy fuck, you're alive!"

"Yeah," she said, stretching like a little girl after a nap. "How long was I asleep?"

But I couldn't answer her, I was too busy crying and squeezing the bejesus out of her. "Kid I didn't think…I don't think…" How do you say to a child that you don't think she can go on a whole hell of a lot longer?

"I'm okay. For now."

And she did sound okay. As if that entire fucking soul spasm hit a reset button or something. Even her skin was a less violent shade of red.

Had I done that for her? And how much more could I do?

Maybe I could save her after all. Even if I shouldn't.

We stayed there for a while, her half in my lap, the two of us taking in the nastiness of the cloudy, bloody atmosphere like we were counting stars.

"There's so much more," Rose said quietly.

"More what?" I ran my fingers through her dirty hair as if it weren't disgusting but the silken gold it had been when I met her.

"More of everything." She sounded content with it, but shit got dark fast. "More memories, more to Hell, more for me to do."

"You know, you don't have to care about it all. You don't need more than this, and you don't have to like, conquer everything. You don't even need all your mem —" But I stopped myself because not accessing all her memories would mean the holes in her brain, those pockets, would take over.

Remembering would kill her and not remembering would kill her.

And would she go anywhere besides Hell when it happened? After what she'd done?

"I can hear your thoughts you know."

"Yup, I can feel it." With her this close to me, it should have been like a punch in the brain stem, but it was softer than that. A slow burn.

"Harpies don't die."

"You're more than a Harpy, though."

"That's right. I am." She stood up, looking every bit as good as new, even her wings folded tightly despite having left sharp bits all around us. She smiled at me, her lips little pink rosebuds still, because she could see into my brain how much I still loved her. Even after all she'd done.

"People aren't just the mistakes they've made," I told her as seriously as I could, because she was in my head, and I had to make every second count. "You're more than the pain, deeper than the things you've done. You can turn this all around, kid."

She dropped her eyes to the ground, swished her bare foot in the blood-blackened hay. "There's no room for me up there. Not anymore. But there's plenty for them," she said, sweeping her arm out over the Wood. "And I can give them choices they didn't have before. That's how I can make up for anything I did wrong. If I did anything wrong. They can stop so much pain up there for kids like me. Us."

Her heart was In the right place, but her mind…

"I'm not crazy," she snapped.

"We're all crazy, kid."

Without warning, blood spurted from her mouth. Her eyes were giant zeroes. She coughed, another spray of blood erupting as she clutched her stomach.

Then her shoulder bucked forward, and I could see what had done it.

A straight razor that had to be as long as my forearm stuck out of her back.

Jumping up, I rushed to rip it out. Her scream of agony tore through every other sound in the Wood.

I wanted to scream too, when I saw the long blade, something from a big industrial machine, jutting out of the middle of her back. It had to have severed her spine. It had to have pierced a half dozen organs. Blood pooled around our feet. It wasn't like you see in movies, it had bubbles in it, and it was dark, as if mixed with mud. I'd seen plenty of blood before, but this time it was a living thing to me.

Again, Rose fell to her knees but I didn't go down beside her.

I dodged a flying butcher knife from above, and saw our assailant. A Harpy, gray wings sprouting from her back, holding razors and a knife in each hand and both claws, baring her teeth at Rose.

Rose was about to be assassinated by her own castoff sharp shit.

I picked up the butcher knife, and threw it like a frisbee at the Harpy.

Not even close.

It fell into the chasm below, and she threw two more, one from each hand.

"We gotta run." I turned to the kid who I expected to be half-dead on the ground. But she surprised me again. And I realized that she was pretty unkillable.

On her feet, Rose's stomach glowed with that searing heat I knew from her, a heat that was thick with the feeling of pulsing organs. Maniacal glee in her eyes, Rose watched her own stomach cauterize its wound, leaving a charred scar in its path and not a hint of pain on Rose's face.

No, the only pain here would be this moron Harpy's, who was sure to pay. Only thing for me to do was get out of the fucking way fast.

The two beasts took each other in until the Harpy screamed—not unusual—but it was when she kept screaming and her mouth opened wider and wider, face cracking like this thing I saw on Animal Planet once, this tiger thing that could open its mouth eighty degrees. She hung in the air, paralyzed as her head was ripped in half. Then she fell to the ground.

Remember how there was never silence in the Wood? True until that moment. And it was full of wondering what in the holy hell could happen next because there were a *lot* of directions this could go.

I didn't expect Harpies to shoot up out of the crowd

from all over, straight up like missiles, covering every inch of the Wood until it blurred black at the edges.

This was planned.

"Rose…"

The one who attacked Rose, she was a suicide bomber.

"Rose," I repeated.

But she was surveying the dozens of Harpies waiting in the air for some cue, some agreed-upon moment, and when that moment came, Rose wouldn't be able to fight them all off. She couldn't. Maybe she could. No, she couldn't, there were too many. And it wasn't a risk I was willing to take.

Think fast.

I did the only thing I could do. The only thing that would work.

I remembered as hard and deep as I could, the feeling of my wings slicing open the backs of my arms as they emerged.

The peeling back of my toenails as talons emerged.

The way the beak took over my face.

The power, the raw power of the sweep of my wings.

When I opened my eyes…

There was nothing. Only me.

Rose had one hand up like she was Force-choking the closest Harpy while simultaneously separating her limbs from the joints. Her arms and legs held on just enough to keep them in the air, enough for Rose to show the rest of them what lay in store. I watched as she committed the cruelest act—slowly, slowly ripped the wings from the Harpy's body, letting her plummet to the ground. I think she was already dead.

The others whipped their heads around, looking to one another, but there wasn't fear in their eyes. They didn't even look particularly surprised.

"Of course they aren't surprised," Rose thought into my head as loud as a tractor-trailer crash. *"They knew I was prepared for a fight."*

And of course Rose hadn't been surprised either. What a jackass I'd been to think she didn't know of the plots against her. No one's mind was safe around her. She wasn't safe from it herself.

"Rose we have to go! You can't hold them off by yourself!"

That might have been the cue they'd been waiting for, because as one they all folded their wings flat against them and dive-bombed toward the cliff where we stood. I screamed at her that I couldn't help her in this fight, and she screamed back that she knew.

"Then why do you want me with you?" I yelled across the deafening wails and cries as the haggard, vicious faces of the Harpies drew nearer with every millisecond.

She looked over her shoulder, smiling, incredulously shaking her head. "Because you're my sister," she said with a laugh.

My sister who was about to die.

The first Harpy hit, the second not a breath afterward, then a third, a fourth, until they'd piled upon her and she was totally unseen. I was calling for her, over and over, but she didn't answer, and not one Harpy looked my way. Because I wasn't a threat.

With a great, guttural howl, I threw my head back, threw my arms out at my sides, hands balled into fists, and cried out until my throat went raw.

But no wings came. No talons tore through my skin. The same kid I was trying to save had crippled me by taking the Harpy away, stripping me of my claim to Harpydom. Even if I'd changed my mind, I couldn't become the Harpy again. I couldn't just *change my mind*. It wasn't my choice.

Shoving the revelation down into my gut, I looked frantically around for some kind of weapon—not that I could do anything with it against all the Harpies, climbing and clawing, kicking, gnashing their teeth, with Rose underneath them all. I dug through hay to finally find a rock that I could bash a brain in with.

They may not be drunk horny dudes at a bar but they might go down as hard.

I jumped into the pile of Harpies, aimed and swung. I connected with the back of one skull, took her totally by surprise. She fell to her side and before the others could catch on, I whacked another right in the temple. "Oh, damn!" I said, despite wanting to keep a low profile in the orgy of maniacs. But the second one went down on top of a few others, and with the crowd thinning I was more noticeable.

"Move it or lose it, bitch!" I cried, regretting my pathetic battle cry immediately. Then I saw Rose at the bottom, and it spurred me on. I struck harder, missed, got clipped in the cheek by a claw. The first one I'd knocked down got up now, and Rose was still lying on the ground, but she was wide awake and smiling. *Smiling.*

"Rose, get the fuck up, what is this?!"

The Harpies, stumbling around each other, losing any grace they had, suddenly were stopping, one by one. Rooted to the ground.

The explosion happened slowly, a show for the others to watch. The unlucky candidate let out nasty sounds, frothing at the mouth, and then the first bone exploded out of her arm. She lifted the other arm as it shook of its own accord, until the forearm split wide open and another dagger of bone came out. Wicked gross.

The grossest was when Rose decided she'd sent enough of a message. Lying on her side, cheek propped on one hand like she was posing for some psychotic magazine cover, she smiled. Loud and clear, we all got it. She could do this fun, easy shit all day. With a roll of her eyes and a wave of her free hand, the rest of the Harpy's bones made one solid *crack*, and jutted out of every part of her body, including her neck which was the worst of it. I mean that shit just stood straight up, all jagged on the end like a little bloody mountain, tilting her head to the side.

Whatever these Harpies thought they were ready for, they sure as shit hadn't seen this coming.

What I knew was that she couldn't keep it up for long. Just long enough to prove a point.

Then she'd die from the effort.

Mission accomplished, the Harpies took off in a messy flurry of terror, in separate directions. And Rose, who'd been trying to play off that she was more than okay by laying in the relaxed position of a lioness basking on a fur rug by the fireplace, collapsed, out cold.

I fell on my ass, stunned. Like I'd slain a giant and didn't know what to do next. This was supposed to be the end of the story. The happily ever after portion. Defeat the big bad monsters and it's over. Except the one I'd saved was the monster, and she was in worse shape than before, I had no way out of this actual Hell hole, and someone would be coming for her again.

Or she'd heal herself, like she was doing right this second, and it would be back to the original girl's night plan: conquer Earth. *Fuck* I couldn't catch a break, just a breather for a second.

Rose rolled around, moaning, her body flickering in and out again, like she'd disappear into a ghost world any second. Magma-orange streaks raced across her red skin in spurts, leaving a charred set of weird-ass stitches in their wake. She convulsed, back arching.

The orange streaks grew longer, reaching up her throat, her cheeks.

Her skull.

Oh fuck. This can't be anything good.

"Kid!" I yelled, shaking her already-shaking body, pulled my hand away burned bright red. Her skin was fucking boiling hot.

The streaks, thick like leeches, wiggled under the thin skin of her temples. Her forehead bubbled as they passed through. They weren't healing surface wounds —they were inside. And this could not be the right way for Rose's brain to heal.

But what the hell did I know? All I had was a sludgy, cold feeling clutching my heart.

Rose's head throbbed, visibly pulsing bigger, smaller, bigger, smaller. Then the leech-streaks stopped moving all at once, leaving an eye of the storm hanging moment.

The cliff shook beneath us, the hay-covered ground trembling.

"Oh shit."

Under the kid's head, a white blossom of light appeared, spreading around her matted hair like a halo. But there was nothing holy about whatever was going to come out of it.

If Rose's most suppressed memories were in there, I sure as hell didn't want to be nearby when they exploded out.

Will she live through it?

I clutched her shoulders, holding her still body, now that all its energy had funneled into this puddle of white light. She couldn't die, not like this, not killed by her own disgusting past. Not alone here. I knew—I accepted—that I would rather die here with her than let her face it alone, unconscious or not.

The ground under my own body ruptured, as if in response to my commitment, ready to open up and take me in.

The Harpies screeched bloody murder, a horrified, excited sound of fright and anticipation. They did love to see the shit end of the stick, and this sure felt like the worst of it.

The white glow around Rose's head took on color. Not one, but many, until the color formed a picture around her head, like she was using a comic book poster for a pillow. But there was nothing restful in this image. Nothing that should have been in her head.

Probably a half dozen different moving scenes showed at once. Some places I recognized from the visions she'd unwittingly shared with me before when her brain let loose: an apartment floor, a white generic carpet. A patch of grass under the trees, hidden from view.

Oh no.

Some places I didn't. A picnic bench with apartment buildings in the background.

A tennis court with a boy looking at me—her—me, in her head—strangely, eyes gleaming.

No, no, no. That was Cody Reese.

He was in every picture as they blended together. And I understood.

The crack under my body blistered up, knocking me sideways. The Harpies scattered in a hundred directions across the blood-red sky, their screams only whispers with the cracking and groaning of the cliff and the ground below it.

I clutched Rose tighter, not giving a single fuck how much it burned. "I won't leave you to burn alone, kid. Not this time."

Rolling her over on top of me to evade the spreading crack, more white light burst forth from it, shooting into the sky, turning the blood-red into a dirty pink. More visions, giant visions, of white hands with dagger-like nails scrambled through the sky in the murky pink, grasping and clenching the pink air, and the air took on the texture of skin, and the skin was a child's and hands were all over it, and it was Rose, remembering that it hadn't been only once.

But the hands weren't just pictures.

They were real.

And they grabbed my feet, trying to pull me out from under Rose. I kicked as they gripped, feeling for her the hands squeezing her soft pink skin and crying out against them all, but more grabbed the sides of my head and pulled in that direction too. All I could do was clutch Rose to my chest on top of me, stare at the nightmare sky, knowing it was nothing in light of what had happened to her over and over with Cody, and then she was torn from me too.

"No! Give her back!"

But she wasn't gone.

I was.

CHAPTER 15

"What in the actual fuck!"

Smack! I landed hard as hell on an ice-cold slab of something. Fast, I tried to get to my feet, slipping and landing on my elbows first. White-hot pain screamed through my arms. Head on a swivel, I did everything I could to get up, digging my fingernails into the ice but it wouldn't give way, rolling half onto one side, trying to grip the ground with tattered sneaker bottoms, but I gave up. I had to give up. I was paralyzed there.

Propped on my bruised elbows, I took in this new place that I wanted no fucking part of, hoping nobody would see me. If there *was* anybody here. It felt hollow, barren.

Black sky. Pitch black, more than midnight. A midnight of the mind, like an emptied soul. Black trees rose up to meet it, close and thick like walls, pine trees like in Plymouth, but there was nothing earthly about this place. Nothing like home here. Following them down, I didn't find a forest floor—I found ice. The same ice I was stranded on. They were rooted in ice and that's all there was, just ice and more ice, so thick it was almost black in spots, and the cold of it permeated everything. A cavernous, deadening cold.

The tears froze on my cheeks.

"Ro…Rose?" I whispered, terrified to get an answer. What could live here? No bird-bitches could survive, nothing remotely human.

I wouldn't survive here long.

Knowing that, I called out for her again, louder. Why not? "Rose! Rose, where are you?"

A voice as rich as Easter chocolate answered. "She is not here. She cannot be."

As piss-soaked terrified as I was, the only thing my idiot brain could muster was, "There is no Rose, only Zuul?"

"What is a Zuul?"

Laughing probably wasn't the best response I'm guessing because real quick I was being dragged by my feet again. The same ghostly hands emerged from mist, shit straight out of a French horror movie, and dragged me through the forest planted in ice. Barely room for my body to clear the trees, I smacked off one here and there, bruising up even more until I was dropped to the cold expanse below. There never seemed to be an end to the trees, the ice, the nothing feeling and at the same time I was waiting for a monster to crash through these woods, one with a velvet voice that didn't match its grotesqueness.

It wasn't a monster I got. I never expected what I got.

Surprise, turns out Hell isn't all fire and brimstone. It's so much worse.

Trees were a theme in Hell. The pines towered in a circle, creating what might feel like a secret nighttime woodland hideaway inside, beneath them where I was. But there was nothing cozy and safe about the field of ice stretched out before me. Not winter wonderland ice, but murky, like a frozen swamp. In a swamp there'd be decaying stumps, lifeless branches reaching for the sky. Here, enormous shards of ice, thick and sharp, jutted into the night, punctuated between by something that chilled me more than the cold air and my numbing feet.

People.

Of course, people. Moaning torsos, pallid blue. Icicles hanging from their face, their thinning, matted hair, their open mouths revealing cancerously black teeth and blue tongues. Those who had arms splayed their hands on the ice entrapping them, struggled to push themselves up and out of it. Their fingernails were cracked, blood frozen to their fingertips. Even the blue veins on the backs of their hands looked cold. Others tried twisting their necks to look at me, but their spines were frozen and they couldn't move beyond the fitful trembling of their heads. One gnashed his teeth until they broke before my eyes, falling to the ice and sucked up by it somehow, as though the concrete-hard swamp needed sustenance.

Worse, were the body parts.

An anthill of a kneecap poking up. An arm above the elbow, blue fingers spasming. A leg cut off at the hip, part of the groin visible, also blue. The toes black with frostbite. A single finger here and there. I gagged when I looked beside my own body to find an emaciated spine breaking the ice like the back of a sea monster, like a mythical dragon's fins as it dives below the surface.

Sucking in my terror, my head on a swivel, I searched for the voice, for the evil that could find it in them to speak so smoothly here. And I knew, deep down, who I was looking for. That what my life had come to was dealing with The Devil.

"So you do want me," his voice purred.

"I...I don't..."

And again I was being heaved, fast, now over the swampy ice water, banging into the souls imprisoned here. Screaming, I closed my eyes until my throat was filled with the ice too, and the sharp pain strangled me. I clutched at a freezing cold hand that grasped my own, as if it could save me, as if it wasn't damned already. I opened my eyes to see a winter-white man, one leg stuck in the ice holding him there. Frost stuck to his entire face but for his eyes, bloodshot-red and brown like the gross water that definitely was below. His white brows furrowed as his eyes met mine. Soft eyes, kind ones.

Eyes that pitied me.

He let me go and I was smacking against other bodies again until I was swiftly deposited in the middle of the tundra. The icebergs rose high here, but not too high that I couldn't see the gleam of their points, like the obelisks I remembered reading about from that time in middle school I went to class. But it wasn't any different here than where I'd been. This getting pulled around shit was just an intimidation tactic, and I was fucking tired of it already.

"I'm already in Hell, you don't need to scare me, for fucks sake!" I yelled, finding my voice and doing my best not to let it shake.

I heard a rumble below the silence punctuated by frightened frozen moans. Then the moans turned to single, ear-splitting, pain-filled cries, as those same ghostly hands plucked the damned out of the ice as if it were pudding and they were gummy sharks, leaving not a hole behind. Dangling arms and legs, limbless bodies and whole ones, picked up and stuck back into the ground in different spots, clearing an area. And then a slick slicing sound as the icebergs slid like chess pieces to either side.

Revealing Him.

This bitch isn't even red, I thought, but holy shit was he scary. The size of him didn't make sense. Massive in every way, taller than the trees but somehow still wrapped in them. Arms thicker than submarines. So enormous that he took up all the space in my vision and yet I saw every bit of him, and it felt like he was inches from me, intimate with me.

Satan was a mottled gray, like a grayer version of the bathtub lady in The Shining. Ginormous bat wings stretched out around him, the points of them leaving spider web cracks the size of a duck pond in the ice where they touched down. I wouldn't have pegged Satan for having a receding hairline, but there it was, with massive gray curls surrounding gnarly, twisting goat horns. His dark eyes were as cold, piercing. But what scared the shit out of me about them was that they were full-moon-round, the whites gleaming, and He looked utterly fucking insane. They goggled around then trained on me like insanity had found a home on my face or something. I forced myself to look away, only to catch sight of His fucking goatee. Like every sloppy beard, food was stuck in it.

And what He ate was humans.

Limbs looked babydoll size as they stuck out of the knotty hair, and as I watched he plucked a body from the ice, which reformed like that same nightmare pudding to fill the space. He tipped his head back and dropped the person into his cavernous mouth. He didn't even chew. He dropped his elbows casually down to rest on the ice after.

"Not supposed to put your elbows on the dinner

table," I whisper-squeaked, making him laugh heartily with that creamy voice.

The lower half of Satan's body was below the ice, the tundra stretched out around him like the rings on whatever planet that was, Uranus probably. So he was trapped too—or he liked being trapped and modeled the rest of the house after his favorite thing.

"Charity Blake. How wonderful to finally meet you."

"Yeah, thanks. Thanks for sending that fucked-up Harpy to make a mess in my friend's hallway, too."

His face dropped, and I hadn't realized he was smiling. I'd thought he was just nuts. "I had to create a creature that had been above, one that you would recognize and that your human mind could reconcile. I made her up," he finished with a flourish.

"Why didn't you just pull me down here if you wanted me?" I asked, trying to get my footing once again to stand up. Suddenly the ice broke underneath me and rose up, formed a highly uncomfortable sort of dinner table chair for me to sit on. "Thanks."

"I want my guest to be comfortable," he said, smile returning.

"I didn't RSVP to your invitation, but I guess now that I'm here, I'd love to know what the hell you want with me."

Assessing me with a death-still stare, he weighed his next words. "Allow me to answer your question. I could not pull you down here, as you say. Humans cannot just go in and out of Hell, as you've seen in your time with the Harpies. However, you were already here, just a touch out of my reach."

"So you made that earthquake thingy in the Wood of Suicides."

"Indeed. And now that you've arrived, I'd like to know just what you think we should do about your friend Rose."

When Satan asks for your advice, I think that's a serious levelling up, no matter what the circumstances. And yeah, I was terrified as a motherfucker, but I knew, I had to keep in mind through my shivering, that this meant I had something he wanted.

"I want to know what *you* think about Rose," I said.

"Do you?" he cooed, leaning forward. I smelled rotting flesh on his breath, his jagged teeth stained with blood. "I think you'll stand beside her no matter what happens, even if it kills you. Even if it damns you."

"Is that a threat? What are you getting at? Or do you just know she's planning to dethrone you and you're what, buttering me up? You want me to take your side. I don't care about this," I said, gesturing to the Devil's Sno-Cone Land. "I care about her, and yeah, I guess I care about the world above." I swallowed. He had something I wanted too, I could feel it.

"We both know there's no going back there for our Rose. She can't get better from here." His eyes lost their crazy and turned to a warmth that seeped into me, almost as if it were real. Goddamn, he had a voice like Ian McShane. "Rose can't outlive the memories in her head. They'll eat her alive, and if they don't, facing them will. She's one of us now," He said, leaning back and opening his arms. "But I can make it right, Charity. I can make it right *for her.*" His r rolled, making my knees quiver.

"What do you have in mind?" I asked, more huskily than I intended.

"I thought you'd never ask." Shark grin. "I have a choice for you, my dear."

"Spit it out, BatBoy."

"I can destroy Rose—"

"No."

"Let me finish," He implored. "I can destroy Rose's life on Earth quickly, painlessly, and allow her to rule the Wood, do as she likes there. She'll die on Earth either way, this time she just gets to have more fun."

"But you're the boss and she wants your job. How's that gonna work?"

"The Devil is in the details and you don't need to know them," He said with a sly smile.

"I don't trust you and I don't think you can destroy her, but whatever. Plan B?"

"I can erase all of her memories. Remove the threat. She'll go back to Earth as herself, with no recollection of what she's been through, and live a somewhat normal life—as much as one can when they remember nothing of their past. I cannot promise that her brain won't recreate these caverns they've made already."

"Okay, that one! That one."

"But…"

"Of course there's a but."

"But when her life ends, she'll come to me. Her eternity will be in Hell, without her memories to torture her. Win, win."

Oh what the actual shit. "But she won't even know why!"

"Fine then, life on Earth, memory-free, but when she comes to me she'll relive all she's done to humanity. Deal?"

"That's not fair," I muttered. I felt stupid having even thought it. Because no, it wasn't fair, and it was totally fair. She'd done terrible things, she needed to pay for them.

"The other option is she can stay on Earth, rip it to shreds for as long as she can, until she burns herself out. She'll get all her jollies out, go out with a bang, then you know, off to Hell she goes, so on and so forth."

"Hmmm. I don't like it, and there's a lot missing in this idea of yours. Tell me what it is. What will make me like this plan even less than I do now? And don't give me the Devil's in the details garbage."

"Don't get too big for your britches, Miss Blake. I don't have to tell you what you want to know."

"But you like me. So maybe you just will anyway."

His smirk was utterly charming in a mesmerizing, catastrophic way. I itched to know his secret.

"You got me," he purred. "She can do as she pleases these last days of her life, but she comes to me as one of them." He waved his claw out to the sea of souls. "It won't necessarily be what you'd call 'a clean break.' Her memories may be...mottled. Regression is non-negotiable. Her suffering may feel...unjust. But you and I will know that she deserves every last breath of it."

"None of these feel right."

"What do you want, an unnatural murdering beast with half-cocked intentions and a penchant for torture to live without consequences because she had a terrible childhood? She's not alone in that."

"It's not a competition."

"And it's not usually a choice, and she's not a usual child. Miss Blake, surely you understand that she is determined to do terrible things! You can't save her forever."

There was that word again. *Charity, your newly realized savior complex is showing.*

"Why are you running this by me?" I said. "I mean, I'm just a person now, what do you care what I think? You've got the whole lot of Hell to pick a lackey from."

"Nine rings of it, to be exact."

"Then why me?"

He laughed at me, not with me. "You may look human but I've never put much stock in first impressions. You don't need claws and wings, my girl. With or without them, you travel through Hell like Dante himself!"

"Don Tay? You know that dude for real?"

He ignored me. "Half the Harpies right now are planning their next attack on Rose, and she'll obliterate them, force the rest to abide by her rules whether they love her or not. And Rose… Well, she's got her next attack ready to go, on Earth."

"Is she awake? Is she okay, you took me from her."

"You'll find out soon enough," He said, and His eyes went wild again, huge and intensely crazy. "When she's done up there, she's coming down here. You know this. She'll level the universe with the power inside her, and everything, everything will be gone *tomorrow.* Tell me, what will you do, Charity Blake? Stand beside me, help me destroy her, finish these great, terrible plans she has and let the universe exist as it always has? Or will you stand beside that child because of your feelings? Help her take over the world, then Hell and what next? What will she do then?"

I had no idea. I pictured just nothingness as far as the heart could fathom, and her floating in the middle of it all. Me tethered to her by my intestines. "How am I supposed to fight her? You can't do it, but I'm supposed to?"

"You never stop fighting, my dear. Your life has been a fight from the moment it began! This girl can't be destroyed physically—she must be *stopped.* You're the only one who can appeal to her now. Convince her to stop this war upon everything living or dead. Convince her to forget her past and live a real life before she damns herself."

This guy was the root of all evil, and he felt like a friend kinda. A straight shooter, but I knew there was something underneath it he wasn't telling me.

He plucked a body from the ice by its exposed foot, pulling her submerged torso out and up. He winked at me as the shivering naked woman dangled there, her own eyes as wild as Satan's.

He ripped her leg off between his thumb and index finger. Held it like a Chinese chicken wing, the gristle of it still hanging from the joint.

"Care for a bite while you think?" He cooed.

"No thanks, I don't eat people these days."

He dropped the leg in his mouth, made a show of chewing. "You still have a taste for blood. There's no hiding it."

"I'm doing just fine actually."

"But you'd be better eating the flesh of the guilty. Wouldn't you?"

"Now if I wanted that, I could just join Rose, couldn't I?" I tossed back at him. "That's part of the plan, destroy the rapists, murderers, monsters up there." It pissed me off how he assumed I'd be so easy to persuade, as if it were just about the taste of meat. "You know, I don't belong in Hell, right? I never did a goddamn thing to damn myself."

Dropping the twitching, unconscious body to the

ice again, where it swallowed up her remaining leg, He said, "You're a killer! Killers go to Hell, Charity Blake."

"Avenger. Not a murderer, an avenger. Righteous killer. And if it were so easy to get me to stay here, you'd have managed to bring me in a long time ago. I'm not stupid."

"Far from it. But hurry with your decision, we haven't much more time. Will you stand with her and attack above and below or will you help me damn her?"

"Well, when you say it like that, I don't want to do either one."

"Which way were you leaning before I said that?" He was tapping one big black pointy fingernail fast.

"What's the hurry?" I asked. "I mean, it feels like you want this right—"

I never got to finish the sentence because I got my answer loud and clear.

CHAPTER 16

*L*oud and clear and hot and red.

Without so much as a warning tremor, Rose exploded through the night sky above. It cracked around her like she'd dropped in through a clay pot. Chunks of solid black plummeted to the tree-tops and ice, crashing through the frozen swamp-lake thing to reveal nasty-ass water below. More ice cracked, broke, and swollen, lumpy body parts rose to the surface. Some of the more alert damned, the ones with limbs still attached, tried pulling the ice apart around them, struggled a little harder than they had been.

A couple broke free. Then five or six.

This whole time Rose, bright red and burning brighter, hovered over us, apparently suspended just by sheer force.

"Making deals with The Devil, are you? Wrong

move, Charity," she said, sending a bolt of pain through my brain. Not even Hell could keep her out of my head I guess. "I can see the makeup of this atmosphere. You're too small-minded to understand but I can take apart what makes it work easier than you can breathe."

I just wanted to breathe and it was becoming intensely more difficult.

While Satan kicked hobbling, limping, crawling and limbless dead people, thunking back into the arena as they tried to get to anywhere but here, Rose put on her show. Waving her hand around like goddamn Scarlet Witch, she disassembled the ice into smaller and smaller pieces, leaving the countless souls untethered to anything. Most sunk to the bottom of the swamp. Some were grabbed by bloated hands and pulled beneath. She went on to take the trees apart, needle by needle, each inner ring exposed. I wished I could count them, see how old a thing got here before it disintegrated or whatever. She turned on Satan himself.

Nothing's scarier than when a creepy kid cocks their head to one side.

Satan put forth a nasty beat of His giant wings, sending a wind colder than anything I'd thought could move without turning into an ice cube. When the icy wind reached Rose, she threw her hands out to the side, her head back, and welcomed the frigidity.

She was so hot, all the time.

The wind hit her skin and formed momentary dots of ice, that quickly sizzled and evaporated.

Rose let out a sigh of relief. I saw her shoulders drop, hadn't even realized they were way up by her ears. Her jaw unclenched. Until the burning began again. It was a metaphor for the kid's whole life. As soon as she got a breather—short fucking breathers, too—she was assaulted again with something freakier.

The ice had completely melted now, becoming a chunky swamp overflowing with paunchy corpses and bobbing extremities. An odor unlike anything natural, unlike regular decay, wafted up from the water. It was vomit and incense, urine, rotten animal corpses, and so much more. The smell of terrible lives and worse memories.

"Kid, don't do this," I said as she snarled and trained her eyes on Satan, who for His part, didn't look afraid. I would.

And I am when she turns on me, spins in the air and growls at me. "You. Left. *Me.* You left me again!"

"You can't be serious! The fucking floor of Hell opened up and swallowed me! And you kinda did it, so lay off. I'm down here pleading for your fucking soul after fighting those Harpies with you, and *your* fucking brain ripped the world apart, not mine. You should be thanking me for negotiating with The fucking Devil on your behalf when I just crashed onto swamp ice chock-full of dead people!"

She blinked a bunch of times, and laughed. My sense of humor wouldn't help me this time. Actually, it never helped me. "It doesn't matter," she said. "You made me face my past and you left me alone with it."

I tried to be sympathetic to the kid, who'd just remembered that she'd been abused multiple times, not just one horrible time. "I can't imagine how you must feel, remembering everything. I wish you didn't have to—but it could heal you completely! It's horrible, but it could be good, we just have to get you checked out."

"It could be *good*?" she said. "You're of the opinion that remembering how I was destroyed would save me?"

"Rose, for fucks sake! This is what *you* wanted! It was ripping your brain apart, you had to remember to survive!"

"Survive," she murmured. "Is that all I'm capable of on Earth? Being tortured and left alone to come to terms with it alone is what survival looks. What if I were to do the same to you?"

It felt like the ice traveled up my legs and into my heart. Because Rose was contradicting herself, blaming me, confused and in more pain than before. And she didn't say shit like that unless she had a reason. A plan.

"What are you talking about?" I croaked.

"Pray you don't have to find out."

"*We do not pray here!*" Satan screeched in a tortured voice. He was clutching his skull, fingers wrapped around his horns.

"Looks like we know how to defeat Satan if it comes to that," I said.

Rose overheard me.

She lowered herself to the ice as Satan recovered. The smirk on her face was so ugly. And she was redder than ever.

"I see you," she said to Satan.

"Rose…"

But she was walking forward, over shattered ice and body parts like it was nothing. With every step, Satan looked more and more worried.

That's when the rings on his building-sized horns began to separate, like the shaving spirals from a freshly sharpened pencil.

To his credit, Satan laughed, this throaty, dare I say hot, laugh. "I can't be taken apart, girl," he said. "I'm all things and nothing." His horns reassembled themselves.

"Rose, maybe not right now, huh?"

But she paid me no attention and kept moving forward, taking his fingernails off his meaty mitts, the skin off his hairy chest. He showed no signs of pain—actually, He was groaning like this was the best sex he'd ever had.

I wondered if Satan ever had sex, considering half his body was frozen.

But the mention—in my brain—of sex was enough to rattle Rose, pushing a sloppy image of Cody Reese's dick into my thoughts.

The black sky split with a white gash.

The gash filled with filthy pictures of Cody Reese,

things a child would notice. This child. Pubic hair. A mole on his thigh. A smell permeated the memory, overruled the stunning nastiness from before.

And Rose's color, her whole being, grew lighter. I'd seen it before, she became *less*, like she was turning into a hologram. Like the memories were becoming more real and she was fading away. As if she didn't notice, she kept advancing, and the sky sliced open with more and more of her memories. Satan kept coming apart and putting himself back together, the bodies kept struggling and failing, and the whole thing was a freakish mobile, a fucked up mechanical scene like a music box nobody would ever open. I was stuck in it. This was Hell, this was a nightmare worse than any I could dream up. A constant surreal diorama of wild eyes, agonized screams, carnival-colored horror scenes that struck too close to home, on a deteriorating, reeking swamp icescape. I felt like if one thing was removed the whole thing would crumble down.

What would Rose do when she got to Satan, right in his face? What if He just picked her up and fucking ate her!

I had to stop her, turn her attention to me.

"Rose!" A slash opened in the sky showing doubled-up pictures of me calling her name a hundred different times in different places. "I know you can hear me! If you do this now and he wins, you'll never know every-thing. You won't know if you've healed, and you won't know if there's anything else to remember. What if there's more? You'll always have been kept in the dark. Is that okay with you?"

It worked. She stopped.

But when she turned on me, every muscle in my body tensed up. The rest of the scene, all movement stopped, transfixed by the radiating waves of red heat from her body, the embodiment of fury.

"You've been hiding something from me," she spat. Not really the case, but I was pretty sure Bob had some tricks up his sleeve.

"No, not me. But your dad is up there, and he knows something." Hard swallow. "Kid, haven't you noticed these memories?" I asked, waving my arms at the scary movie playing overhead. "They aren't anything you recognize. I can tell, I'm in your head, too now." It was true. She'd breeched something, drawn our minds together with the constant digging around in there she'd done, and let me tell you—I'd have done about anything to get out of her head.

That stillness might have been worse than the carousel of insanity. No, actually.

Rose's face softened, and I let out a breath so hard my chest ached. "See, Charity? This is why I need you. Even though I can see everything, you see everything *else.*"

"And the more even-tempered one," I said, because she could hear my thoughts anyway. "No rash decisions from me, nosiree Bob. And speaking of Bob, let's get the hell out of here, go have a chat with him."

She nodded once, turned to Satan. "This isn't over," she said.

"Not by a long shot," He replied.

~

*B*eing torn through a portal from Earth to the Wood of Suicides and back is one thing. Hard, but it's a straight line. With Rose—Harpy, human, inexplicable *other* thing, child, murderer—and through multiple levels of Hell, is different. I was peeled like a banana from my toenails to my heart, and put back together in pieces. Then spit out on the Facility floor.

"Charity!"

Cleary was lifting me off the floor, making me aware of the instant bruises and the pain when I fell on both knees. Never noticed that stuff as a Harpy.

"You're burned," he said incredulously. He was right. The nice clothes Theo had bought me had been through a fire it seemed, and char spots showed underneath the holes, my skin like charcoal briquettes. The rest of me was a stiff, tender hot pink.

"Where's Rose?" I tried to say, but my throat was on fire.

Cleary understood. "She's with her father." Fear littered his words.

A Harpy nurse, wings exposed, came in with aspirin and a glass of water on a tray for me. I thanked her, which was weird because thanking Harpies wasn't something they got a lot of, and guzzled that water in one gulp, then asked for more. "And some Jack Daniels, please!" I shouted after her down the hall.

Mr. Cleary helped me to that same sitting area with the big ol' windows for those on death's doorstep to look out of. It was nighttime, not long after sunset. Boston has an ability to *look* cold. The streetlights shine on ice patches, the cobblestones get snow drifts between them, the number of skull caps and blowing scarves increases. Pedestrians, huddled into their long coats, had shopping bags dangling over their arms, hands tucked into pockets. The Salvation Army guy rang his bell, sitting on a low brick wall. And a giant Christmas tree glittered with white lights.

"Right, it's almost Christmas," I said.

"It's tomorrow," Cleary replied.

"Tomorrow? It's Christmas Eve? Wait a second. What the hell? The Facility is in some dead zone, what the hell happened? How are we here?" Panic rose in my voice, making him put a gentle hand on my own to calm me. It worked.

He chuckled. "Rose, of course. Once she saw that the ruins of the Facility had been found out, and by the mob at that, she changed things, moved things. Moved it, in time."

I didn't even have questions. Of all the lunacy I was involved in, this was the least surprising.

Elbows on my knees, I lifted my hanging head to

ask him the question that made my heart squeeze tighter. "What's she gonna find out in there, Cleary?" I asked, voice hoarse. All hope drained out of me through those words.

He deflated, too. Not a good sign.

"I did as much as I could to get her out of Satan's face," I said, waving his mask of confusion and horror away so I could finish, "but I used like, the stupidest playing card and said she should make sure she learned everything about her past to be sure she was healed. But what the hell will happen next if she finds out even more? I mean, Bob is a super secrety, what the fuck else can she dredge up? I might've ended the world bringing her back here."

The Harpy nurse returned with a pitcher of water that I drank straight from and actually took the aspirin this time, and the bottle of Jack I'd requested. Drank that straight from the bottle, too. No need to play games, not now. I passed it to Cleary, and to my surprise, he took it. Wiping a sheen of sweat I hadn't noticed from his forehead with the back of his sleeve, he took a giant slug, like at least two adam's apple bobs, looked at me like he was going to answer me, but then just drank again.

"How about this one: Is Dr. Mortimer okay?"

Pulling the bottle from his mouth, he scoffed, spittle flying. Shit, if he was in this condition, did I even want to know what Mortimer was like?

"He's alive. He's…alive."

My heart pounded so hard that my hand flew to my chest. "Where is he?"

"You can't just go and get him, Charity. Rose knows everything. She knows we're together, talking, right now. She knows you're on both sides of the fence. And yet, she doesn't want to know some things, even if she pretends she does." He took my hand, squeezed it, looked into my eyes, showing me his were bloodshot and manic. "When she hears what Bob has to say, it's not going to go well." Tears fell. "There's nothing more I can do for her. I can't do anything for anyone at all."

I took the bottle, felt good about having drank less than him. I turned more toward Cleary, took his hands in mine forcing him to turn my way. "I know how much you love her," I said. "I love her too. She's…well, I don't need to tell you. And I thought I could take care of her. I couldn't do it for Maggie, but I could do it for her. I could."

"Maggie?"

"Long story. But the point is, we both love her, we both want what's best for her, and the truth is, nothing is good for her. Nothing can bring her back the way she was. Nothing will ever just *work out* for that kid. It fucking sucks it, but it's time I said it. Time we both realized that she's the only one who can take care of herself, at least now."

He closed his eyes. "What do you think we should do now?"

"I don't think it matters," I answered.

"Then let's go get your friend, Dr. Mortimer."

~

The same Harpy nurse took us to Psychiatrist's room, but she sure wasn't happy about it.

"Rose won't like this."

"Pretty sure Rose doesn't like anything these days."

"She isn't finished with him," the nurse snapped, showing pointed teeth.

I got right in this bitch's face because of all confrontations I needed today, this wasn't one of them. "Listen. You're probably on the winning side of the fucking bloodbath we're all about to walk into, yeah? So fuck off with your chastising. You're not my fucking mom. Bye now."

She seethed, like a real growl, opened the door in this dank-ass hallway, and left us there. But not before spitting, "She'll kill you and I hope I see it."

"Bitch, I'll gouge your eyes out first."

Cleary was already in the room. But I was scared.

A smell of body odor came from the room, and no light shone from inside.

"Charity?"

"Psychiatrist!" I ran into the room after hearing him speak so clearly, but I wasn't ready to see him this way. He sat on a hospital bed, crisp white sheets and fluffy white blankets, the whole bit, but the rest of the room couldn't be less hospital-like. Or sadder.

Nothing like the giant, well-lit room I'd been in, this one was painted a pea green, with only one window way up high letting in precious little sunlight. The gray tile floor, though clean like the bed, was so drab it was hard to look at. No cobwebs to be seen, but the feeling of age was overwhelming, stuffy, claustrophobic. This room was sanitary—but created to emotionally drown someone. If there was any question that this place was meant to break him, the wall décor proved it.

Haphazardly, everywhere, were pictures of Rose's childhood. Her shining yellow hair, her bright smile, her knowing eyes, her sweetness. Her mother, carefree, and with a strong chin that defied authority. Her dad—Bob—younger, cradling Rose as a baby, then carrying her on his shoulders at a fairground. Drawing pictures with her as they lay on their bellies in the Boston apartment. They faded into pictures of a dead seagull, parts removed and fanned out in a circle. Of Rose's hands dug into the dirt like she was trying to touch the core of the earth. Of Cody Reese, bouncing a basketball far below the Prestons' window. Of the nook of trees that shaded Rose and her tea party.

Then the pictures became darker.

Cleary was at one wall, running a shaking hand over one picture of Cody Reese sneering into Rose's little face, pulling her head back by her hair.

"These are her memories," he said. His voice broke.

"But these…" I started, going over to the wall near Mortimer's bed as he watched with a dazed grin. "These are Psychiatrist's family." Happy pictures of him with his arms around his two kids from a swimming pool in some tropical place. Pictures of the boy in a school play dressed like a floppy-eared dog. Mortimer in a tux, his laughing wife in a midnight blue evening gown.

The contrast between Rose's life before, Rose's life after, and Mortimer's life before I'd known him were overwhelming. Just like she wanted him to feel. That he'd had a life and lost it. Hers had been taken before she lived it.

Mortimer stood up, and boy did he look like he'd been through the wringer. His little chubby belly was gone, and his face was gaunt to go with it. Big circles wound around his eyes. His breath smelled like a garbage truck when he got near me. For as much of a mess as he was, he had this maniacally happy gleam in his eye and a never-fading smile that was just plain unsettling.

"Charity!" he exclaimed like I'd come over his house for a visit. "How have you been? I believe you've missed several appointments."

I looked over my shoulder at Cleary who only shrugged in response.

"Hey, Psychiatrist, good to see you too. Now listen, I think it's time we left this place, don't you? Get some sun? A cheeseburger?"

The smile faded quickly. "Oh no," he said, backing away from me. "Rose wouldn't like that at all. And she's suffered so much already, I couldn't disappoint her that way." His eyes roved over the pictures of her, in sequence, of losing her childhood and her mind.

"You don't deserve this, Doctor," Mr. Cleary said gently. "Psychiatrists can refuse patients whenever they like, drop patients whenever they deem necessary. You are not responsible for this child. Do you understand me?"

Mortimer gave him a pitying glance. "Deserving has nothing to do with it. Making amends, putting my wrongs right, that's what matters now."

I hissed under my breath at Cleary, "She's breaking him down. He won't give her the memories that he knows will turn her even more—whatever—and she's breaking him down, making him think he has wrongs to right. He didn't goddamn do anything. If we leave him here, who knows what she'll do to him. He can't know anything that Bob doesn't, after all."

"I know," Cleary said solemnly, watching Mortimer run a loving finger over a picture of Rose in a sundress with Hello Kitty on the chest. "She won't have need of him anymore. He has to get out of here."

"But where? She can find him if she wants to, really, really easily."

"When she finds out the things Bob has kept from her, none of us will be able to hide from her fury anyway."

The oppressive room, the senseless babbling from Mortimer, the hopelessness of coming out of this mess unscathed, the fear of Rose and the Harpies, and Satan, were almost enough to make me crawl under the white bed and hide. But when Mortimer began to cry silent tears, giving them away with sniffles, I forced myself to move.

I took him by the arm, bare in his Facility-issue johnnie, and pushed a pair of terrycloth slippers toward him that he'd obviously worn a lot. My heart hurt for him—but I would *not* let myself think that I was responsible for his condition. This one wasn't on me, but I could be the one to help him out.

"Where are you bringing me?" he asked, combover falling across the bridge of his nose. I pushed it back.

"Let's go outside for starters, huh?"

"Oh, I'm not supposed to leave, Charity."

"Says who? Rose? You don't owe her, Psychiatrist." I pulled him along but he shook his head fast, looked down like a dog being sent to his crate. "Dr. Mortimer," I said, so he knew I meant it, "you may have had part in Rose becoming this way, but you did what you thought to be right in your professional opinion. And that professional opinion, and your caring so much, is what made me *better*. I would have been—who knows what I would have become without you to listen to me and make me understand myself more? You cared about me, at least on paper, and it was enough to help me survive the life I had. And now I'm better. You see that?

Trust that you've done what you can here and Rose is responsible for what she does now. You made your choices, and now she's making hers. It's okay. It's time to move forward. You told me that many times, now you do it."

The poor basket case swallowed back tears, but when he spoke it sounded like the clear-headed Mortimer I knew. "You dear girl. I know when to take advice, and when I need help. Lead the way."

Taking him by the hand, I did just that, with the two men right behind me. Oh, how the tables turn.

"Charity, he's naked under there," Cleary shouted up to me from behind Mortimer as we ran down the hallway.

"I don't think they carry cords and sweater vests in the Facility gift shop, Cleary, deal with his ass for a moment, would you?" Fuck I wished I had my phone on me, but who knows where it had gone. I needed Theo to come and get Psychiatrist, get him somewhere momentarily safe.

Safe. What a joke.

On cue, the scream began. I say it began because it lasted and lasted and lasted.

I fell to my bruised knees, just paralyzed, praying it would stop, but I knew it wouldn't. Not until everyone had paid.

Rose's wailing was a thing of devastation like a mother in a movie who finds out her son died in war. But it never stopped with the sister rushing to her side, or someone getting her a glass of water. It went on and on, until all of us were crying with her. Mortimer was outright sobbing, sitting on his bare ass on the tile floor, rocking back and forth.

That was when the walls began to break.

One after another, the crashes and littering of the floor with rubble could be heard until it happened right beside us. An explosion of concrete that rained down on us in crazy huge chunks. Odd chairs here and there pelted off the floor.

"Cleary!"

Trapped under a broken wall that was still crumbling, a support beam fell next, hitting him square on the head. I couldn't look. I couldn't see how much blood there was.

Through the cavities that had once been walls, came Rose. Slowly she glided in a red glow, turning the dust-filled air behind her hot pink, rusty razor wings still as death. Her blonde hair waved like octopus tentacles all around her, but did nothing to cover her naked, thin body. Her clothes had to have sizzled right off her. Now not only was her skin the same lobster sunburned red but her eyes—her eyes brought bile into my mouth.

No pupils, no blinking. Nothing but hot coal red, staring through everything in her path.

"Ro…Rose," I managed. She snapped her head to look at me, answering my question of whether or not she could actually see with those red orbs, but said nothing. "Help Mr. Cleary. I know you can."

She was on him in a second, having of course taken apart the rubble crushing him and dismantling the beam with a glance. He moaned and I let out a sob of relief. Until I got a glimpse of him. The gash on his head showed a fair bit of skull. That he was even alive was a miracle.

His legs were obliterated. Flat as a pancake. Bones jut out from the sides like they'd been blown out from the seams. Mortimer stopped blubbering just long enough to keel over at the sight of it. "Jesus Christ," I muttered.

I bounced back from my annoyance, replacing it with awe. Rose with a softness I didn't know she had any longer, had removed the debris with her hands. And she ran her slender scarlet fingers over the wound in his head, cauterizing it with her body heat.

The real wonder was how she fixed his legs. Because there was so little left. Nothing to heal. Nothing to take apart and put back together.

A faint dizziness breezed through me, a thrown-back bottle of champagne of the brain. My lip twitched in a smile. It felt *good*. The buzz amplified, my dizziness extending to Rose it seemed. Her body hummed like a machine, flickering in and over itself a thousand times over. The connection between our minds shuffled, a deck of cards of experiences and feelings and moments. Dimensions. Timelines. Worlds. All breached in a heartbeat.

When we returned, Cleary stood over Mortimer, rousing him from his ladylike faint.

"What was that, Rose?" I said in a breath, turning to her.

Rose had changed in that time, in those worlds.

Her body not only lost that demonic red, but had been drained of color, making her a porcelain that was almost translucent against her yellow hair. Those eyes remained red, even more haunting in her paleness.

"Time travel doesn't work the way you'd think," she said with a colorless smile.

My heart pounded and slowed a few times, unsure of how to feel.

"What does this mean, kid? Are you…back?"

But her face hardened, skin so pale I could make out the grit of her teeth beneath it. "This changes nothing except him," she growled, pointing at Mr. Cleary.

"Well, fuck."

CHAPTER 17

The kid could transform into a thousand different things it seemed. I couldn't keep up anymore.

Harpies, without an ounce of the grace Rose had, carried Bob through the chasms in the walls, flapping their wings more like insects than birds. Bob looked okay. Groggy. As if he'd been through Hell, which I'm sure Rose had seen to.

"Fuck me, what is she doing now?" I muttered as she went to him, walking like a regular person, wings dragging behind her. They reminded me of tin cans on a "Just Married" car.

She did nothing to him though, just looked at him. I couldn't help thinking it was for one last time.

It was me she turned on. Me she trained her blood-ball eyes on, but not before I mouthed to Cleary to get out of there, motioning to bring Mortimer with him. Of course they didn't.

"You don't know what it's like," she said without an ounce of anger in her voice. Made it scarier. "You can't understand how it feels to have someone who you thought would do anything for you abandon you, because you never had anyone."

"Low blow. Not nice."

She smirked. "My father…my mother told me how much he'd done for us, and how much he suffered being away from us. I loved him all these years, and feared all this time that he was so ashamed of me that I'd never see him again. Then I thought he was ashamed of himself more than me. Then to find out he built this place to *contain* me, like some wild animal. You know what else I know now?" She paced back and forth, either summoning the courage to say it out loud or adding to the tension that almost had my brains blown out anyway.

Her voice roared. "He wasn't ashamed. He was afraid. My own father. Not of what I'd become, but because of what I would see. I'd see that he was a coward!" Her eyes burned, shimmered the air, glowed horribly. "Ask me why, Charity. Go ahead."

Too afraid not to, and morbidly curious, I did. "Why is he a coward?"

"I thought you'd never ask." Kid took my sarcasm to a new level. "Lots of reasons! The first one, and this won't surprise you, was that he was too *weak* to kill the boy who destroyed me. Who unmade me. Who, in his own words, would 'take me apart from the inside out.'"

She waited for me to respond, but what could I say? We'd been over this, but she was setting up for the big reveal and I was paralyzed with terror, loathing, hopelessness.

"It gets better. Doesn't it, Daddy?" she said, smacking his foot as it hung above her. The Harpies laughed. Poor timing, if you ask me. "You hid something even more damaging. That the one time, wasn't the only time. In fact, he babysat me once or twice, because Daddy wanted to 'give the mess of a kid a shot.' That's what he told Mom, right?" Another slap of the foot. "Cody found me outside more than once, too. And that day that you found me was just the cherry on top, so to speak. *And he told you.*"

The memories that poured between the white gashes no longer were Rose's—she pulled them from her father. Astounding. Astounding is the only word to describe that she could play it for me so clearly. As if it were her own memory. Then again, she felt as though they all belonged to her.

Bob, his hand on Cody Reese's throat. Him, still a kid himself. I hated that I could understand not being able to kill the kid, even though nobody would miss him and it would bring such satisfaction.

I remembered those kinds of kills myself. Murdering the ones no one would miss, making the world a better place without them. How they made my blood burn and my heart pound, exhilarated.

The memory changed as Cody burst into tears. It was soundless, but I knew what he was saying as though I'd been in the room.

Cody Reese confessed, though Bob had never asked. He confessed to molesting Rose many times.

As if that weren't bad enough, Cody couldn't stop there. He blurted out to Bob how much he'd been abused, too. How worthless his life had become, that it had all been taken away from him. How much he wished he could die but he was too scared. Too worthless even to do that.

Bob dropped him.

And then he sat next to him on the messy living room carpet. Cody's apartment. Looking around, the place looked…well, not a whole lot unlike the place I'd *grown up*, but this one had carpet. The occasional needle. A beer can or thirty. Full ashtrays. But this place was empty, where my house always was full of people ready to hurt me.

Cody was curled on his side, and Bob hesitated, but he put a hand on his shoulder, and rubbed, shaking him in that reassuring way. Probably the most nurturing thing Cody had ever experienced.

I didn't have to imagine how that made Rose feel. Castoff. Worthless. Unavenged.

Unavenged.

Was it my place now, was it *my* place to avenge her?

Would I if I could? Did Bob's weakness—because that's what it was, weakness to not do anything for that kid—make him worthy of being torn to shreds by Harpy claws?

I didn't have to ask, because it happened before my eyes. The Harpies holding him tore him completely in half. And Rose didn't bat an eyelash.

~

"Jesus fuck, Rose!" My voice didn't sound like my own. My head swam, my heart thudded like a hammer.

She looked at me with her nasty red eyes, shoulders totally relaxed. She actually *shrugged*. "There's no room for the morally ambiguous," and with a glance at her father's entrails in a puddle, "or the moral cowards. In our world, everyone will have the courage of their convictions."

"It's not just about the rapists and pedos then, huh? Everyone has to check off awesomeness boxes with you to survive?"

"And why shouldn't they?" one of the henchmen Harpies scoffed. She sounded so human, but she looked total trailer trash run over by that trailer. Dark skin bloodstained, claws longer than any Harpy's I'd ever seen. Her body wasn't half bird, half woman, it was a mixed collection of both, like she'd been put together with glue.

This was the quality of creature that should take over Earth, I guess.

"Where is Dr. Mortimer?" Rose drawled, tone low, foreboding.

"You've done enough damage, kid. He's gone. Like, from here, but also his brain is baby food." My anger welled more and more as I thought of him, how good his intentions were, but how sadly he'd failed. I'd never even found out where his wife and kids went. Just that he rattled around that nice house alone. Now he probably wouldn't even recognize it.

Super fast, Rose was in front of me, even faster her hands on my throat.

"You. Tell me where he is," she hissed. The fucking eyes though, they burned into mine. It fucking killed.

"Take shit apart and find him yourself," I wheezed out, clawing at her wrists.

She could find him in the blink of an eye. This was a power play, to prove that I was her right hand. Her pet. Slave laborer. But I would be nobody's stomping ground ever again.

Tossing me to the ground, where I smacked my head on a pile of debris, she snarled at me. More animal than Rose. Obviously she knew what I was thinking. I'd never get used to having no privacy in my own mind, especially when my own thoughts were used against me.

Her red eyes teared up, which was so gross I couldn't even deal with it. "You forced me up here. I was happy to defeat Satan, it would have been nothing for me. I could have!" she screeched, having heard me think, *Don't think so, kid.* "Because of you I learned things about my father that I didn't want to know."

"Nope, no way, no how. That shit's on you. You had him brought here, you tortured the shit out of Mortimer to find out what he knew because you were too scared to face your dad still. All I did was give you a little push. If it was too much for you, well, look at what you're doing. Nobody has a chance. I don't feel bad for you. You aren't a victim anymore. You're not a child anymore."

A stab of a memory seared through my brain of a little old lady telling her that she was more than a child once.

It sent Rose right over the edge.

"You want to know what facing your past feels like, Charity? *Hazel?*"

Oh fuck no. That name didn't translate past the Queen who just loved playing with it.

"Don't call me that."

"What did your mother call you?" she asked sweetly, tilting her head to the side.

My stomach flipped as a million feelings that I'd shoved into a pit rolled over me, tore into me. Feelings I'd escaped for all the years since I'd run from "home," my mother who gave zero fucks, Carl Painter. Even when I'd seen the bastard with my own two eyes in the Wood, I hadn't felt this mix of being ready to shit myself and sob and claw my own eyes out and anything I could do to escape that *hurt.*

Rose was putting those feelings *into* me. Forcing them on me again.

"You think that's all I can do?" she said, utter joy in her voice.

"Please…" Goddamn it, she'd gotten me to beg.

"Look what I've been stashing away for a rainy day," she said. And madness gripped me.

~

Harpies flooded the world outside the hole where windows had once been. So many I couldn't see the sky.

But that wasn't what scared me most. I'd seen them before.

Once again, two Harpies, new ones, one with the head of an eagle entirely, brought a figure into view. And I was a weak, fragile, nothing kid again.

"Mmm…mmmom?"

But this woman was *healthy.* Harpy-smacked around, but her bones weren't jutting out from forgetting to eat for days. Her hair—dyed rich-girl auburn with goddamn highlights—was long, and *thick.* I recognized the twisty cowlicks at the bottom from when I was little. Before I remembered that I remembered them. I hadn't seen her hair thick and shiny since I was tiny. The tatters of her clothes were as conservative as Jen's had been, though less soccer mom and more stylish. Like, J. Crew shit.

I zeroed in on all these details, in case I needed to repeat them to myself later. In case I didn't believe it. If I was still alive and if this moment went away before I could make sense of it.

The woman's bloodied lip dropped open. Full lip. Barely parched. I bet she had good lipstick.

"It can't be," she gasped. "Is that you? What's happening, Hazel?"

She spoke to me as if knowing my name meant she knew me. Psychiatrist used to do it as a tactic, a put-on, but eventually he warmed up to saying it. This bitch wouldn't get the chance. "I wouldn't tell you the fucking time if you asked me."

"Put me down, please," she said gently to the Harpies. I hadn't heard her be gentle for a very long time. I hadn't heard her ever sound confident. I hated it, I ached with how much I despised it.

The Harpies looked to Rose who watched this whole thing like she needed a fucking bucket of popcorn, and she nodded. They put my mother down.

My mother.

She stumbled a little once—her heels were broken— but walked to me with grace, her head held not high, but not drooping. Not like she was ashamed at all. Not at all.

Sonofabitch, once she was in front of me I could

smell her expensive perfume through the blood and wreckage.

"Hazel, you look…"

"Shut it, bitch. Don't you fucking dare tell me I what, look good? We aren't bumping into each other at the fucking bank. What the hell have you been…" I gestured to all of her. The clearly doing-well all of her. I noticed the needlemarks had faded.

"Yeah," she said, laughing awkwardly like we really had bumped into each other at the bank, "I cleaned up. Got a job. Got married," she said slowly, looking anywhere but at me.

"Really?" I laughed, embodying the phrase 'dripping with sarcasm.' "Let me guess, have a kid or two? Living the All-American, huh? Does your husband like your track marks? Does he play connect the dots while you giggle? Does he think your past makes you *so strong* and *such a survivor*? Does he even know I exist? Never mind, I don't care."

She reached out to me. I slapped her hand away. A flood of light streamed through the wall-hole as the last of the Harpies poured into the sky.

"What are these things?" my mother said. Her voice warbled. I swear, she was like a well-to-do lady in a horror movie. I hoped she'd get killed first. By me.

"Harpies. Vicious bird bitches that rip the hearts and guts out of predators like all your boyfriends, and just maybe you." *Here it comes.* "How could you let those guys do that to me?"

"I wasn't in any condition to know what was happening then."

"But now that you're all clean and pretty yourself, you got *yourself* taken care of, you still never bothered to look for me, did you? You let me go."

"Exactly! I let you go! I let you leave that terrible place, I was no mother to you! You deserved—"

"What I deserved was for you to think of me first."

"Well," Rose interrupted us, "what would you like to do now, Charity? Or should I say Hazel? Who would you rather be the person you've chosen to become, this common woman? Or the master of vengeance that you were and could be again?"

Outside Harpies swooped through the afternoon air like eagles, proudly. Well, some of them. Others flapped wildly, shellshocked to see a sky that wasn't the color of an open wound. Who knew how far they went, what they were doing?

The screams didn't take long to begin.

I pulled my attention from my mother—my distraction—to appeal to Rose, get her to call this massacre off. "Kid, look outside, listen to the pain out there. You can't tell me the Harpies know what they're doing, they're just slaughtering people! All the people."

"I don't care," she said, shrugging. "For now, let them do what they want. Nobody can run from pain forever. This is their time to face it. The Harpies deserve some respite. Some lawlessness."

My mother took the opportunity to run, kicking off her broken heels.

Rose quirked an eyebrow at me.

"Mom!" I yelled, guttural, a you-better-get-back-here-or-else voice. But she kept running.

Rose's henchmen hovered, waiting for direction.

Or I could go get the bitch myself.

She was nearly at the elevator, but joke's on her, there was no way that shit worked after what the building had been through.

Outside gunshots echoed through the air, and Harpies scattered.

This wasn't about my mother right now, and to pay her any attention was just proving that I couldn't move forward. I couldn't be better even if I wanted to. I kinda got it. As a Harpy, I was stuck. I couldn't change or move forward. Being that monster was the best I could do then. I'd chosen to be stuck then.

My mother banged on the elevator doors, sobbing, looking for a way out and failing at that too.

I had my own way out.

I turned my back to her, let the banging and crying echo. I didn't know if she'd get out, come back, get ripped apart. I realized that I'd never looked for her either. I didn't need her to make myself better, and she could be all dressed up, but she was more stuck than I'd been.

"What are you doing? She's getting away!" Rose said, waving an arm at the elevator.

I mimicked her shrug. "I don't care."

She scowled, childlike, pouty. "You think you've had a victory."

Oh, that sounded loaded. "It doesn't mean anything between me and you."

Her chest heaved with a silent laugh. "It means everything. You think you're better than me."

"In no way do I think that."

"My brain is dying!" she shouted out of nowhere, and I found myself shaking my head in confusion. "Finding my father, remembering everything, it didn't help. And *you* think you can just get better."

Swallowing back some emotion I didn't want to feel. "I wish it had, kid."

"How does your victory feel now, Charity?"

"Goddamn it, stop with the ominous shit and the nasty moves to prove it! Who are you fighting exactly? What are you trying to win, or do you even know anymore?"

"Nobody wins!" she screamed. Loose rubble fell from the ceiling, cracking the few remaining hospital tiles. "Nobody. Wins. But at least the Harpies can be free, just for a little while."

We both looked outside, listened for the gunshots, the crashing cars. Watched smoke billow up. The smell of blood swept through the air like a skunk spray as Harpies zipped past. For once, the smell made me sick.

I was glad I couldn't see the street below.

CHAPTER 18

She let me walk away. I went down like six flights of stairs until my thighs burned, and when the bottom floor was finally in sight, I plopped my ass down on the bottom step. How could I go outside when I had no more ideas, no more plans, and not a care in the fucking world? And nobody was on my side now.

No one to care about. No one who would survive the shitstorm out there.

Rose hadn't let me walk out. She'd given me a head start.

Tears poured down my cheeks, finally, finally I could let them. I wasn't about to run. I'd wait, but I wasn't about to run.

Rose had said the Harpies could be free, for a little while. My first and final on the subject was that they should be. If murdering was the only thing that brought them any amount of happiness now, they deserved it. Didn't everyone be happy once in a while? Especially if, as Rose said, nobody was going to win in this fiasco.

"This is really it," I murmured as the Facility shook. The metal railing I'd left my hand hanging on screeched away from the wall, the gray cement cracking. The concrete stairs beneath me shifted.

In little tiny steps, I would die on the steps. I chuckled at my own joke.

I pictured the aquarium. The concrete here the same shade as there, the blues not so much different if I just unfocused and let myself half-drift off.

"She's here!" I heard whisper-shouted from around the corner.

Soft slapping of feet without shoes, like running at the side of a pool. I waited where I was, no energy to go anywhere else, no need to.

Cleary came up on me, with a patched-up Mortimer limping behind him.

"Holy shit, what are you guys doing here? Where are your shoes?"

Viciously brought back to the present, I took the two of them in. Castaways hiding from the zombie horde outside, like a horror movie that Robbie would've liked.

I wondered what movies Meat Matt had liked. I never asked. I always just talked about myself.

"Charity," Mortimer said, reminding me again who I was, "you thought we'd just leave you?"

Cleary seconded it by just staring at me, puzzled crease in his forehead.

"Yeah, I totally thought you'd leave me. I wanted you to, dummies. I mean, I thought you'd be dead right away, but yeah."

Mortimer hobbled forward, held out his hand, which I took because what kind of an asshole wouldn't? We were all about to die anyway. Maybe a little running out of the building final scene and evading murderous monsters would be the icing on this shit cake.

"Psychiatrist, you should have run while you had the chance," I said as we rounded a corner, narrowly missing a Harpy eating what looked like another Harpy. We slammed our backs against the wall, Cleary going down into a crouch, finger to his lips like we needed to be told to shut up. "The world's about to end," I whispered to Mortimer. "Rose is…breaking. Nobody's getting out of here, and especially not you."

That pissed him off a little, which kinda surprised me. His beat-up face hardened. "You're pretending that Rose has all the power here so that you don't have to take responsibility. You can save us, Charity."

That pissed *me* off. "You know what, fuck you. I'm not pretending shit. You've done plenty of pretending yourself, though. You wanna talk about running from responsibility? You had a responsibility to that kid and you were so *scared* that you abandoned her. While she was fucking *dying,* you pretended she never existed. Now look what happened."

"Shhhhh!" Cleary hissed.

"I'm only a man, Charity!" Mortimer snapped, fists clenched at his sides. "I've faced horrors that no man should because of her and you—"

He cut himself off.

"Oh no, please go on. Did we cost you the family? Did that happen before or after you threw Rose to the wolves? Was it before or after she grew up in a mental facility or whatever the fuck? Was it our fault you had to go to a nuthouse? Look, I'm real sorry if our problems came home with you and your picket fence got destroyed," I said, grimacing, feeling nastier every second, "but some of us never had the picket fence. Me and Rose are more likely to get impaled on one."

Cleary was quiet, the defeat on his face too heavy for him to look up. "Rose might be saved or she might not. But you're the only chance the rest of us have," he said. "Dr. Mortimer and I, we failed. We—I—did my best, but it wasn't enough." He lifted his head, looked me in the eye from the crouch he was in. "You've survived so much, only you understand her truly. Your connection is one she feels on a different level. *Use it.*"

"I tried, dumbass. I failed."

"And you got back up again," Cleary said. "Seems like you always do."

"It's not the point that I get back up. It's the fact that I can't stand upright on the regular."

Cleary stood up, grabbed both my hands. Theo had done it just like this once.

Theo. Was he out there somewhere?

I peeked my head around the corner at the growling and scrabbling noises to see more Harpies had joined the cannibal feast in the destroyed hallway. We'd have to go a different way. I pulled Mortimer along by the hand in the opposite direction, obviously being the one with a level head here.

Mortimer was wheezing, and when I glanced his way as we snuck down the hallways, avoiding Harpies like this was fucking Jurassic Park and they were raptors, I saw that his eyes were unfocused. That he was smiling off and on, like none of this was as scary as it really was. Like we weren't running for our lives.

"He's been like this," Cleary murmured to me as we stopped for a break. "Lucid one minute, then…"

Out of sheer assholery I refused to admit it when accused, but me and Rose had done a number on him. It was totally all our fault. My fault. Yeah, he'd left Rose to die, but here I was, dragging a feeble-minded Psychiatrist through the bowels of the freakshow Facility, back and forth from and to his death. Toting him along through the belly of the bitch. I pretty well was the reason everything had gone to shit.

Didn't matter anymore.

Rubble rained down upon us, more walls collapsed.

I couldn't tell if it was structural integrity issues—shit, did that feel good to say—or Rose, cracking, crumbling and bringing everything down with her. Harpies, fighting, fell through the concrete, clawing and ripping at people and each other. There was no plan here. No reasoning. Just violence. Rose's violence made real.

And still, him and Cleary had hidden in this nightmare, took their damn shoes off to be quieter, waiting for *me*. The craziest, most insane thought raced into my head.

What if there were more people out there who'd have waited for me and I just hadn't found them yet?

I whipped Mortimer around, making him stumble into an overturned desk, and got right in his face. "I'm sorry. I'm really, really sorry," I said.

I threw my arms around his neck.

His arms came up around my back.

Wicked unprofessional. I was definitely getting him fired.

Mr. Cleary put a hand on my shoulder, said quietly, "Come on, kid."

My breath caught in my throat and I didn't think I'd live through it.

We ducked into a room quietly under the nose of a giant Harpy, bigger than any I'd ever seen, its head touching what remained of the ceiling, stalking like a murder ostrich, clucking to itself, twisting its head and sniffing the air. I closed the door with shaking hands.

Cleary had sat at a desk in this remarkably unaffected office, while Psychiatrist rested in a crappy chair.

"Think you're gonna find yourself on that side of the desk a lot more, Psychiatrist," I said as I picked up a stack of papers on the desk.

They were all blank.

I whipped open a file cabinet drawer, chock full of manilla folders slipped into hanging green ones. Every one was brand new, not even bent in a corner. Everything blank. Because nobody was checked into this place but Rose.

All that blankness in an office made for nothing but show—and to nobody, at that. Nobody was coming looking around here. Nobody was looking for Rose. Bob hadn't even been looking for her, this was all made just in case she got anywhere near the truth. To hide from her under as many layers as he could muster. To protect his own ass.

It was all fake, just to bury her memories. And the horrid realization that she'd re-created this place, or moved it, or whatever, and it was still exactly the same... She wanted it buried again. Maybe she didn't know any better, for as smart as she was, for as different as she was.

Cleary had stuck his head out the door, and was giving us the all-clear.

Finally, we came to a glass door that went straight outside, like at a 7-11 or something. Rose's Facility design was weird.

Outside it looked like hurricane five footage. Innocent people under rubble, covered in powdery dust as buildings crumbled before my eyes. Shadows of flames climbed up brick walls on side streets in the darkening daylight. SWAT dudes in black uniforms ran in formation right by us, guns drawn. More gunshots rang out in the distance. A woman huddled against a smashed glass door across the street, crying.

We're the bad guys, I thought. We, as in the Harpies.

But that wasn't me anymore, and I didn't want it to be. I wanted to be *people.* Like, I really wanted to. Not just going through the motions, not running from my bloodlust, looking for raw meat, not trying to be one while all the time thinking they were less than me, and not wearing fancy clothes and starting a new family and pretending my past wasn't part of me. A real life. A real person.

I wasn't part of the Harpies' *we* anymore. A momentary sadness drenched me.

One that felt like leaving Maggie Painter behind as I ran away from her father and my mother. Knowing I'd get better. Knowing what it cost.

A Harpy who looked just like Margot Robbie, I swear, but with like, fur instead of feathers—no wait, that was human hair stuck to her with blood—smacked the sky and opened a portal that dripped red goo. She jumped through it, and it sucked her inside, quivering like a human organ.

As policemen and guys who thought they were

heroes wrestled with Harpies, some saw what Margot did and tried to open their own portals. But Harpies aren't all able to do it. I knew that. It was a special thing. I used to be that kind of special. Most of them failed. One got sucked into it halfway and left her bird legs behind. Two guys grabbed them and tore them apart. Beasts. And now there were more officers and army guys out there than there were Harpies. But it was ugly as fuck on both sides.

Harpies were heaped, bloodied and mangled like roadkill, but they'd been killed on purpose. Gunshot wounds leaked into puddles of black blood. An arrow stuck out of one. Others were beaten, visible in their black eyes and swollen jaws, but they were dead now. Piled up.

It dawned on me.

The fires on the side streets. They were burning Harpy bodies.

I had to look away and the only place to look was at Mortimer and Cleary. "I don't know where you guys planned on going. Judging by that lady hiding in a doorway, there's not far to go without mass destruction in the way. Rose is up here, Harpies are out there. If the building weren't about to become dust I'd say stay right here, but the fact is there's nowhere safe for you that she can't reach. She's only let us get this far because she has better things to do."

"What are you proposing?" Mr. Cleary asked.

I didn't want to say to go back the way we came. I

didn't have the fucking energy anyway, even if I thought we'd get there. Jesus fuck, we were going in circles. No, I was sending us in circles.

"I'll ask her to protect you," I nodded out the window, "from *that.*"

"What am I missing?" Mortimer asked. "She's the one who caused *that.*"

"No," Cleary said hazily, getting closer to the door to get a better/worse look. "They're out of her control."

"They don't have any control at all of themselves either," I said. "They don't know what the fuck they're doing up here, they're moths to a lightbulb."

Cleary muttered, "More like sharks to blood."

"Yeah. Right. This shitfest will only last until it doesn't. Right now Rose feels like none of it matters, she's lost some hope, but it won't be long before that turns into the same goddamn fury she usually plays with, and then who knows what."

"Get to it, Charity," Mortimer hissed.

"Fine," I hissed back.

And I pounded my way out into the middle of the apocalyptic street.

~

Rose was looking down from up above, flying high over all this mess. The building had been reduced to little more than the bottom couple of floors, like the rest of town as far as I could tell.

She spotted me quick. As if she'd been waiting. She cried out some weird-ass bird call and the Harpies scattered. The ones that could, anyway. Then she descended to me. Coming down to my level. That was a good sign, I supposed, until tires screeched in my head and everything became white fuzz, nothing making sense, everything static.

It cleared up in a snap as soon as Rose spoke. "Come to your senses, have you?"

"That—shit—in my brain just now, that was you?" No answer. Which means she didn't do it on purpose. *Is anything in your control anymore, kid?*

Again, no response. She couldn't see in my brain, and I didn't know if that was a good or bad sign for her, but it sure felt good for me.

"Are you with me?" she asked in a tiny voice.

"Yeah, kid. I'm with you." I reached out, brushed some dirt out of her hair, let my hand land on her shoulder.

She loosened up, rolled her neck like she was about to say she'd had a long day and was going to bed. "What do you think we should do next?" she asked. Like this great bitch-bird release was step one and not a complete fucking blunder.

"Question is, how can I get you what you want next?" No answer again. She was perplexed.

She was tired.

Pulling her in close for a hug, I said, "Let me take the lead here, so you can rest that head of yours.

Because if you don't…I don't want to know what will happen." She pulled away, eyebrows knit like she was doubting me. "Let me get you what you want while you stay quiet, so you can run things the way you want when they're yours. Okay?"

It took a minute but she nodded, and her head fell forward.

When it did, I saw that parts of the sky behind her had turned Wood of Suicides-red.

~

"Nope. Not until our work is done."

"When our work is done there will be more work."

Rose stomped her foot in a mini-tantrum—which was about all she had energy left for. She took a big sip of her drink, making tons of noise with the straw.

We were at an only slightly destroyed McDonald's. I sat on the drink counter, throwing ketchup packets in the air and kicking them. My aim was just okay. Rose leaned one hip against the same counter in front of the soda dispensers. She was wearing velour sweatpants in an ungodly shade of Christmas green that we'd taken from the totally demolished and looted Walmart. Regular pants hurt her skin now, she said.

"I'm just asking for a little time with him before I do what comes next, Rose."

"And what is it that comes next, *sister*?" she said, all

snooty-like. Not her usual power behind it, just teenager irritation.

"You'll find out when I get what I want, too."

Her eyes, in her exhaustion, had returned to her normal sparkly blue, but the whites were bloodshot. The fire that burned in them, all that ambition and rage, it had cooled off. Part of me thought that I could just wait her out, that her power had been so used up that she'd never recover again. Then we—I—could kill her.

But I convinced myself that she was too smart not to see that coming and too strong for it to happen. Best to stick to my original idea.

Rose before would've asserted her dominance, argued with me. This one thought about it, but instead filled up her cup again, this time with orange soda on top of the Pepsi. So I kept going.

"I want to see Theo, have a somewhat normal Christmas for one, simple day. *Simple,* isn't that what you always wanted? Hmm?" Nothing. *Keep pushing.* I inched closer. "If you could have just one perfect, simple day, wouldn't you? Come on, kid. I'm asking here, but remember—you're the one who said I was in charge for a while."

"Watch it, Charity. I said you could take the reins but that does not mean you're in charge. It's temporary. Do you understand that?"

There was a little of that fire. "I do. And that's why I'm asking."

She glanced out the smashed front wall. Nothing to glance out of, really. It was gone. "Do you even know if he's alive?" she said.

My stomach turned. I got up to grab a cold burger from the smashed warmer. This time I was the one with nothing to say.

CHAPTER 19

The Harpies had ravaged much of Boston and who knows how far outside of it. Every time I thought there couldn't be more of them, that the Wood wasn't big enough to hold any more, a new flock tore through some shitty portal, one that would never work both ways. Or a few would regain consciousness and suddenly were rolling with a few new friends. I didn't know where they were coming from and I couldn't get an answer from Rose.

What mattered right now was that Mortimer and Cleary were safe, put up in a luxury hotel somewhere that I didn't need to know the whereabouts of. Or so I was told. And it was Christmas Eve.

The city smoldered in the snow like a wood stove. Smoke curled up, licking the sky, twisting like magic through the blue night sky, sparkling stars swirled into it. And my total solitude was suffocating me.

I needed to see Theo. I needed to see my bird. I needed normalcy for this one night before the shit really hit the fan.

For someone who hated the phone, not having one sucked it, and of course I didn't remember Theo's number. I couldn't remember if he'd even given it to me. A car just always *appeared*, he just always was there… What it taught me was that people in shady business always have more convenient means. Going forward, in this actual human life, I needed to be in some shady business myself. If I survived in any way, shape, or form.

Highly unlikely.

Rose busted into the room with zero grace. She'd plopped us into an office that had managed to stay nearly intact, or at least parts of it—500 Boylston Street. I only knew because it was plastered over the entrance.

"There's a car down there waiting for you," she said, all sulkiness and annoyance.

"What? Seriously?"

She smiled, which was weird, but my excitement was obviously infectious. "Yeah, he wasn't hard to find."

I knew what she meant. She was looking healthier. More *able*. It hadn't taken long. I'd slept here in the office once. Two days? And she was back to being able to take stuff apart enough to find one man in a trashed city.

She got me down there with her big-ass nasty

wings, straight out of a smashed bunch of windows. If her taking over Earth actually worked and hadn't turned into a massacre and demolition, people would pay thousands for her to do this.

The same driver, even. Different car. "I should probably know your name by now, huh?" I said to him. But his tight-lipped smile told me he disagreed. "You can take me to him? He's safe?"

"He's safe, miss. You'll be with him in just a few minutes."

A few minutes was all I needed to see the havoc Rose's *master plan* had wreaked. Imagine my surprise when the aquarium came into view.

"Holy fuck, are the fish okay?" I yelped at the edge of my seat, smacking the driver on the shoulder with one hand.

"Miss, please wait a moment."

He sped up to get me there, and pulled up right in front of the abandoned place. My heart sank to see the glass tank that held the seals smashed to nothingness, the water drained out. I made a choking noise and tried to hide it but the driver noticed.

"It's okay, miss," he said, leaning his head close to mine and pointing out. "They live in the ocean right there."

I wiped a hand across my face. "Right, yeah. Thanks, of course."

Theo had run to the side of the car from inside the building, that looked pretty okay. He looked pretty okay, too. But not untouched. He whipped the door open before the driver could even get to my side of the car. He pulled me up into his arms, wrapping his around my shoulders, hugging me so close, closer than I thought I'd ever be held again. Not just physically close but the kind where it seems like we'd been separated for so long that being together again was a sort of healing.

"I can't believe you're okay," he whispered into my hair.

"You can't? I'm so much tougher than millions of nightmare birds."

I could feel the creases in his face when he smiled. The way every line was a laugh line. "Yeah, you are," he said, pulled away and turned my face in one smooth move to kiss me full on the lips, both hands holding my cheeks, until the ash and the snow were the same falling from the sky, and the rubble underfoot and the cobblestones were the same and it didn't matter if we were in this world or Rose's. We were together.

"Merry Christmas tomorrow," I said.

That smile again. Even now it didn't falter, even though the world was ending. And I had like, a lot to do with it.

A Harpy swooped, screeching bloody murder, making us both duck. A reminder of how little time I'd been given, I thought. But she wasn't here for me.

She plunged into the harbor, sending boats tossing

all around her. She emerged from the water with a seal in her claws, working hard to carry it away.

"You fucking bitch!" I screamed, and it was distraction enough for her to drop him. The seal twisted and was too heavy for her to begin with, and he dropped back into the water.

The bird-bitch was fucking irate and she made it obvious that not all Harpies ravaging Earth cared whose side I was on or about maybe much of anything except being free to destroy things. She landed on the dock, spun on me holding up human hands with the shape of long super chicken claws, screamed at me and revealed black, sharp teeth below her demony eyes. No human eyes for this one, they looked straight demon, cat-eyes with the weird-ass pupils that always unsettled me. In her anger, she turned her claws on herself, ripped at graying, nasty hair.

"Now's a good time to run," I said, snapping Theo out of his fear.

Dodging ripped-up cobblestones and monstrous hunks of glass, we bolted for the entryway. The tarp overhead covering the ticket booth and walkway and stuff got shredded as the Harpy dove down through it, and now three or four more had joined her crusade. The tarp smacked into my back, knocking me onto the pavement where I skidded on my fucking knees. Theo pulled me back up, yelling something that I couldn't hear over the loud bitches, and we ran like fucking

Olympic medalists through the once-glass, now-empty entrance, and dove out of sight to the left.

Bostonians weren't stupid. They built the shit on the wharf to last New England winters. The inside of the aquarium hadn't been bothered. No lights, but whatever.

"We gotta keep going," Theo rasped.

"No, rest, it's okay," I said, pulling him back down by the arm. "We were convenient then. They like meaner, uglier prey than us, trust me."

The way he looked at me, not horrified, but more impressed, made me tackle him to the hard floor and kiss him harder than ever. I didn't want to think about it, but Robbie popped into my head, kissing him, how sweet he'd always been.

But how I always felt like a rescue mission with him. And how I'd been strong enough to not need rescuing. The question was where did I want to use my strength. For now, it was right here on the aquarium floor.

~

"Wow," he said for the hundredth time, staring up at the giant shark hanging overhead. "Wow."

I rolled over onto my stomach, no longer caring about how hard the floor was and how many bruises

I'd acquired, because I felt too goddamn perfect. "Yeah, that's a big shark."

He poked me in the side, and I did care about the bruises then. "Gah, shit," I moaned, clutching my side.

"God, I'm sorry." He straightened me out, rubbed my side, hovering over me. The most pleasant thing that had hovered over me in a good long time. I pushed his floppy hair behind his ear, did all I could to remember every inch of his face. I thought for a second how nice it would have been to see him under the blue neon aquarium lights then, but I always had liked darkness. He brightened it plenty.

"I have to tell you something," I said. Why did I do this shit? Why did I ruin everything as fast as I could, as soon as I didn't know what else to say next? I had so few good things to talk about, and now was definitely not the time to bring up how I'd love there to be at least a near-future with him. Not marriage or some shit, but just some *time.*

"Go ahead, anything," he murmured.

"I gotta go to Hell. To stop this, all of this. I really am the only one who can do it. And my chances of coming back are poor at best."

His eyes stayed glued to mine while he thought of what to say. "I believe you. You're the only person I can imagine being able to stop the apocalypse," he said, laughing. "And I find it really hard to believe you won't be coming back." He kissed me quickly, and jumped to his feet, holding a hand out for me. "Give yourself a little credit, Blake," he said.

The lights flickered, once, twice, making us both squeal like kids. Then they finally stayed on, the basic ones, and then the neon blue. It was magic. No reason for them to come on, nobody was working on power lines. It was almost laughable how fast a guy in a cherry-picker would have been eaten up.

"It's a Christmas miracle," Theo joked, eyes wide and blinking. "God bless us, everyone. Come on," mischievous grinny. "Sun's coming up. It's Christmas."

Indeed it was. The naked entrance revealed the winter sun bouncing off an ice-cold ocean, the gray air brightening with it. The seals were croaking, unafraid. I pointed one out bobbing not far from the dock.

Theo pulled me away to the aquarium gift shop. "Gift shop is the best part," he said. Having it all to ourselves, I busted into a pack of gum to handle my atrocious breath while Theo put on a New England Aquarium baby blue sweatshirt. While I looked for one of my own, he popped up behind me with a little black box held in front of his smiling face.

"I didn't get you anything," I said.

"I didn't ask you to."

I cracked it open to find a black cord inside with a big shark tooth pendant attached.

"Is that real?" I gasped, letting it poke my finger.

"One hundred percent authentic Great White," he said, taking it from the box and coming around behind me to put it on my neck. "Almost as dangerous as you," he said into my neck, making my breath catch.

We didn't have a lot of time. Rose wouldn't let that happen.

I spun and gave him a kiss with all the good energy I could muster, and it was a pretty fair amount now.

"You can do this," he said, nodding. "Whatever it is you have to do, you can do it."

"I know," I said.

"You can make it back, too. Or this goodbye would be a lot longer. Charity, I believe in you. Come home when you're done."

I let out an inappropriate laugh. "I think the kid burned my house down." And the question I should have asked right away, the question that I hadn't thought of because I'd been my usual fucking selfish self, finally climbed its way up my throat like puke. "Speaking of houses…your place…" But I didn't care about his place, not really.

"Keegan is at my driver's place," he said. "He's fine, I got him out in time. He's not happy, though. He misses you. Won't eat much. You need to come back. See my new apartment."

"You already found a new place?"

"My family is good but not that good," he said with a low laugh, but shoved his hands in his pockets. "I actually haven't heard from my dad in days." His face went unusually blank. It hurt to watch. A face with that much expression should never be blank.

"I'm sorry."

"Not your fault. And he might be fine, just laying low, right? Could be something else entirely. He's not exactly in the business for high profiles, but he's a good guy and…"

"You don't need to justify that he's a good guy because he's in the mob, Theo. People aren't just good or bad. People have reasons. Nobody horrible could create a kid like you."

It made me think real fast of my own mother, and I shoved that shit right out the window.

"Hey," he said, rubbing my arms. "I hope you're talking about yourself, too. You've always had reasons. Everything that's happened to the world, it is not your fault. You're a good person, Charity."

I surprised myself by saying, "I know."

With that smile bigger than his whole face he said, "Then go to Hell."

CHAPTER 20

Going to Hell isn't as easy as The Bible might make it out to be. And if I'd had questions about whether or not I was a good person, it was proven when Satan had a hard time getting to me. Sending his gross faux Harpy that melted like the Wicked Witch had been his best attempt. So getting down there was a plan all in itself, and I needed Rose for it.

As requested, I shouted her name in my head, but it barely took that for her to know I was thinking of her.

She was getting stronger every minute. The effort of bringing the Harpies above had put her down, but she sure as shit wasn't out. It made the reality of what I had to do even more solid.

"Leave here. Rest now."

The words came into being in my mind—but they weren't meant for me.

She was speaking into the Harpies' minds. She hadn't been able to do it before, I was sure of it. No, she'd come back stronger after getting back on her feet. Which meant she was allowing the Harpies to destroy the planet like this. She was letting them.

This was not her plan to begin with.

I went outside, where yes, there wasn't a Harpy to be seen. And I waited in the stillness, Theo watching me from the aquarium, for her to come.

Wind whipped around me, stirring up pieces of the tarp that had been shredded, stray papers, sand, making a little tornado.

And Rose touched down in the middle of it, smashing what remained of the walkway in front of me.

"Done some upgrades overnight, huh?"

Her wings had been repaired, shiny and new. No more rusty blades and broken razors. Silver and gold that blinded me with the sunlight, perfectly aligned and whirring like some store-bought steampunk slicing machine. And at the arch of each wing, where it came to a point, a giant scythe stuck out. A nauseating show of power, such an obvious threat and so aggressive, it felt like they'd cut me in half with fear.

"I have," she said, turning to show me the monstrous size of them. I don't know how she could hold them up. Facing me again, she said, "Let me show you what I've done."

"No," I said, backing up. The slickness of her voice,

the glint in her bright blue eyes was enough to make me quiver with terror.

But there, smacking into my mind was the memory of her, her own memory, slicing through my brain. And yeah, she was feeling better all right.

I could see Rose standing in the courtyard of 500 Boylston, making great swooping circles with her arms. With every movement, the pieces of her wings detached, floated through the air, spread out on the ground, and she simply *looked* at them. That's all she had to do was look at them, and the fixing began. Different for each one. Some blades began to glimmer again, as if being shined with an invisible cloth. Others seemed to go backward and forward in time, showing the phases of their deterioration and being built sharpened and tightened again. Red, red heat blazed on more than one, welding themselves into shape. It would have been beautiful in any other situation. If Rose had been the Rose I knew once.

"Okay, that's enough," I said. "Here we go, kid. You stay out of my head, right? I can't take you stirring shit up in there while I'm trying to negotiate, okay?"

"Done."

"I get this for you, and you call off the Harpies up here. Let them come above just for *specific* reasons? Earth stays Earth, Hell stays Hell. Right?"

"Right," she said a little more reluctantly.

"Then let's go."

I hadn't known that Rose's ability to get in and out

of Hell stopped with the Wood of Suicides. I didn't know that until she created a gaping portal, a hungry thing with red, ragged edges, as though it had been torn out of the skin of the Wood. Rose jumped in like it was a swimming pool in the dead heat. I sorta clambered in after her, and it felt like climbing in through an open wound. Warm. Wet. Smelly. Fleshy.

I think I'd been climbing for six hours. Or six days. Definitely until I prayed for death. It was disgusting. The lower intestine of fucking Hell.

It shat me out right in the middle of the Wood of Suicides. A fairly empty Wood of Suicides. Loretta had stayed, I saw. I waved, but she didn't wave back.

"Great, here we are. Here."

Rose had been there waiting for me, and she was walking in circles, shaking her hands like she was psyching herself up for a fight.

"Kid, we aren't fighting today. We're just talking."

She stopped, looked at me like I was the biggest moron in existence. "I'm always fighting," she said. "To get there…I don't know another way to get there, even though I can see it."

"You're not…"

"Be ready," she said.

She let out a horrific scream, a hybrid battlecry and cry of submission. And then the images plastered themselves across the sky. I let out a long breath, tried to ready myself for it, but poor Rose just twisted and sobbed, moaned, just pure torture to watch her.

Still, the earthquake never came. And I was starting to wonder if this whole plan—which was about as much of plan as I'd ever come up with—would work.

Then the images changed.

The white streaks where the memories played out grew darker. The color of old wood. Of wood paneling.

Fuck.

These memories were mine.

Maggie, her bare feet tapping on the floor, waiting for her father.

Painter, his laugh, shuddering through the house with zero happiness to it.

Me, my back against the bedroom door, pushing it with all my might as he howled on the other side.

My mother laughing as she dropped a used needle on the floor, having gotten what she wanted from it.

Then it was just feelings. The feel of his hands, the feel of watching a helpless child be hurt, the feel of anger that I was in so much pain, the feel of cigarette burns the day after they'd been made, the feel of helplessness that I would ever get out. The absolute feeling that this was all there ever would be for me. The feeling of utter hopelessness and acceptance of that hopelessness.

"God fucking dammit, I was too young," I sobbed. Then, "Rose! Stop it!"

But the harder I yelled, the more of my memories found their way out of my brain, through hers, out into Hell, whatever the fuck they did, they found *me.*

And when I saw my mother, over Painter's shoulder as he pinned me down, and that pig *shut the door*, leaving me in there, that was it. That was all I could take.

There was no reason to scream when the feathers burst out of the backs of my scarred arms.

It didn't hurt when enormous talons split the skin of my mutilated toes, my toes burst through the stupid sneakers, enormous talons having split the skin.

I didn't cry when the flesh on my legs hardened, scaled over.

Finally, I had no reason to hurt anymore.

~

When I threw my head back to scream out all the pain I'd endured and all the guilt and anger that came with it, a wild *cawwwwwww* erupted, and shook the ground I stood upon.

And for the briefest second, I thought, *I could do this all on my own. No Rose. No Satan. No humanity, no Harpies, nothing but screaming in Hell.*

Oh, how simple that would be.

But simple wasn't what I was meant for. The voice in my head sounded different than it used to when I was a Harpy. Maybe it was the same and I was different. But I didn't resent that simplicity wasn't for me.

I gathered up all the physical power I'd been missing as a human, and did something I can only describe as an ultra rocketpunch into the ground. Once, twice, three times until it cracked. Which only made me hit it harder, gleeful and giggly about it. Until Rose saw what I'd become.

"Hoooowww did you do thiiissss!" she moaned. I didn't get it at first—she wanted me to see what I was missing, to beg her to give me my Harpy wings back. But then I got it—I did it without her help. I hadn't proven her right.

"Oh can it, kid, I don't plan on staying." I jumped up, flipped my wings out with a resounding *crack* and dove at the break in the ground, willing it open further, inching closer and waiting for it to expand, hoping I didn't knock myself out and then

I went through.

~

*T*he ice welcomed me like an old friend.

I was so *hot*, just so hot and never noticed. The heat of the Wood and the redness of it always did offend me, but it felt like I deserved it. I was sure I did, and that was why I belonged there. This… this felt like a beautiful relief. Darkness. Cold.

Everything had become Rose-tinted red and this place had none of that.

It did have living corpses, half-frozen and never resting. I ran a talon over a broken femur with skin sloughing off of it. This place felt like death. It didn't just feel like torture. It felt like dying over and over again. Which I'd have to guess might be the best part of some of these bastards' lives.

The ability to fly again was delicious. Delicious. I didn't waste time getting to where I needed to be, but I sure did smile against the chill wind as I ripped through the trees. And I landed with a satisfying *thud* on the ice with Satan towering over me.

"Place looks good," I said. No evidence of it being torn to shreds before.

He flapped his mountainous bat wings—which did give me a twinge of jealousy—and a fresh sheen appeared over the ice from the cold wind. He could put on a show, but all he did was dig himself deeper into the ice. Interesting.

"I want to know why you've come," he said in that great, booming voice.

"You don't know?"

He smiled—ugly as hell—and when he did I could see a person in his mouth, still alive. Reaching out to me, making eye contact. Didn't like that shit at all. "It's…problematic…to distinguish between your intentions and your friend's."

"Yeah, so she's not able to come, but I'm here on her behalf."

"She's making quite a mess on Earth. It's delightful. Chaotic. But it will not last."

"Exactly," I said, pointing at him. "You nailed it. I'm

here to discuss long-term options. Whaddya say, big guy?"

He swallowed the person he'd been chewing, rolled his massive head on his neck, eyes closed, savoring it. When he opened them again I could see so much *hunger* and need behind them, I didn't know if he'd eat me too. "I cannot wait another second to hear your ideas, Miss Blake. My delicious Miss Blake," he crooned.

"She's promised to let me handle this. It's just us." He wiggled his eyebrows at me and for chrissakes it was grossly hot. "Frankly, I'm a little pissed you didn't mention the big change," I said, playing to his hotness and weird sexuality.

"Oh no, sweetheart, this isn't a change. The thing you did before, becoming human, now that was a change."

I wouldn't bother answering that. "Let's get down to business. Rose can't stay on Earth, and she wants to take over your place here. Did you know that?"

"I could have guessed."

"What would you say to letting her be your right hand?"

"She won't go for that, she's too powerful. And I have ruled this place for far too long to accept a partner."

"Ruled it?" I scoffed. Probably stupid to do to Satan. "Looks like you're stuck here, babe." *Oh my god why do I say things like this.*

It had the effect I thought it would. He flapped his big ol' batties hard, and a bitter wind swooshed through Hell, getting moans from all the lucid corpses. "How dare you," he growled.

"Just sayin', Rose can take stuff apart like that," snapping my fingers, "and this is just ice. I mean, she could free you—for a price."

He went totally expressionless, impossible to read. Super fucking scary. "To rule with me?"

"Yeah, sure."

"I won't allow it. Tell me, what do *you* want for the child?"

"Fairness," I said without hesitation. "It's something she's never had."

"You speak of this fairness with such haughtiness! My dear," he drawled, "fairness is an illusion. You find childhood to be fair? Some born with the assistance of multi-million dollar doulas and others dropped in fast food bathrooms. Fairness is an idea invented by the very people who denied it to Rose. Now, survival of the fittest, *that's* real, the age-old standard, and Rose has claimed that one all for herself."

I narrowed my eyes at him. "You say stuff that makes sense. I don't like it. Keep going."

He laughed, so disturbing. "A survivor herself, she's taken the illusion of fairness and turned it on its head! Now *she* determines what fair means, and she has taken those survivors like herself to re-order the world that created such foolish ideals. And yet—now don't take this the wrong way—you feel as though she needs you to bargain for her?"

"Someone has to look out for her."

"No. No they don't," he said, his face turning stony and wild. I'd made him angry in that split second, it seemed.

I could use that.

"Well, maybe I don't have to, but I am. Don't you wish someone would look out for you once in a while?"

"What? I need no one, this is my domain."

"Yeah, but…" I waved at his ice prison.

His whole body—well, torso—shook with rage, the ice cracking all around him. For a second there, I was like *oh shit*, but the angry breaths through his nose came out cold, freezing the ice over and over again as he broke it.

"You speak to me of fairness?" he growled. "It's something I have never known, but I have *survived*, and claimed my ground like your demon child is doing as we speak."

"Right! She's upending shit, yeah? You're a resourceful guy, why don't you think this over, work with her to get what you both want." I had no idea where I was going with this, but gotta start somewhere.

His turn to narrow his freak eyes at me. "Yes. Yes, indeed. This is why I like you, young lady."

Here it was. I'd been hoping he'd offer something, I mean he's well known for making deals, right?

"She frees me, and I allow her to flex her muscles, so to speak, as my temporary stand-in."

He was also famous for giving two-faced deals.

"Give me the flip side, Batsy."

"When I'm not...on vacation," he said with a mischievous grin, "she stays here with me. I won't eat her, of course, that would be silly. But she can't leave. She's mine. And so are her Harpies."

The icy sea of horror, forever.

I reminded myself that I was here *because* she wanted to be in the ice prison. Wanted to own the goddamn ice prison.

"Where will you go? If you're free?" I asked.

He leaned forward, templed his claws under his goaty chin. "Why don't you stick around and find out?" he said, voice a menacing, sexy growl.

Gross, he's nasty. Get a hold of yourself.

"Nah, I'm gonna human it up until I die."

His eyes rolled out to the sides, lazy eye-like as he said, "You'll do exactly as I say. You're a creature of Hell through and through. What makes you think you can traverse The Inferno like the streets of your garbage town? You have belonged to me since the beginning."

He had me until that last part. "Sounds funny that you've owned me all this time when you couldn't get me down here without a homemade Harpy muppet and still only one of us is here now. And actually... aren't you the one who can't go anywhere? Seems like I can go wherever the fuck I please. So why don't you get off your high horse—if you have a horse under all that ice—and let me name my terms. Her…terms."

"What does she want?" Satan spit out, emphasis on every t and d.

"You work for her. You do as she says. All of The Inferno is hers. You're allowed to exist."

All of his many upper body muscles tensed to the point much that the ice cracked all around him, but the furious flapping of his bat wings cooled it back to freezing immediately.

For the record, his bat wings didn't scare me half as much as Rose's scythe-tipped ones.

"And if I say no?" he drawled.

"Well, that's easy. She doesn't make the same mistakes twice. She'll tear you apart one way or another, and I'm betting you won't like how it feels."

"You're threatening me," he said, nodding slowly as if assuring himself it was true.

"Yup. Threatening Satan. Go big or go home, right?"

He laughed, long and hard and enough to shake the surrounding trees. Then he stopped, caught his breath, and laughed long and hard again. He said, "Charity Blake, you *are* home."

ose slipped into Satan's ice lair undetected. "How long have you been listening?" Satan asked her with a how-was-your-trip tone.

"Long enough," she said, glaring between the two of us. "You two get along nicely."

"Which should make you happy," I said, "but I'm not getting that from you at all."

"I don't *like* when conversations get friendly behind my back."

"Okay, we can start talking shit then," I joked, making Satan laugh and Rose…not laugh.

"You'd never bow to me," Rose said, disappointment dripping in her words to Satan. "And you," turning to me, "still think you can joke your way out of your treachery?"

"Treachery? What the fuck? I just cut you a deal with fucking Satan, Rose!"

"I can't trust either of you to follow through."

Shit, she was getting really upset, and nothing went well whenever Rose threw a tantrum. Problem was that Tantrum was the only language she seemed to speak anymore.

"Rose, listen to me," I said as calmingly as I could. "You release him from the ice. He gets to play on Earth for just a little while, a day maybe, which is all he ever wanted. Hell is already up there. When you say it's time to come back, he brings the Harpies with him and you've got everybody where you want them. You leave Earth behind, you rule The Inferno, Satan is your right hand—"

"I thought you were my right hand."

We fell silent, looking at each other expectantly.

"I want to be normal," I said. Wrong words. "I want to be human, I mean. A normal human."

But even as I said it, I knew there was no way I could keep my hands out of Hell for long. That Rose would never be happy as long as she didn't control everything she could think of, including me. I don't know where she'd go next, but she wouldn't stop at Hell.

"I would, too," she said, tears filling her eyes. "I'd stop here if you were with me. We weren't meant to be up there, Charity. And this place is a world of wonders. They might be terrible, but we can change whatever we please! We can make real change down here. Stay with me. Be more than human."

"Oh, I think you're mistaken," Satan piped up, tapping one claw on the ice. "Nothing changes down here. Eternity is eternity, my dears. If it were that easy, plenty of powerful men have come before you that might have done it."

"Men can't do anything right," I said.

"I do believe the terms of our agreement need amending," he replied.

Rose said, "I don't think there's any agreement at all."

"You would not have lasted this long if there were no agreement, Miss Preston," Satan said. "We agree on one thing: power. We both have it, and we both want more of it. And we both have very specific vulnerabilities."

She weighed that for a minute and I thought my face was going to crack from trying to stay still.

Because I was in no way powerful, not like the two of them.

And also, *what the fuck was I doing here?*

If I was no longer necessary for negotiations, what then?

"You can't live with your memories," Satan said. "But you could live without them."

I could see Rose scanning him, trying to read him, get a leg up. But Satan was basically made for this shit.

"Go on," she said once she'd given up.

His goat eyes went out of focus. "If you'd eavesdropped properly, young lady, you'd have heard. I can give you a life up there, free of your memories. A fresh start. And when your life is over, you begin a new one. Here. Just where you wanted to be."

And like a child that sees exactly what she wants to, she lost one half of that statement. "You can make me forget?"

He smiled wide, a gash in his monster face, and her face lit up in response.

"Rose, it's not that easy," I blurted.

She whipped around on me. "Don't ruin this for me!"

"I'm not ruining anything. Not this time. But hear the whole thing, kid."

"She's heard enough," Satan warned.

Why was I pushing her to think it over? Didn't I *want* her to live a real life on Earth, even if it meant spending eternity in Hell with Satan?

Wasn't she bound to end up there anyway, one way or another?

She'd thought enough. Rose got on her knees and splayed her fingers across the ice, feeling for a weakness. Laying her cheek on the ice next, she closed her eyes and I think she was listening to it. No, not listening to the ice.

Listening to the bodies beneath it.

The cracks started appearing next, and then ice chunks separated entirely from one another, revealing decaying, soggy bodies underneath, long-dead and still fighting for the surface, even harder than when it opened before.

As if they were answering a call.

God fucking dammit, Rose never stopped surprising me. I was almost proud.

At the same time, a beat of Satan's wings iced the bodies over again, and Rose's head snapped up, viciousness just seeping from her expression.

"Stay still!" she growled at The Devil.

"I could not even if I wanted to, else I would have escaped the ice long ago, fool child!"

"Then you're weaker than I thought," she said. "And I think my vulnerabilities are the last thing we need to talk about."

"You. Cannot command my souls," he shot back. "They belong to me."

This was getting out of hand. Satan was pissed off, and that was nothing I wanted to be present for.

"Hey, hey, hey," I said, "let's all be friends here. Things were going well for a minute there, why don't we all just calm down? Talk this through. We all want out of this in one piece."

"Your girl likes to cut things into pieces. I don't think she can see past it," Satan said. And fuck me if he wasn't right.

The bodies were banging on the ice now, definitely pissed that they'd been trapped again.

"Tell me what the catch is," Rose said. "Tell me everything about what you're offering, Devil."

"I did," he said. "You live without memory. You die and come here. That's it."

"I come here as one of your souls, not as the master of this place as I should be. Look at me!" she shouted, shaking. "Why should I choose a petty life when it's unknowable how much more I could become!"

"Rose—" I interrupted, and immediately regretted it because she whipped on me in this like, fanatical, drink-the-Kool-Aid freakout. "Rose, you aren't becoming more. You're not." Why the fuck do I ever speak? "This is *happening* to you. You aren't in control here. When do you burn out? In five minutes? Ten years? I think we need to ask not what more you could be, but what more you can take."

Shit, that sounded pretty good. I was damn proud of myself. For a second.

Because her memories fired up. The moments were too fast, unrecognizable to me, but the faces were sometimes familiar, and the big message was plenty clear.

Everyone underestimated her.

"You think I can't handle myself," she said, her voice singsongy, as if she couldn't quite believe she was still hearing this shit. Approaching me in slow, gentle steps, "You never believed in me. You don't want to be my guardian and my partner, you want to be my overlord. You want to quietly control me, like everyone always has."

"Nope. Nope, I don't want any part of Hell anymore, kid."

"DON'T CALL ME 'KID' AGAIN!" she roared, and I fell over backwards onto the ice. Which cracked under my newfound chubbiness. Cold, mushy fingers wrapped around my arms and thighs, and I was in it. The fucking dead swamp ice water.

~

It was a while. I was under there a while. Until I couldn't feel my fingers. Until my vision finally went black and saved me from seeing yellowed, wild eyes, boring into me as their hands clawed at my face and sunk into my skin, tore the feathers from my body.

Nobody was coming to save me. Everyone I'd saved, and nobody was coming to save me.

Wait. Feathers.

I swept my arms out with my last bit of strength, sloughing off the bodies clinging to me, letting the wings bust out. I'd forgotten all about them.

There's probably a life lesson there but at the time I just wanted actual life.

Breaking out of the ice, I projected myself into the air, taking an enormous breath and then coughing my fucking lungs up. Probably didn't make for a great superhero entry, but I was no hero and I'd already been here. When I finally caught my breath, I was absolutely fucking boiling angry.

"What the fuck, Rose?! You were gonna let me die! I could've spent eternity under the ice, for fucks sake!"

She stared at me, blank, but not without feeling. Like she didn't remember who she was anymore or what mattered. "I don't know," she said.

Satan piped up, "You cannot afford not to know if you intend to take my throne, young lady."

"I don't need your advice, old man," she said, waves of heat tingling around her. "As a matter of fact, I don't need anything from you."

"You don't know what you need! You're spectacular, without question, but you are a child at heart and you think like a petulant, selfish brat, not a ruler."

Rose grew darker and darker shades of pink to red, then her skin burst into flames, glowing hot. Shit got real.

"The Devil," she said snidely. "So feared, so *powerful.* Right?" She fanned her wings out, glided over to him, just a speck against his size and yet he was stunned. "I can see what makes you what you are. Yes. I see it now. You're nothing more than a collection of souls." She tilted her head to the side and that never meant anything good.

To my surprise, she focused first on his wings. The great bat wings that were in no way as scary as hers, and in a shackle-freeing moment, had stripped the sleek bat skin, leaving only the bones. Which she then took apart like Lego bricks as Satan's head swiveled, looking in awe back and forth. In a matter of seconds and a look from a child, the timeless evil incarnate had changed. In a place that he said could never change. Sure didn't make him look all-powerful to me.

But Rose sure as shit seemed to be.

In only a few more seconds, the freezing wind stopped blowing through the trees and across the field of ice.

And it wasn't long after that when the heat from Rose's body melted the first chunks of ice from under her. Once the melting started, it spread fast, and boy was I glad I had wings for a while. The bodies without anything to cling to in the swamp water, clambered all over each other, a whole new lot of moaning and angry, unintelligible yelling. While they all re-drowned each other or whatever, the melting ice had reached Satan.

I expected to see his bottom half all waterlogged and emaciated and stuff, but when he busted out of the ice he was all muscle under his gross goat legs, you could just tell. And huger than I even realized.

He was close enough to the treeline to jump into a damn tree, bowing the whole thing over, while the souls underneath began to give up their attempts to get on solid ground. Not so bright after living—or being dead in—ice, like cavemen. Whereas Satan popped out of the ice more like a smelly, evil Captain America. He threw his head back and bellowed, a sound that they had to have heard on Earth, and I couldn't help but look for a place to hide.

Rose had been waiting for this moment. God, the kid had freed him on purpose just so she could smite him down. Sick.

Dwarfed by the giant Devil, Rose rustled her blade-feathers in a show of dominance with a great *shing!* The scythes—making her perfect for a Judgment Demon or some shit—gleamed brighter than anything else in Hell.

"Does it feel good?" she asked Satan sweetly.

"You..." he rumbled, bending forward from his perch on the tree, "you freed me. A beast that could never be free. You are a god." And he laughed hard, a sound like the world ending.

"I am," she said. "And I'm far more powerful than you."

But Satan, so excited to be out of his prison, wasn't paying attention to Rose. He just plucked struggling bodies from the fetid water and dropped them down his gullet in celebration.

I had no idea what Rose's next steps might be. She was entirely unreachable, our brains on totally different playing fields, and since she'd tried to let me die a short time ago, I was pretty sure she wasn't looking for my input.

And yet here I was, the only person who could stop her. Or so everyone said. Even though any plan we had went out the fucking window and I was stuck in Hell with the scariest fucking monsters in history.

What the fuck am I supposed to do but wait at this point?

The Devil rubbed his giant belly and came back to reality. "And now, child, you want something from me. To rule at my side and become the most fearsome, unprecedented beast who's ever lived."

Boy, he didn't know her the way I did.

"I don't think I like what you've done with the place," she said, and flicked her wrists out in front of her.

Streams of blazing heat rippled between them.

Satan screamed like a little girl when they hit him, but it totally wasn't the sudden burning after eternity in ice that hurt. It was the snakelike twisting of the flesh on his stomach, like two thick worms wrestling, that had to hurt.

Rose sent out more heat, pure energy, and more of the wriggling things rose from beneath his skin and hair, all over him. His arms, his neck, until every visible part of his body but his head was a mass of scrabbling larvae.

Veins burst out of him like exploding water pipes, spraying black and red blood all over the place.

The worm-things had broken the skin now. They wiggled out, carving giant trails in his flesh, chewing their way out in ragged holes ringed in blood. Globs of something *else* seeped out, too, some horrible organs only The Devil must've had. They fell with a splash to the water below and then, so did Satan. The impact was a cannonball at the shittiest pool party ever.

Bodies fucking tossed as high as the treetops. Corpse water drenching the trees, and me.

The bottom of the swamp was black silt and the monster maggots tunneling and squirming out of Satan's body almost glowed against it.

"Oh, fuck no."

Hot bile filled my throat, my mouth, my nose, when I got a look at the wormy things against the blackness. I couldn't hold it in, projectile-vomited on the silt far below.

Where the white came clear as more of a translucent pinkish. Like thin dead flesh.

And the worms had human fucking faces.

I couldn't stop moaning. I felt crazy weak with the puking and having been in the air for so long after not being in the air for over a year, and if I had to land on that fucking human-worm land down there… Well, I'd rather die. This was way worse than being trapped in ice, if you ask me.

Satan bounced back, though. The human worms spasmed outside of his body, but he looked much the same, if not for a bunch of nasty jagged holes all over him.

"You think you can take me apart that easily, girl?" he shouted up at Rose. "Take the souls, there are always more! I've consumed souls since the beginning of time, it will take more than the loss of these to kill me. Face it, child—you're stuck with me."

Rose, for her part, hadn't seen this coming. I was pretty impressed myself, that he was able to survive the de-worming, but Rose wouldn't give up now. If anything she'd be more driven and ruthless in her exhaustion. The kid didn't know how to be told no.

Satan started waving his meaty hands around, mumbling to himself, some mystical evil shit. If he was summoning someone, I hope I never know who.

"Rose, it didn't work, just end this, okay?" I pleaded. "Take the damn deal, live a quiet life, something simple. You don't have to come here…until you have to come here. You know?"

But the kid was still in flames, and that said everything.

The bodies had gotten their bearings again, and had climbed back into the empty swamp, surrounding their king. They lifted him up with their mangled, bloated bodies in an ugly parade thing. Rose got really antsy at this, watching him still waving his hands, mumbling words and things started shaking. I was so tired of things shaking. Such a pissing contest.

"Rose, *please*. Go back home, or, or take the spot beside him, you can rule Hell with him here still, but please Rose," now there were tears pouring down my face because this was the last time I was gonna see her ever again, I could feel it, "even if you win this fight, you'll lose, don't you see that?"

I was pulling on her arm, no attention to the flames

licking up my own arms. She paid attention, though. Removed my hands and patted the flames down, absorbing them back into herself. Meeting my eyes, she showed me that she had heard me. She did know I wanted her to be okay.

"I know what I need to do now to win this, Charity," she said so quietly I don't know how I heard her over the sounds of the souls carrying The Devil. "I know exactly how to take him down."

"Why does it have to be about taking him down? Not everyone is against you!"

She laughed good-naturedly. "Charity, he's *Satan*. He's against everybody."

That made me laugh too. "I can't convince you. Not fast enough. Can I?"

She shook her head with a sad smile.

"Then tell me how to help."

The time didn't work in Hell. There'd been a reason for it in the Wood of Suicides—time doesn't move forward when a damned person can't change. I'd learned that being damned didn't always mean you had to change into something or someone else.

I had all these thoughts and this conversation with Rose while Satan rallied his corpse-souls—because that's what they were, I figured out. Souls. Soul worms and soul corpses. Rose was way ahead of me.

And here I thought I could do something to help her. I never did.

Narrowing her eyes, her upper lip curling, Rose leaned her head forward in concentration. The flames around her head brightened, brightened. Then when they couldn't get any brighter, when they were blinding, the flames turned black. It was actually really beautiful, her red skin and blonde hair with the black flames all around her in the night sky.

The Satan parade had gotten much closer to her, and he realized that she was different. Didn't bother him any, though.

Rose whimpered. It was like an avalanche of sadness in the tiniest sound. She so rarely sounded frail.

The black flames flickered. And the white streaks of memories exploded in the sky, but these weren't Rose's memories. These were like some ancient god's story, creatures I'd never seen before and so much viciousness. Dark. Then they went actually dark, black, but when they got so dark that I couldn't see them anymore, Rose still could.

And the whimpering grew.

Pain had her body contorting as she clutched her head, her wings faltering. But she still forced her eyes open, baring her teeth. Her head jutted forward as she pushed with all her might into Satan's mind. His head punched back like he'd been punched in the face. When he lifted it again, though…

Three faces looked back.

Same head but bigger, with three hideous faces. The one I knew was almost the same, now stretched nearly flat, the eyes goggling around like something over a carnival funhouse.

The next rounded the side of his head, the eye I could see looking so hard out the side that half the pupil disappeared. Lipless, all teeth, no eyelashes or eyebrows, at least on the eye I could see.

The last was flesh but doglike, long nose, slathering mouth with dripping canines that had to be as long as my arm. I could *smell* the waste falling out of its mouth as much as I saw it, the body parts and organs that stuffed it to overflowing, its cheeks lumpy with them.

We got a damn disgustingly good look at all of them when The Devil's head spun slowly in a circle, a carousel of unthinkable ugliness, each revolution revealing more details until I thought I was going insane, that nothing was real and everything was real, and all of it had to be my imagination but the stench of the souls beneath and the wriggling of the bloodlessly pale worms with human faces, scowling and insane themselves, told me this was nothing even I could think up.

A word, scrawled in thick, viscous blood was slapped on each of the faces across various features.

Betrayal.

Malice.

Dread.

Their demonic eyes trained in turn on Rose. They spoke as one, a sound like a thousand missiles crashing into each other, like the breaking of a million bones. It assaulted the ears like fists crashing into helpless children's jaws, enough that I couldn't even feel the blood rushing from my ears, only feel it, hot and thick, my head reeling.

"You wish to use my memories against me?" Satan said. **"My memories are those of the endless souls of the damned. AND NOW YOU RELIEVE ME OF THEM."**

Everything hurting me disappeared. Time stopped. I could only turn my head to look at Rose, as terrified as I was to do it.

God help me, she was only a child in my eyes no matter what she'd done.

Hanging there, she didn't return my gaze, only waited for Satan to do his best on her. The kid had every intention of taking all the memories of the evil souls he'd consumed. I hated to admire her intent. It would end her.

Deadly quiet and stillness blanketed everything. I couldn't read Rose.

"Rose, stop fighting him!"

Her voice busted into my head, stronger than I'd heard it in a long time, clearer. *"If I don't do this, I'll never know what he knows."*

"You don't have to! Take what he's offered, kid! Live a simple life up there—"

"That *is damnation, Charity*," she said, not unkindly. *"Living without memories would eat me alive. I speak from experience. I'd rather be damned my own way."*

I wanted to plead with her. Take her little body in my arms, no matter how unrecognizable, and tell her how much I loved her, despite it all. Same as she'd have said to me.

Instead I fumbled around my body, found a pocket on my butt and breathed a sigh of relief. Pulling out the pack of Zebra Stripe Gum, I removed a piece and unwrapped it with trembling fingers, put it in front of her face.

"You always knew I wouldn't make it out, didn't you?" she said.

"I did."

"You'll burn here with me, Charity, go now."

"Meh," I said, hoping she didn't notice my voice crack. I popped a piece of the bad gum in my mouth. Purple. "I've been burned before."

"Thank you for not leaving me alone."

I just nodded.

I watched the blood pour from her eyes, her nose, her ears, soaking the blonde hair in its path.

I watched her scream, not because of the pain but because of the defiance and determination. I saw the flavorless gum on her tongue.

I watched, dumbfounded, torn apart, as the first hole opened in her skull. I couldn't hear my own screams, only feel them.

The hole opened wider, swallowing one bloodied eye and a chunk of her head, leaving nothing there. Nothing.

After that it was fast. The Devil's memories ate her alive from the outside, no different than her own had done from the inside. It was almost too perfect. Clicked together too smoothly. Hard to deny fate exists at that moment. To believe that there's a higher power. Stood to reason, if there was a lower one, right?

The next wave of Satan's memories overtook her, but not without a fight. Kid was a live wire, hadn't known how to fail since I'd known her.

But when her own memories of murdering innocent, undeserving people punched into view before us, all the death on her hands up close… She blinked away the freshest wave of blood in her eyes. Looked at me. I saw how she knew that she'd been so unforgivably wrong.

Raising her arms above her head, she grasped at the sky, as if she could take the memories down like bad paintings. I both did and didn't wish I could see what she saw. I hoped it wasn't all the wrong she'd done.

Before another hole engulfed her face, when she was still herself—to a point—a gut-shaking *whoooooooomp* echoed throughout Hell, an almost elegant sound of finality. A big orange plane, like the rings of that one planet, but made of sunlight and magma, sliced through everything I could see. A super-nova of energy and heat leveling everything it touched.

When it was gone with a sonic boom Havoc-from-X-Men-style explosion, something else took its place.

I whipped my head around and around, blinded but still *seeing*, knowing.

I saw that Satan had returned to where he'd been. Blinked into vision that the ice had re-formed despite what Rose had done.

Looked down to see that the ice wasn't swampy like it had been, and that visible below it, like another layer of a horrid cake, was a new place. An entirely new place. It *felt* new, and it felt like history.

My wings took me through the ice to this new not-place. A creamsicle-colored sky. An endless flat plane of pinkish matter. Not like a desert exactly—mushier. A vein of blue lightning jolted under the fleshy surface, then another, Frankenstein's monster anti-life energy. The electric impulses began arcing out of the bumpy pink stretch, leaving holes behind.

Holes.

No. No.

I brought myself closer.

The faint traces of images, like ghosts, peered back at me from deep in the holes.

I reached down, let my fingers graze a ridge of the pink tundra, feel the warmth of it, the life in it.

"Rose?" I whispered.

Down in the hole, I saw Rose and I eating fish and chips on the waterfront, our legs swinging over the harbor.

A memory.

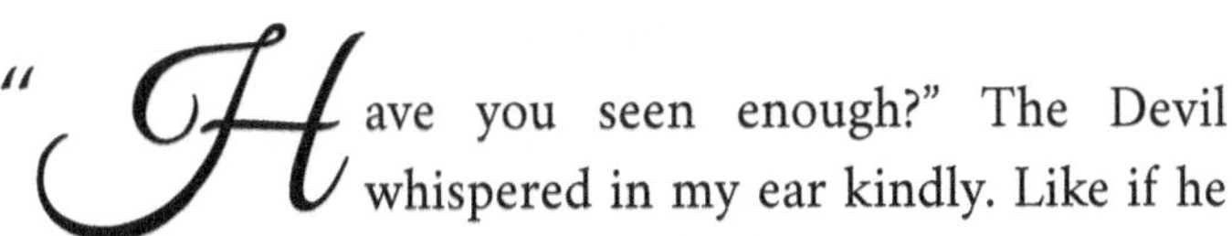

"Have you seen enough?" The Devil whispered in my ear kindly. Like if he could he'd put one of his big ol' paws on my shoulder to reassure me.

"How long have I been here?" My voice was something other, outside of me and bigger than voices. A dream of a dream of a Dali painting. That's what this was, me looking out over a surrealist nightmare below, the people little more than ants. Like God herself.

I didn't know art, but I knew Dali. M.C. Escher. Minds as fucked up as my own had been but had been able to put it on paper.

"Time is nothing here. Time is nothing anywhere, I'm afraid," Satan said.

"What's happening?"

"Rose was never meant to rule Hell, or to be consumed by it. She was meant to become it."

I fixed my eyes through my mind's haze on a person, naked, falling from nowhere above and into a hole in the fleshy wasteland. The screams came shortly after.

"Then it's true. This is her."

"Yes."

"What's in the holes?"

"You already know."

The bodies would fall now and again from an unknown point in an orange sky into a hole, while others wandered, stumbling over the brain desert.

"Are they her memories or theirs?"

"Both."

"Will they ever come out?"

Satan sighed. "Not for long."

As he spoke a naked man climbed out of a hole, sweat glistening on his bare back. Just as he reached the top, he ignited in sunset orange flames, tapering gold into the creamy sky. Seconds later the same man fell from the sky, blonde hair blackened, burns all over his body. I averted my gaze only to see another man in the distance plunging into a chasm, body burned all over, hairless, screaming. Always with the screaming. The pink, gold, orange of the place would have been beautiful, if it weren't so *ceaseless*, and burning and burning, pockmarked with lies and betrayals and cruelty.

"She is her own Circle of Hell now," Satan said with a note of finality.

"You think I'll just accept that, move on?"

"Have you not always done that? Accepted the horror, moved on with the scars? Is there any other way?"

I laughed. Felt hollow here. "I have a Psychiatrist who'd say that acceptance is the first part of growth. Then I came here—to the Wood—and because I couldn't accept shit and move on, I thought I was damned."

"Ah, yes. Growth must of course equal salvation, to the Big Guy. Learning from your mistakes. Because of course, you must always be wrong in some way if you want to go to the Good Place."

"So that place is real too, huh?"

"Never read Dante, I'm assuming."

That guy again. "You know," I started, "what if I chose not to grow? I chose to be a Harpy. Here I am again. But I feel different. Bigger. I never was in the market to change, I'm not the one who needs fucking changing, you know what I mean? It's the dicks of the world who need to change for me. Maybe damnation isn't just staying the same, never changing. I'm pretty fucking happy with who I am, all of it." I swallowed as I watched a memory of Rose's reach up out of its brain hole, carve its way through with a rusty razorblade. "I think I'm good just helping some others find the change they want."

"And do you think damnation is the change Rose wanted?"

"I'd say given the choice between forcing her into the world that destroyed her with a bunch of assholes she could literally see through to all their ugly dirties and here, where all their ugly dirties already existed, she'd have chosen this." I swallowed hard, hard enough to hurt my throat and remind me that I was human. "Yes. She'd have chosen this." But this…this wasn't what she wanted. This was an unholy punishment, not repent, and the kid's mind had been so distorted her entire life, she couldn't possibly understand what repentance even was. Shit, I don't know if I did either, but nobody deserved to *become* their worst choice for eternity. Damnation wasn't a lifestyle, and it wasn't what she needed. It surely wasn't what she deserved.

What she deserved, she *needed*, was forgiveness.

I was never one for letting bygones be bygones. I'd held Robbie's murder against her because yeah, she murdered him. But she didn't want to. She didn't. There was barely anyone left who could forgive her, and Rose wouldn't be seeing any of them anyway, but I could be the first one.

Then it dawned on me. The whole salvation bullshit was just that in my opinion—bullshit. But it bristled The Devil and that had to mean something, a bargaining chip. I didn't know how to play it yet, but I wanted Rose out of Hell and somehow I had to make connections.

"That Big Guy you mentioned," I said, rolling my eyes upward, "He's been strikingly quiet during Hell's restructuring, hasn't he?"

"We don't talk as often as you might think," Satan said.

"But—and correct me if I'm wrong—he likes to keep you—"

"He does not *keep* me!" The Devil roared.

"No, no, I know that, come on. *I* know that, but He's built kind of a whole thing on keeping you in your place. I mean, yeah this is your place, but...well, it's probably just me, but I get pissy at being told I'm not welcome. I like the chance to show off what I can do, you know? It sucks to be treated like an outcast, right?"

"*The* outcast," he sneered. "He is The Creator, but look at what I have done." The Rose level of Hell flared up, screams piercing the air. I wanted to say that maybe he hadn't actually created the new ring of Hell, but why piss off Satan? "You're a smart cookie," he said to me suddenly.

"I know. You're a good conversationalist."

"I know," he crooned. "Where do you see yourself going now?"

"I'm not staying to be Queen of the Wood of Suicides, so don't offer it up."

"No need," he said.

I whipped my head around, got really dizzy. "Why's that?"

He grinned, and I sure could see how he was The Devil then. "It's gone, my dear."

Blink. Breathe. Do something, dumbass. "Wh—what do you mean by that?"

He leaned back, where I got a good look at him. One face again. Out of the ice, hovering in the peach sherbet air with me. Not really him. An astral projection. Any stupid supernatural TV show'd tell you that.

"I can't say for certain, but as the lord of the manor, I'd say that when Rose created a new Circle of Hell, one got taken away. Would you like to see?"

"Uhhhhh…."

Suddenly the image was before me, this nightmare fucking movie theater, showing me Harpies plunging into the Wood, just like these souls were plunging into the brain holes now. Wings, torn from their bodies, dismembered and mutilated as I'd seen happening on

Earth. They landed in clumps on the bloody hay and never moved again. Those who'd been there to begin with cowered. I wondered where Jen was, what was happening to the trees, and the people I didn't want to think about. But it was answered for me when the great leveling happened, the supernova that was Rose turning into something unimaginable.

Then the Wood was gone. A blank space. As if it had never existed.

"Are you sad, Charity Blake?" Satan asked, real concern lacing his voice.

That was a fair question. Jen, Loretta...Evan. Painter. All the trees, the Harpies that were born there, the ones that had been made. "Not at all," I said.

He gave me a patronizing look. "Do you think they've been Saved now?"

"I think they've been ended and that's good enough."

"And who are you to decide what's good for those beasts and prey?" he said, playful glint in his normal-for-now-but-still-goat eyes.

I felt like I needed a really smart answer to that one or somehow he'd turn it around on me. I smiled for him. "I'm Devil's Advocate, right?"

The hearty laugh was so genuine, shaking his belly and everything, that I laughed too, and it felt so good. It was gross, it shouldn't have felt good to have a laugh with The Devil—but then again, who says? I didn't give a shit what anybody said. Satan wasn't all bad.

"I should be so lucky, to have you by my side," he said. "I imagine you've fulfilled your purpose now. So tell me, Charity Blake," Satan breathed down my neck like a lover, "do you feel *Saved?*"

I ruffled my wings—but nothing was there.

"Fuck Salvation," I said. "I want spaghetti and a beer."

CHAPTER 23

It made sense—if there was no Wood, no Harpies, no wings for me. But that didn't bother me. What bothered me was something Satan said.

"I imagine you've fulfilled your purpose now."

Not only was I brimming with restlessness to get Rose the fuck out of Dodge, in my own interest, I didn't like the idea of just being *done.* Like nothing I did mattered anymore because I'd done the big thing. I'd done a lot of big things—I had plenty more to do. Maybe even some good stuff.

And I sure as shit didn't like the idea of being done because someone else decided it. If you ask me, Salvation is a choice, and I chose to do whatever the fuck I wanted. Psychiatrist said it was a much healthier way of asserting my independence of spirit. He was all proud of me, now that he'd made it back to normal-ish.

There wouldn't be any more psychiatristing in his future, but he was good for a cup of coffee once or twice a week. He loved to talk about how far I'd come. Sometimes even Mr. Cleary came along, if he was in the mood. But he never, ever asked about Rose.

Keegan chirped from beside me on the couch. Little guy was just sitting there, in a wildly dangerous place if anyone else was here, watching Ozark with me. I handed him a tiny piece of a corn nut. I'd taken to eating them lately. I'd taken to eating a lot more than I even had been before lately, but fuck it. Skinny had never been a fashion choice for me; it was a running stance. And I'd been running even when I was sitting down for most of my life.

That shit was over now. My choice.

Theo sure didn't mind the extra rolls, that's for sure. He'd just been glad I made it back in one piece from Hell. Got real emotional about it and all that. He wanted me to move in with him in Boston, said after what we'd been through together he wasn't sure he wanted to be without me anymore at all. I told him he was taking it a little too fast, but it felt goddamn delightful to be that wanted. And it felt really fucking great not to be judged every second. I mean, he's the kid of a mob boss, and I'd be lying if I said I wasn't looking forward to meeting the Family. Theo took my "maybe" with that enormous grin of his, and said he'd give me some space as long as I didn't go too far. But my traveling days were over.

It had been a lot easier for Satan to put me back on Earth than it was for him to get me to Hell. Safe and sound in my apartment—which Rose left standing when she killed my adorable landlady. Her granddaughter moved in downstairs while I was gone, said I could stay which was cool.

Obviously, it didn't feel the same. It was nice to be home, but it hadn't felt quite right without Butter, and definitely not right with my view of the butcher shop. Every time I passed the window my throat closed up, broken down in tears. I couldn't stop looking at the fucking window no matter where I was in the apartment until I'd just sobbed on the floor for hours. Hours. It didn't feel any better. It wasn't even that I missed him, which I did—but that he was gone. It was my fault. No other conclusion could be drawn. There could be no punishment enough for me, no way to ever feel better. Mortimer said I didn't deserve more punishment, and yet I continued to give it to myself. He hoped that I'd give myself something with more growth underneath it than needling destructiveness.

Forgiveness.

He asked me if I thought people who did terrible things deserved forgiveness, and I said yes. But did people like Painter deserve forgiveness? Nope. I knew someone who did though. Someone who didn't understand what forgiveness felt like.

I missed her. Maybe I even missed the Harpies.

I sure as shit was done being a Harpy, though. I'd

even gone vegan. The idea of meat and Matt… Yeah, I'd gone vegan.

And I was happy to be back on Earth. Boston had made it back, like Boston always would. The news chalked Rose's remake of The Birds up to a terrorist attack and genetically engineered human hybrid monsters. Was a real easy way to stir up hatred, bring Americans together in their anger.

I'd never felt much at home before, no matter where I was. How could I have been when I'd never felt like a part of anywhere, and when I'd always been thinking of the next place to run, the next time I'd have to be afraid, the next person I'd lose or push away or kill? It could have just been that the temptation of the Wood was gone, but that's not how it felt. I mean, Hell is where you make it, I think. It felt like I'd chosen a place.

Still sorta wanted a vacation spot though.

Satan's words, that I'd fulfilled my purpose…they rang in my ears like I'd been knocked in the head by Tyson. I hadn't loved being kicked out of the club. I didn't like being cut off from a place. A new feeling, that I didn't like failing, infiltrated too. Maybe I just didn't like failing Rose. "Fulfilled my purpose," I muttered.

"Why don't you go back?"

"Can't. No wings, no Wood. No Wood, either."

"How are you overlooking such a glaringly obvious path?"

"Did you just Captain Obvious me?"

"Well…yes."

"Listen here—"

Wait.

What.

"Wait. What?"

Keegan turned his little head to me, tiny feet surrounded in corn nut crumbs. "Everything has changed in Hell," he said in this lovely, lilting voice. "Will you let an Employees Only sign stop you?"

I hung my head back, put my hands over my eyes as the glare from the window inched across my face. I'd seriously fucking lost it. This was it. This was why killing myself actually was a good option after all.

The tickle of itty bitty nails on my knee made me uncover my eyes.

Keegan sat there, shifting back and forth the way he did on his perch. His tiny beak opened. He spoke. He *spoke.*

"What the fuck is happening?" I gasped out.

He tilted his head. "It's still me," he said in that melodic voice. "I'm a messenger for Satan, the Great Unholy Beast." Then he chirped, all cute.

"How long have you been able to talk? Is that a British accent? Are all canaries British? I feel like I'm in The Devil's Bee Movie. I mean, what the actual fuck, Keegan?"

"You love that blasted movie," Keegan said.

"Holy shit, you really are my bird still."

"Yes," he sang. "But I'm also an unclean spirit now. The wings of The Devil on Earth! It's quite exciting, really!"

"You stop that, you're the most perfect little thing in the universe, you hear me? Now, while I'm going fucking nuts, you might as well tell me what He has to say."

"In fact I am *more* perfect, infused with His greatness, so thank you, my friend. He is excited by the change you've made in Hell! Decimating the Wood like that? Truly inspired."

"Whoa, whoa, that was not me."

"It couldn't have been without you, though, now could it? The Devil tasted delicious freedom for a moment because of you. He spoke his evil without judgment from you. He could use you, to make more changes."

"Oh no, this is some Rose shit right here. Talking about making changes in Hell. You can't tell me The Devil is interested in doing good and easing the suffering of souls." But underneath—not even that far underneath—this was a chance to get my foot back on The Devil's doorstep. Near Rose. Location, location, location.

"Certainly not! That is not his role. The question is, what will yours be, sweet friend?"

"He's letting me choose?" I scoffed. "I doubt it."

His soft voice softened even more. "You speak of The Beast as if he has not known suffering himself. He knows nothing of escape or growth. Nothing of choice. Yet you bring him change. " He laughed, an indescribable little sound. "Certainly you could help Him keep things in order. After all, there is a new level of Hell that needs overseeing."

"And what do I get in return?"

"Oh, I would not dare to bargain for the Great Evil, my sweet. But certainly, there must be *something* He could provide for you…"

I found myself petting his fiery pink feathers with one finger. The silence that between us could have taken up a room. He broke it.

"She calls out for you, Charity," he said solemnly. Painfully.

Sunlight from the window heated the back of my head. "Heading right back to where I came from, huh?" I muttered. Going backwards is the new forwards.

The bird hopped up onto my chest where it spilled over my bra. "It's not where you came from, friend," he said. "Hell is what you've left behind. What you've survived, and what you've created in part. To be beholden by such a place and to become more powerful because of it! *You* decide what moving forward will be. Perhaps for more than just yourself." That laugh again. "It seems to me that damnation for you means having nothing to do."

I shook my head, but I was crumbling fast. Not sure I had much of a wall to crumble. "You think I should go back to Hell because I'm bored?" But my wheels were already turning. They had been since my last sharing and caring time with the Big Boy Downstairs.

His voice took on a less sentimental firmness again, like he really did work for Satan and had an agenda, even if he was my friend. I supposed it could be both. "You did create a bit of a mess down there, dear girl," he said, using Satan's own pet name for me. "You helped eliminate an entire realm of monsters."

"Monsters? The Harpies weren't all monsters. Not always."

"Don't fool yourself. And surely you know in your heart—there are always more monsters, waiting to be made."

~

If pink lemonade was as warm as sunshine and smelled like dandelions and that could be made into a wind tunnel, that's what it was like traveling to Hell with Keegan. All rainbows and roller skates and picnics and orange soda in one weirdly retro trip through light the color of his feathers.

"Hi, Beast!" he greeted Satan as we landed softly in the newly-formed trees in the ice desert.

There was Satan, right where he'd been when we first met, stuck in a sheet of ice as thick as a giant's toenail and the same color. Half-eaten souls stuck out all over the place as usual.

"Sure doesn't look like much has changed to me," I said.

"Change is on the inside," The Devil said with a mischievous smile. "The ice…it's thinner."

"Yeah, okay." I shrugged. Let him think I wasn't impressed, which I wasn't. "So, what's up? You've got a business proposition or some shit?"

I tried to play over the fact that I could sense Rose all around me. This wasn't her level of Hell, but her pain permeated it, a ghost of the battle here. And the mere thought of her sent a sliver of ice through my brain, an echoing cry for me. *"Charity!"*

"Fuck," I yelped, grasping the tree branches for dear life, but I fell anyway, hitting the ice below. "Owwwwww. Thanks for nothing, Keegan."

"I can't carry you down here!" the bird said defensively.

"Whatever. Anyway, you missed me, huh?" I said, turning to Satan.

"Indeed. And I'm not alone," He said.

"Charity!" the cry came again, reverberating into my bare feet through the ice. I moaned.

"Nobody fucking said I'd be haunted by the kid!" I yelled. "I'm not one of your damned souls, I don't deserve to be fucking tortured with her voice—"

"Does she deserve to be in eternal pain? Does she not deserve the companionship you promised her?"

"She made her choices," I growled, but even I didn't believe it. I'd made mine too.

"And for that you won't ease her pain?" he asked.

I'd been talking shit to myself about forgiving her. Not that I thought I'd break the spell or whatever, but I had to do something.

"Rose!" I hollered. "Rose, I need you to know something. You might not deserve it, and I might only half mean it right now, but I'm trying, kid. I forgive you, for all of it. I forgive you for Robbie, and Butter, and—" I couldn't say it. "Well, I can't forgive you for Matt, not yet. Maybe never. But it's a start. I forgive you."

I expected her to call me again, but she was silent, wherever her plane of existence was. The Devil watched, face alight with curiosity. Probably never saw the Forgiveness, Live show before.

"What can I do?" I whispered, head hanging, staring at nasty grass poking through the ice between my toes. I wanted Satan to think I was really desperate, but I wasn't pretending to be disappointed that she didn't burst out of the ground or something, all angelic and glowy with her sweet little smile and grant me wishes and shit. Part of me did think my magic moment of forgiveness might actually do something for her. "What can I do?" I repeated.

"Ahhhh, I thought you'd never ask," He said. The Ian McShane voice didn't make it any less nerve-wracking. "You have given me new wings, change I never thought possible. And though yours have been taken, I have given you new ones as well." He nodded to Keegan who chirped like the little sweetie I took home from the pet store so long ago. "I'd like you to use them. Travel between The Inferno and Earth. Usher souls to me, and in doing so perhaps you can give them some reassurance, some hope for change still."

"You want the damned souls to change?"

He laughed and it shook me, rattled my teeth. "I want them to hope for it," He said, and his eyes did that goddamn circus-twirling thing they did that was enough to make me squeeze my eyes shut against the nausea.

It was what He wanted, but it didn't have to be what I gave him.

"Charity..."

"I get to be with Rose, whenever I want?"

"Whenever you want," he assured me, holding his hands out wide.

"And so much more. Decadence in every form you'd like. Powers that—"

"Let me finish that for you. Powers that would fucking consume me until I don't know who I am anymore? That would get everyone I care about killed or make them hate me? Been there, done that. You leave Theo the fuck alone, too. I don't want him sprouting wings or going batshit, you got it?"

"Only power that you ask for!" he pleaded, the focus returning to his eyes. "Or what you agree to, for I can offer you so much more than you could imagine."

"I. Am not. Damned. You understand me? Being

Satan's ticket taker doesn't mean I'm going to Hell one day myself, you got that? I'm not your bitch."

He laughed, but it wasn't that all-powerful shit he usually did. It was one of concession. "Miss Blake," he said, low and sexy, "do you not see that you're the one with the power here?"

The souls around me were oddly quiet, as if waiting for my response. I glanced to Keegan, where he perched like a little gentleman in the tree. He nodded once.

"I never was the one with a plan," I said to myself. But I did have a way with "people." I'd negotiated this far, and yeah, it got out of hand, but like The Devil said —I was the one with the power here. Probably just what He wanted me to believe, but sure as shit, I did believe it. I was human, but walked the Inferno like Don Tay. Hell would never have changed without me. And I could change it again.

For her.

"You say I usher souls, huh?" There was a couple of different directions souls could go in.

"Lots of traveling. Plenty of benefits," Satan said with a wink.

He was joking, but I wasn't. I trained my eyes on him. "What benefits? What do I get?" But before he started with his money, cars, women spiel, I shut him down. "I'll tell you my price. I'm working off Rose's debt. I give you enough souls—you name the amount— and this thing she's become, it's over. She goes back to

Earth, new Rose, new life, with or without memories, I don't give a shit, but she's free of you forever."

He sized me up, one claw stroking his goat beard. He was amused. I wasn't. And I knew He was just playing with me, pretending to think about it. I knew what a true jerk was, and we never let someone else name the terms.

He finally said, "That seems…*fair.*"

Oh, well-played. He liked a good theme, and polite tradition.

"Shall we shake on it?" I said with a smile.

With a boisterous laugh, he said, "No such pleasantries are required, but I appreciate the formality. This is merely an agreement, my dear, and that's all it needs to be."

"You'd cross your claws anyway," I said, winking at him. "An agreement then."

We sat together in companionable silence, looking out over fates worse than death. I don't know what he saw, but all I saw was Rose. How much more she could be. How much more I could do for her.

"It's quite beautiful, isn't it, what she's made?" Satan said of the creamsicle nightmare.

"Change always is," I said, eyes straight ahead, owning my ponytail-phase philosophy.

"I didn't—" he started, but caught himself. When I turned my attention to him, he finished. Chalk one up to becoming a confidant to The Devil. Tuck that shit away for a rainy day. "I didn't know there could be any more to this place," he finished, sadness dragging his voice down. Almost like he'd lost hope—and had it rekindled.

Now that I can work with.

"Rose and I do enjoy stirring things up." I sat up straighter. I raised my chin. I tried to hide a smile. "Who knows what else could happen?" I leaned closer to him, conspiratorial, with my most seductive narrowing of the eyes that made most men scream. "I bet you and I could change things that would make even—" I pointed up, "—jealous." Big smile for the Batman.

The Devil's desire burned, in the clenching and unclenching of his claws, the way he leaned forward as if needing the new Hell level to touch his skin. I knew what aching looked like. He had fire. Ambition. A twisted send of hope. I'd seen it in Rose herself. That kind of craving could only claw its way out, incapable of restraint. I had a little experience with that. The itch to go places one shouldn't be and places one had been cast from. With the right whisper in His ear, The Devil could get some real lofty ideas. The kind that would benefit from having an usher to traverse all the places death could reach.

I'd found my way into Hell so many times I'd lost count, and someone always found a reason they wanted me to stay.

My way with "people," and my newfound skill at playing both sides of the board with this whole Rose situation just might work to my advantage. A foot in the door in both Heaven and Hell was just what I needed to get the kid the deal she deserved, and just maybe secure myself a decent ending to boot.

I couldn't tell Satan that. He'd love the idea of trying to weasel into Heaven one way or another, but He'd never give Rose up, or me. He'd use me for the fun of it and turn our agreement on its ass just for tricks.

The Man Upstairs was probably less shady.

Layers of a plan clicked together, and I was ready to have purpose again.

But first, I had to dazzle The Devil.

I met His creep-ass goat eyes, and couldn't help but smile at his eagerness. "So. How many floors are in this shitty hotel, anyway?"

RESOURCES

If you or someone you care about are experiencing sexual violence, RAINN provides support, live chat, hotlines and ways to help the cause 24 hours a day:

About the National Sexual Assault Telephone Hotline | RAINN

If you suspect child abuse, please take action. Contact info by state in the U.S. is here. State Child Abuse and Neglect Reporting Numbers - Child Welfare Information Gateway

For quick, in-depth info on abuse, abusers, who's at risk, and more a one-page reference from the Cleveland Clinic: Child Abuse: Definition, Signs, Child Neglect, Emotional Abuse (clevelandclinic.org)

Child abuse can come in many forms:

Physical: Slapping, pushing, punching, kicking,

shaking or burning a child or not allowing a child to eat, drink or use the bathroom.

Emotional: Frequently verbal, involving insults, constant criticism, harsh demands, threats and yelling.

Sexual: Rape, incest, fondling, indecent exposure, using a child in pornography or exposing a child to pornographic material.

Medical: Intentionally trying to make a child sick or not treating a medical condition.

Researchers have noted certain characteristics in children who have experienced abuse. Some behaviors may be more noticeable, such as:

Acting out sexually in inappropriate ways.

Chronic belly pain, headaches or other physical complaints.

Return to childish behaviors such as thumb-sucking and bedwetting.

Running away.

Self-destructive behavior, such as cutting and self-harm.

Severe behavioral changes.

Other characteristics may be harder to identify, such as:

Anxiety and depression.

Difficulty learning and concentrating.

Evidence of post-traumatic stress disorder (PTSD).

Lack of emotional development.

Poor self-esteem.

Recurring nightmares.

Suicidal thoughts and/or attempts.

Physical signs:

Looking unclean or neglected.

Unexplained bruises, welts, sores or skin problems that don't seem to heal.

Untreated medical or dental problems.

Pain in the genital area.

Vaginal bleeding other than a menstrual cycle (period).

Unusual discharge or pain.

Emotional signs:

Fear of one or both parents or caregivers (including babysitters, day care workers, teachers and coaches).

Fear of an activity or place.

Crying often or in situations that seem inappropriate.

Regression (returning to behaviors typical of a younger child).

Behavioral signs:

Acting different from other children, especially if it's a sudden change.

Frequent absences from school.

Being withdrawn.

Bullying peers or younger children or being bullied themselves.

Trouble learning and paying attention.

Avoiding physical contact with adults, peers or older youth.

Overachievement or being overly eager to please.

Unusual sexualized behaviors or comments, especially ones that seem more mature or pornographic.
--From MyClevelandClinic.org

ACKNOWLEDGMENTS

David Purse, because of you, THE HARPY became a trilogy I'd never thought of. What started as friendship, then wanting to collab because you loved Charity, has become a new world for me and a partnership I never knew I needed. Thank you for being my kind, encouraging darling and bringing my favorite Hell to new dimensions.

Thank you for reading THE HARPY 3: DAMNATION! If you enjoyed the book, I would greatly appreciate it if you could consider adding a review on your online bookstore of choice.

Reviews make a huge difference to the success or failure of a book, especially for newer writers like myself. The more reviews a book has, the more people are likely to take a shot on picking it up. The review need only be a line or two, and it really would make the world of difference for me if you could spare the three minutes it takes to leave one.

With all my thanks,

Julie Hutchings

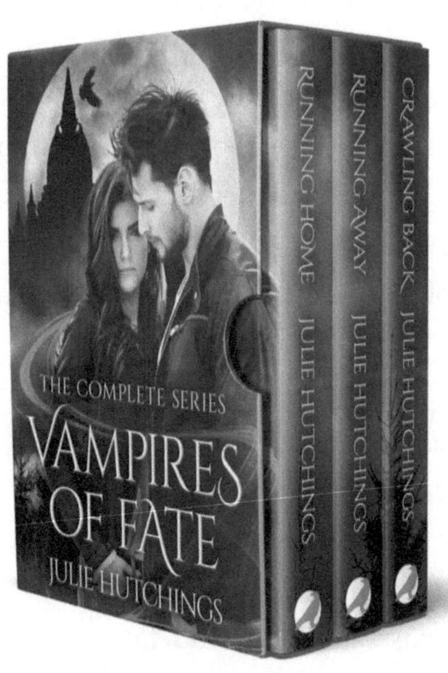

THE VAMPIRES OF FATE SERIES
BY JULIE HUTCHINGS

Death seems to follow Ellie Morgan. Now someone's out for blood.

Tucked away in rural New Hampshire, awkward booklover Ellie lives a simple life, keeping herself detached from others. With just a single friend in a world that has taken her family from her, a part of Ellie longs for something more than nights on the couch and dull days working in a gift shop.

Enter Nicholas French.

Something about the new guy in town sparks a burning desire within Ellie, something more than his rugged good looks and piercing gaze that can see into her lonely soul. Fate has led him to Ellie's small town, and Nicholas' interest in her is more than undeniable attraction.

As Ellie learns more about Nicholas' dark yet noble nature, she discovers a part of herself she never knew existed, and why the threads of her destiny feel intertwined with his. But Ellie's chance at a new life comes at a cost, and in the end, fate may be the one to decide if she'll live or die.

RUNNING HOME is the first book in the dangerously passionate and deeply romantic Vampires of Fate series, where not all monsters are evil, and love comes with a bite.

Get your copy of the complete three-book collection today and delve into the compelling trilogy that has readers thirsty for more!